A GRAVE OPENING

BY

JEANE HARRIS

Bywater
BOOKS

Ann Arbor • New Orleans
2005

This book is for my daughter-in-law,
Sarah Ann Clem whose love for the natural world
is surpassed only by her devotion to
her family, her husband and God.

Acknowledgments

The author would like to thank the following for their love and interest during the writing of this novel: my sister, Jill, my son, Christian S. Harris, my dog, Sweetie, and my all my friends in the CWOD NA group, (especially my sponsor, Terri R.) who loved me until I could love myself and who continue to encourage me to take it one day at a time. Without them, I would never have finished this novel.

Three women prominent in the lesbian publishing and writing field have played a crucial role in my development as a writer: Katherine V. Forrest who edited my first two books and taught me about writing by her insightful comments on the manuscript; Jean M. Redmann, mentor, novelist and editor whose friendship has been an unexpected blessing; and Barbara Grier, founder of Naiad Press who published my first two books, *Black Iris* and *Delia Ironfoot*. Barbara encouraged me to think that I could be a writer. Depending on your opinion of my writing, you may praise her or blame her for her encouragement. My best friend and magic guy, Sir Guy Lancaster; my boss, Chuck Carr, chairman extraordinaire, Nat and Brandi, secretaries par excellence, and my friends at The Edge coffeehouse, Anne and Paul Williams who feed me everyday. And finally thanks to Kelly Smith for her invaluable suggestions about the plot.

I have taken some liberties with the geography of northeastern Arkansas. I have taken even greater liberties with the archaeological periods and artifacts of the Central Mississippi Valley. Every effort has been made however to portray archaeological procedures accurately. The following sources have been incredibly helpful to me and I wish to acknowledge them:

Colin Renfrew, *Archaeology*
Robert Silverberg, *The Mound Builders*
David Hurst Thomas, *Archaeology*
William H. Stiebing, Jr., *Uncovering The Past*
Stephen Williams. *Prehistory of the Americas*
Bill McMillon, *The Archaeology Handbook: A Field Manual and Resource Guide*
D. P. Wick, *Decoding Ancient History: A Toolkit for the Historian as Detective*
Stephen Williams, *Fantastic Archaeology: The Wild Side of North American Prehistory*
Brian M. Fagan, *Archaeology 6th ed.* and *The Time Detectives*
Jane McIntosh, *The Practical Archaeologist: How we know what we know about the past*
Bill McMillon, *The Archaeology Handbook: A Field Manual and Resource Guide*
Dan and Phyllis Morse, *Archaeology of the Central Mississippi Valley* Anyone who wants to understand Central Mississippi Valley archaeology and culture reads this book.

Chapter 1

Delia Ironfoot realized how utterly exhausted she was as they crossed over the Mississippi on what everyone in Memphis called the "Old Bridge." Her flight from Salt Lake City had been delayed by thunderstorms over the Rockies, which had caused her to arrive in Memphis two hours late. The physical labor she had performed on her uncle Robert's farm, in the weeks before her trip, and the stress of flying converged on her; now in the truck she leaned back against the soft leather headrest and closed her eyes.

The faint country music from the radio was not enough to fill the silence between her and Kevin, a tall, gangly young man with curly dark hair that stuck out from under a battered Memphis Red Birds baseball cap. Though her great aunt Eunice assured Delia during their telephone conversation yesterday that she *had* met Kevin at her grandmother's funeral, in truth, she held no recollection of him. But there had been so many people she didn't know at the funeral, that the passage of time effectively erased their names and faces from her memory.

However, Kevin seemed to be a pleasant kid, and she felt obligated to at least chat with him on the hour and half drive to Crowley's Ridge in northeast Arkansas where her late father had grown up and where most of his relatives, including her grandfather, still lived. So she spoke, though she kept her eyes closed.

"I hope it didn't inconvenience you to have to come down here to pick me up."

"No," Kevin reassured her. "I wasn't doing anything."

"Well, I still appreciate it," she told him. "So . . . do you have any idea how this accident with Granddad and the tractor happened?"

"You mean besides the fact that the tractor fell in a hole?" Kevin asked.

"Yes, Eunice told me that part. She just didn't go into any detail about *how* it happened. She said Granddad was banged up a little."

"He's banged up some," Kevin told her. "He broke his wrist and split his head open. Fractured his cheekbone." He chuckled. "Doc wanted to admit him to the hospital overnight, but he wasn't having any of that."

"Uh-huh, Eunice told me he wouldn't stay in the hospital after they treated him."

"Nope, he went on home. He's tough as an old boot. Stubborn too."

Kevin flicked his brights at an approaching truck and then asked, "Is there some trouble between you and your granddad?"

Delia turned her head to look at him. "Why? Did he say something to you?"

"Not to me, but I heard him and Miss Eunice talking about you."

"And?" Delia asked. "Did he say there was trouble?"

"Nope, he didn't say anything like that," Kevin replied.

"Then why did you ask me if there was trouble between us?"

Kevin shrugged. "He told Miss Eunice he wasn't sure you'd come even if he asked you. I figured . . ."

"I understand," Delia sighed, deciding she wasn't going to discuss the subject with a young man she had just met and barely knew. "No, there isn't any trouble between us. I just think he and Grandma were disappointed that after my mother died, I didn't want to stay here with them."

"But that was a long time ago. You were just a kid."

"Yeah, and I did stay with them for a little while," Delia said. "But I missed my dad. I wanted to be with him."

"That makes sense," Kevin admitted. "But like I said, he's never mentioned it to me."

"Well, I don't know if that's all," Delia said slowly. "I've always felt that maybe he was ashamed or embarrassed with all the publicity surrounding my getting fired from the university—and all the other stuff that came out."

"You mean about you being gay?" Kevin asked.

Delia was startled. "How do you know about that?"

"Everybody knows about it," he said matter-of-factly. "It doesn't matter to most folks I've ever talked to."

"I find that hard to believe," Delia said skeptically. "This *is* the South, after all."

"We're not all ignorant rednecks." Kevin glanced over at her, grinning. "Now it's true that a couple of my cousins have Confederate flag decals on their trucks, but you'd be amazed. Most people I know have somebody gay in their family, even if they don't know it."

"That's true," Delia said. "I'm just a little surprised."

"You're his kin," Kevin stated. "That's what matters most around here."

"Hmmm," Delia said. "Well, Granddad and I do need to talk about some things."

"Sounds good to me," he said, slowing the truck and turning onto the road that would take them up the ridge to the small farming community where her grandfather lived. They drove in silence for a few minutes and then he spoke again. "There was one thing your granddad told Miss Eunice that you might want to know."

"Oh?"

"He said he wanted you to come and look at what he found in the hole where his tractor ended up."

Delia sat upright. "Eunice didn't mention anything about that to me on the phone."

"Well, don't get worked up," Kevin said. "Because I don't know anything else. They clammed up when I came in the room. I'm sure he'll tell you now that you're here."

"Yeah," Delia said. "How much further is it?"

"'Bout forty-five minutes."

Though she was still tired, Delia found she was enjoying her talk with Kevin. "This sure is a nice ride," she said. "Is it yours?"

"Nope. Wish it was though." He shifted his body in the big leather seat. "It belongs to my second cousin, John Ed."

Delia thought a moment. "I don't think I know him."

"He's the jailbird—just got out of prison a while back. Says he 'forgot' there wasn't money in the bank when he wrote those checks."

"His fortunes must have taken an upswing since then," Delia noted wryly. "Or do they give away F-350's now when you get out of prison in Arkansas?"

Kevin laughed. "Not hardly. John Ed can afford it though. He's got a good job over in Marmaduke workin' for a rich guy...Bob Noland."

"What's he do?" Delia asked idly.

"Who? John Ed or Noland?"

"John Ed," Delia said.

"He works at Noland's truck dealerships...says he unloads and details the new trucks before they put them on the lot. Sounds believable, I guess."

"He *says* he unloads them? You sound like you're not sure," Delia remarked. "Is John Ed not known for his honesty?"

Kevin laughed heartily. "Not so's you'd notice. I mean, it's *probably* the truth. I'm sure that's how he could afford this nice 350...Noland likely gave him a discount. But...well, there's a story behind Noland."

4

"Tell me," Delia said, relieved that she had found something Kevin wanted to talk about that didn't involve explaining her feelings for her grandfather.

"Oh, it's just what I've heard, mind you," Kevin cautioned. "It all happened about ten, eleven years ago...I was just a little kid then."

Delia smiled. "How little?"

"I was only nine," Kevin told her.

"Okay. Sorry I interrupted. Go on."

"Well, like I said, it's old guys sittin' around the courthouse tellin' tales. But it's mostly true. I've heard my dad and his friends talk about it. It was a big deal back in the day, you know? This place hasn't ever been jumpin' with excitement."

"Okay, I'm intrigued."

"When Mississippi made casino gambling legal, Noland, who'd made a bunch of money from his dealerships, and a guy he'd grown up with and had some money too, bought an old riverboat. Fixed it up and turned it into a casino."

"Uh-huh," Delia said. "How'd that work out?"

"My dad said that the guy was kind of...I dunno what you'd call 'em—'a yahoo', I guess. One of those guys who make their own commercials for their cheap-ass discount furniture stores. Know what I mean?"

Delia chuckled. "Yeah, we have some of those out in Utah."

"Okay, so after Noland and his buddy got the casino up and runnin', his partner got into some trouble with the cops over drugs. I don't know if he was cookin' it or sellin' it or whatever. But anyway, the cops busted him and he went to jail. So the guy got out on bail before his trial, but the prosecutor's office kept pressurin' the guy to make some kind of deal...give 'em somebody more important."

"And did he?" Delia asked.

"He didn't have a chance to," Kevin said. "A couple days after he got outta jail, he up and disappeared."

"Just like that?"

"Yep, nobody's seen him since."

"So, the police thought maybe the people he was going to give up got worried?"

"Maybe the police did. Opinion's divided whether he's dead or running. And the running camp's divided: half say from the police, half from the people he was going to talk about."

"And who was he running from—besides the police?"

"Probably Noland," Kevin said. "There was talk that drugs were pretty easy to find around his casino."

"Okay," Delia said. "Then what happened?"

"Well, then Noland got jammed up with the State Gaming Commission somehow. I don't know the details...just that one of the commissioners went after him for violations of the State's Gaming Code. I think maybe he had hired some ex-cons to work in the casinos, as muscle, to collect money from people who got in too deep at the tables or the private poker games they had goin'."

"That doesn't sound good," Delia remarked.

"No. Anyway, one of his goons meets with one of the commissioners and beats the holy shit out of him. Put the commissioner in the hospital."

"Did it work?"

"Nope, the commissioner got pissed off and went to the county prosecutor who's had a hard-on for Noland since the partner disappeared. So they wired up the commissioner when he got out of the hospital and set up a meetin' with Noland. The commissioner said he was retracting his charges and investigation, but he wanted some money."

"Blackmail?"

"I guess so. Anyway, something happened...I don't remember what and the prosecutor didn't get anything on Noland or the even the guy that beat him up. And then, the commissioner disappeared."

"You're kidding!"

"Nope, just like the other guy. Vanished into thin air."

"For good?"

"Nobody's seen 'em since," Kevin told her. "Here's the weird part. A couple days later the county prosecutor goes on TV sayin' how he'd get whoever was responsible for whatever happened to the two guy, blah, blah, blah, and said he was going to bring in Noland for questioning."

"God, the suspense is killing me," Delia said. "Then what?"

"He disappeared too."

"You're *kidding.*"

"Nope. Never found him either. They're either buried somewhere in the woods or on a beach in Tahiti. Conspiracy buffs think the three disappeared guys were in cahoots."

"Jesus," Delia said. "Three people disappear, and they never find any of them. That's pretty intense."

"Yeah, the cops couldn't prove a damn thing. They tried to, but they never found the bodies."

"Or traced them to Tahiti," Delia murmured. "Could somebody else have done it?"

"Maybe. People were always sayin' before gambling was legal that it would bring criminals into the state. So, who knows? Maybe it wasn't Noland. Maybe it was, I don't know, like the Mob...or organized crime. Something happened though, because Noland got to keep the license for his casino. Whether it was because the other commissioners were scared, or he paid them off...like I said...nobody knows."

"Wow, that's some story," Delia said.

"Yeah, biggest thing ever happened around here." He glanced at Delia. "Listen; don't say anything to your granddad. Okay?" Suddenly his voice was tense. "He doesn't like Noland *at all,* and he's told me to stay away from him. He calls Nolan a killer and says John Ed is gonna end up back in prison if he keeps workin' for him."

7

"What do you think about that?" Delia asked, taken aback a bit by his vehemence. "Is Noland a bad guy or not?"

Kevin hesitated. "I don't know. I don't judge people by what they've done in the past, you know? Lots of people make mistakes." He shrugged. "John Ed's not a bad guy. I mean, he lent me his new truck." He grinned. "And I know it's not stolen 'cause I made him show me the registration."

Delia laughed. "That's good. And you're right—it was nice of him. But you didn't answer my question about Noland."

"Well, he's givin' John Ed a chance to work...which a lot of people around here wouldn't do."

"Good point," Delia acknowledged.

"Yeah...see, here's the thing...I went turkey huntin' with John Ed last year at some huntin' club west of Hardy that Noland owns. He let us use his bird dogs. Those were some *nice* bird dogs. I really took a shine to one of the bitches we hunted with, and John Ed told Noland how much I liked the dog. So when she had a litter last year, he gave me one of her pups." Kevin paused. "You know, it was kinda nice of him to give me the pup since I never even met the guy."

"Hmmm," Delia murmured noncommittally. "What's her name?"

Kevin looked puzzled. "Whose name?"

"The pup."

"Oh," Kevin looked sheepish. "Spaz."

Delia laughed. "She a little excitable?"

"She's a mess. Got the attention span of a gnat." His voice softened. "If I had any sense, I would've drowned her by now."

"Right," Delia said, and then asked casually, "So where does this worthless animal sleep?"

Kevin mumbled something.

"What's that?" she asked. "I missed that."

"On my damn bed," Kevin said over her laughter. "Under my

goddang armpit most of the time," he admitted. They continued talking about dogs—Delia told him about Sam, her old dachshund and the Rhodesian ridgeback, Neji, and the llamas she used for her wilderness trekking business in Utah. Kevin seemed genuinely interested and under his questioning, soon she found herself sharing the story of her and Beth Collins's near death experience with drug dealers in the snowy wilderness of the Uinta Mountains. She finished her tale just as Kevin pulled into the gravel driveway behind her grandfather's house. The back porch light was on, but the rest of the house was dark.

They sat for a few moments in the truck, letting the silence settle around them. Then Kevin said, "Wow! That's some scary shit," he said admiringly. "You must be one helluva gunslinger." He shook his head. "I've never shot at anything that could shoot back."

"Yeah, it's amazing how focused you become when someone is shooting at you," Delia agreed.

"Well," Kevin said as he opened the truck door and got her bags from the back seat, "I can pretty much guaran-damn-tee you that nothin' that exciting will happen to you while you're here. I mean, there're some brain-dead meth-heads cookin' up dope in their trailers in the woods. Luckily, about half the time, the idiots blow themselves up."

"Good," Delia told him. "That experience was exciting enough to last me a lifetime."

As she and Kevin stepped up onto the back porch, Delia heard a muffled bark from inside the house, and when Kevin opened the door, a large yellow Lab was sitting right inside. The dog woofed again, but Delia noted his tail was wagging.

"Hush, Wally," Kevin said quietly and pointed at the kitchen table. "Go on now. Lay down." The dog obeyed and went to lie under the table. Kevin carried her bags through the kitchen and set them down beside the staircase that led to the upstairs. As

Delia followed him, she saw a note on the table and switched on the overhead light so she could see to read it. It was written in her grandfather's hand: *Dee, Stayed up as late as I could but this medicine they gave me makes me sleepy. There's some fried chicken Eunice made in the icebox if you're hungry. She made up the bed in your dad's old room. I'll see you in the morning. Granddad.*

"I'm surprised he even took the damn medicine," Kevin said softly when Delia showed him the note. He glanced under the table and said, "Look at that. Dog knows there's gonna be food on the table pretty soon. He's just hangin' out, see if he can talk you into some."

"Why don't you stay for while and have some with us then?" Delia asked him.

Kevin grinned. "Hell, I never say no to Miss Eunice's chicken." He opened the refrigerator door, removed a plate of chicken covered in plastic wrap and put it on the table. "If I did and she heard about it, she'd be pissed."

They found plates and glasses in the dish drainer and after setting the table and getting glasses of sweet tea, she and Kevin ate in companionable silence while Wally waited for any scraps thrown his way.

Delia watched in amusement as Kevin put away four pieces of chicken.

"Miss Eunice is famous in three counties for that chicken," Kevin told her when he finished eating. He smiled at Delia and asked, "So, has the place changed much since you visited the last time? How long ago was it?"

"Not that long. When Grandma died. I wasn't here very long though. Just a couple of days. Before that, I was here when the university dedicated the wing of the earth science building and named it after Dad."

Wally came out from under the table and nudged Kevin's hand. Kevin rubbed the dog's head and gave him some scraps from his plate. "If you don't mind me askin'—how come you don't visit your granddad more often?"

"Oh, I don't know," Delia said tiredly. The late hour and her forgotten weariness were clamoring for her attention. "I've got a lot of stuff going on most of the time." She paused. "My trekking business . . . and I also help out my uncle Robert with a little farming. Speaking of farming . . . what in the world was Granddad doing on a tractor in the first place? I didn't realize he still farmed."

Kevin snorted. "My dad leases some land for duck huntin' from some guy who's gotta be ninety. The old dude still farms some." He frowned thoughtfully. "Your granddad grows some alfalfa for some of his kinfolk and neighbors who raise some cows. Not to sell, you know . . . just for their own use. They butcher 'em and then give him some of the beef."

"So . . . he was plowing?"

"No. Miss Eunice told me he'd gone over to the new property to bush-hog."

"Ah," Delia said. "Okay, so he was just clearing the brush."

"Yeah," Kevin answered. "Probably makes him feel good to get out once in a while and do some real work."

"You said *new* property? Where is it?"

"It's on the other side of the river," Kevin informed her and then said: "The Big Right Hand River? The one that divides your granddad's property from the Buck's."

"Kevin, I don't know the Big Right Hand River from the Little Left Hand River. As a matter of fact, I couldn't tell you the names of Granddad's sisters and brothers . . . except for Eunice." She paused. "I've only met my Dad's two brothers a couple of times. I wouldn't know my first cousins, let alone my second or third cousins, if I passed them on the street."

Kevin said nothing for a moment and then said, "See, most people around here don't get that. They get you bein' gay better than they get you not knowin' your family."

"Well, it wasn't exactly my idea not to know this side of my family," Delia informed him, a little defensively. "My dad was a paleontologist—he hunted dinosaur bones. He took us wherever he went. Most of the time, those places weren't anywhere *near* Arkansas. I wasn't even in the country during most of my childhood."

"What about after you grew up?" he asked. "Why didn't you visit after your Dad passed?"

Delia sighed. "I'm too tired to have this kind of conversation, okay?" She reached across the table and put her hand on his arm. "I'm here now, right? They called me and I came. Let's talk about this later...after I have a chance to see Granddad and to sort things out with him."

Kevin nodded. "Sure. I didn't mean to stick my nose where it doesn't belong. I didn't mean nothin' by it."

"It's okay. Tell me about this property Granddad bought from...who'd you say?"

"The Bucks," Kevin told her. "Well, not both of 'em. Old Man Buck...hell, I don't even know his first name. He died a few years back and, after that, his widow...can't remember her name either...Marlene? Arlene? Whatever. Anyway, she sold it to your granddad."

"Hmmmm," Delia mused. "I didn't know that. So why did granddad want to buy it, I wonder?"

"My dad told me that, a long time ago, the property belonged to Whitakers. Way my dad tells it, your granddad's granddaddy ran up on some hard times way back and none of his sons was much interested in farmin'. Anyway, the family sold that piece of ground to their neighbors across the river. Don't know who they were back then but, somewhere along the line, the Bucks bought it."

"I didn't know that either," Delia said. "No reason why I would, I guess."

"Well, he didn't get to buy it right away. After Buck died there was some kinda legal dispute over it. Anyway, it musta got cleared up because your granddad did buy it." He paused. "Damnedest thing, huh? He buys back the family's property and, right after he buys it, it tries to swallow up him and his tractor."

Delia tried unsuccessfully to stifle a yawn. "Yeah, I'm anxious to hear that story," Delia told him. "But right now, if I don't get to bed, I may just fall asleep here on the table."

Kevin looked at his watch. "Damn, it's late." He began cleaning up. "I'll be outta your hair in a minute," he promised; and five minutes later, after hugging her warmly, he was gone. Then, with Wally following her, Delia carried her suitcases up the darkened staircase to her father's boyhood room.

Chapter 2

Struggling to awaken from the dream, Delia was amazed at how vivid the images remained even after she was fully conscious. Finally, she opened her eyes and saw Wally, sitting by her bed, staring at her. The door to her bedroom was partially opened and through it, Delia saw that her grandfather's bedroom door, across the hall, was also open. Delia noticed that his bed was already made, and then she heard the clatter of dishes from downstairs and smelled coffee and bacon.

"Did he send you here to wake me up?" Delia asked the old dog as she got out of bed. Wally shook his head violently. Delia imagined that her great aunt Eunice had probably tried to banish the dog from her grandfather's bed. Delia could imagine her stern voice. "You keep that dog off the bed, you hear? Don't want him jostling your arm, or trying to lay on you. Won't hurt that dog to sleep on the back porch."

Delia smiled to herself. The chances of her grandfather making Wally sleep on the porch were as likely as him making *her* sleep there. He had found the Lab in a ditch right after her grandmother died. Someone had hit the dog and left him to die. He had picked up the injured animal and nursed him back to health. She remembered him telling her during one of their rare telephone conversa-

14

tions, "Never have to use a leash with him. He's a smart one."

As she made her bed, Delia considered her dream: a lone woman standing atop an earthen mound overlooking a burning city. Not a modern city though. A city of round, thatch-roofed houses in concentric circles that stretched as far as the eye could see. The woman had been holding a staff or a spear; there was something strange about her face, as if she were disfigured in some way. Other images came to her from the dream—a snake with an egg in its mouth, coiling and uncoiling. She walked over to the window, searching her memory, but the dream was fading. As she looked out at the autumn-stubbled fields, however, the sunrise made her recall one last image from the dream: The red sky above the flaming roofs—above a city of burning circles.

A strange dream brought on by her unfamiliar surroundings, Delia thought. Looking at the farmland below, she thought of her uncle Robert in Utah and wondered whether he had finished storing the hay she helped him cut. She knew that, in her absence the twins, Tawny and Will, would help him with the work she had left undone. She imagined the golden foliage of the aspen trees that surrounded her home at Half Moon Lake this time of year, the trees a transitory blaze of color that would soon be stripped by the cold winter winds sweeping down the mountain—a stark contrast to the flat land of the Mississippi Delta they had passed through last night.

A sharp pang of homesickness stabbed Delia as she thought of her home in the Uinta Mountains of northeastern Utah. She imagined that her friend and business partner, Shawla, was probably feeding the llamas and horses or relaxing on the front porch, drinking coffee; Neji and Sam were undoubtedly sprawled at her feet. Delia chided herself; she had only been away from home for a day and already she missed it deeply. Her homesickness was foolish, for she had already begun to pack up her belongings for the annual trip to her maternal grandmother's home in the canyon country of southeastern Utah. She spent the summer months, and part of the autumn, as a wilderness outfitter and guide; however, during the winter months she lived with her maternal grandmother, cousins, nieces and nephews on the Navajo Reservation in Mexican Hat.

She shook her head and turned away from the window: peeled off her flannel sleep pants, T-shirt and socks. Opening the bathroom door, she noticed a full-length mirror; and, as she waited for the water to warm, she appraised herself in it—a rare occurrence. A few months shy of her forty-fifth birthday, she was a solidly built woman of medium height with shoulders broader than most women. She had a V-shaped scar on her cheek, the result of a gun battle with drug dealers in the Uinta Mountains a few years ago. During the shootout, a stray bullet had gouged out a piece of wood from Wild Rose's front porch and embedded itself in her cheek. She had been lucky though. Rose had been shot in the thigh before her half-wolf dog had saved their lives by tearing out the throat of one of the gunmen who would have surely killed them. She had other scars, less visible but just as real. However, she rarely examined them anymore. She had decided long ago that living in the present was challenging enough. Her ghosts were there, but they rarely showed themselves.

Long dark eyelashes fringed her hazel eyes. Her mouth was small, and her bottom teeth were slightly crooked. She considered her nose too large. Her thick wavy hair was still predominantly dark brown, though some were gray now. She kept it cut short in the back and on the sides; it parted naturally on the left, usually falling across her forehead. She had the nervous habit of combing it back with the fingers of her left hand, which made her hair stand up in odd places as if she had numerous cowlicks, or simply never combed her hair. She was usually oblivious to her appearance; it was something she rarely thought about. When she did think about it, she was surprised at how little she cared. Her friends teased her, remarking that she was a rarity among most women in that she cared far more how she felt than how she looked.

As she showered and dressed, she recalled the conversation she had with Kevin last night. Now that she was more rested, she mentally pieced together what he had told her with the conversation that she had with Eunice, her grandfather's sister, two nights ago.

She had just arrived at her uncle Robert's farm, in the Uinta Basin, to help him cut hay: as she had every year since moving to Utah. Pulling into his driveway, she had seen her uncle's wife, Lilah, on the front porch, waving frantically. She quickly parked her truck and hurried up to the house. Lilah was standing in the doorway with the telephone in her hand.

"It's Eunice," she told Delia. Delia's heart had sunk; the last time she had received a phone call from her great aunt, it had been to report the death of her grandmother. Eunice had tried, mostly unsuccessfully, to take care of her oldest brother since then. But, according to Eunice, he had mostly resisted her efforts.

She took the phone from Lilah.

"Eunice?"

"Oh, hello, Dee. Lilah said you'd just pulled in."

"What's wrong? Is Granddad all right?"

"Well, that depends on what you mean by 'all right'," Eunice said in her characteristically brisk, no-nonsense tone. "He's still stubborn and won't listen to reason."

Delia chuckled. Her grandfather and his youngest sister carried on in a continuous verbal battle, their attempt to disguise deep affection from each other. "Well, besides that . . . what's the matter? What's he done?"

"It's a long story, but to put it plainly—he fell off his tractor."

"What was he doing on a tractor?" Delia asked.

"Actually the tractor fell out from under him," Eunice replied cryptically. "What he was doing on a tractor is the long story. You'll have to hear it from him."

"Is he in the hospital?"

"Lord, no! Even if he needed to be in a hospital, I'd have to call the sheriff to put him in handcuffs to get him there. He broke his

17

wrist and he's pretty bruised on one side, but for an old man who fell off a tractor and into a hole, he's doing fine." She paused. "But..."

"But what?" Delia pressed.

"He wants you to come here and see him," her great aunt said.

"He's going to be okay, isn't he?"

"Of course he's going to be all right," Eunice promised. "He's as cantankerous as ever, but he'll be fine."

"Did he tell you why he wants me to come?"

"Dee, he wants to tell you about it himself." She sighed. "I know this is the time of year you usually go to the reservation." She paused again. "I know it's a lot to ask..."

"No, it isn't, Eunice," Delia said firmly. "If he wants me to come—for whatever reason—I'll come. I'd try to come tonight, but I have to take care of a few things first. If I can get a flight from Salt Lake to Memphis tomorrow, I'll be there tomorrow evening. Can someone pick me up in Memphis? Or should I call when I get there?"

"Yes, you call me back when you know what time your flight gets in," Eunice told her. "One of my grandnephews—Kevin—said he would," Eunice assured her. "He's a good driver."

Now, as Delia descended the staircase to the kitchen, the dream she had about the lone woman under the red sky came back to her, like a tendril of smoke from a distant fire. But the smell of coffee pushed the images from her mind as she entered the kitchen.

Her grandfather, Hollis, was sitting at the table reading the newspaper, a cup of coffee beside him. Delia stood in the doorway, hesitating a moment, feeling the apprehension she had avoided talking about to Kevin the previous evening. Just then, her grandfather looked up from his newspaper. Delia noted the black stitches over his left eye and his swollen, bruised cheek. His left wrist was encased in a bright purple cast that ended mid-forearm.

"I wondered when you were gonna come down," he said, rising

18

from his seat, an uncertain smile on his face. "When you didn't wake up after I put on the coffee, I figured I'd better send that old dog to wake you up."

"So—who won?" Delia joked as she embraced him and kissed him lightly on his cheek, careful to avoid the bruise.

"When you tangle with a John Deere tractor, the tractor usually wins," he said.

Delia looked around. "Can I make you some breakfast?" she asked.

"I don't want to trouble you none," he said.

"I'm happy to do it," Delia assured him, as she began gathering food from the refrigerator.

"Bacon, eggs and toast all right with you?"

"Suits me," he said, folding up his newspaper and putting it on the chair beside him.

"Sorry I didn't wait up for you last night."

"It's okay," Delia said, putting some bacon in a frying pan. "Do you like your eggs fried or scrambled?"

"I like 'em fried . . . over easy."

"That's how I like mine too." Delia put some bread in the toaster and put the butter on the table. "How are you feeling, Granddad?"

"Aw, I'm all right. No permanent damage done." He paused a moment and then said, "Count yourself lucky, Sis. If Eunice was here, she'd be bitchin' about cholesterol. That woman is obsessed with what I eat." He shook his head. "She drives me out of what little mind I have left."

Delia continued to fix breakfast, deciding that if her grandfather wanted to complain about Eunice instead of telling her why he had asked her to come, she would not press him. When the food was done, she slid eggs and bacon onto his plate and put the remainder of the food on her plate; then, she poured herself a cup of coffee and sat down.

"Where is Eunice?" Delia asked.

"She's not coming until tonight, thank God. I told her to stay

19

away until then," he said, dipping his toast into an egg yolk. "She got herself a job working at the university, in the audio visual department, half-days usually."

"Sounds like she's doing well," Delia said.

"Aw, she'll probably fill you in on all my transgressions—how I won't eat right or sleep right. How I don't go to church anymore." He snorted derisively. "The only good thing that happened after your grandmother died was that I didn't have to endure sittin' on those hard oak pews in the Methodist church anymore. And I'll be damned if I'm gonna eat some kind bran flakes that taste like cardboard just because my baby sister is worried about my cholesterol." He snorted again. "Funny damn thing—before folks knew about cholesterol and all that nonsense, nobody had a by-pass or other such thing. You were either healthy and you lived, or you were sick and you died." He looked defiantly at Delia. "I guess you think that's craziness."

"I think that's an interesting point," Delia said tactfully. "I'm sure that Eunice is just concerned about you; she wants you to stay healthy."

Hollis Whitaker drained his coffee cup. "Humph," he said. "If I wasn't around, she wouldn't have anything to complain about. She's tried to get me to stop drinking coffee too. And, whenever I have a beer, she frowns at me like I'm sixteen years old."

"How long has she been doing all these things, Granddad?" Delia asked.

"She's been bossy since she started talking," Hollis said. "And she started talking at two."

Delia chuckled and began buttering her toast. "When did Eunice start working at the college?"

"Oh, about a year, year and a half ago," Hollis replied. "She's also taking some courses. History, psychology—what have you. She's having a high old time."

"I think that's great," Delia said sincerely, pouring herself a glass of orange juice.

Hollis shook his head. "It's an interesting notion—waiting to go to college until you're practically senile."

Delia smiled at the idea of her quick-witted great aunt being senile and studied her grandfather. His blue eyes were clear and alert. And though pink scalp showed through his thin white hair, his voice was still firm and vigorous. He looked younger than his nearly eighty-five years, but his face was pale. Perhaps his fall from the tractor had taken more out of him than her great aunt and Kevin had led her to believe.

Her grandfather finished eating and pushed his plate away. He cleared his throat and when he spoke his voice was strong, but Delia detected nervousness in his tone.

"I know you must be wondering why I asked you to come here—right when you were fixin' to go visit your grandmother. But something has happened, and I thought you might be able to help—you being an archaeologist and all."

Delia frowned thoughtfully. "I can't imagine what an archaeologist could help you with, Granddad, but I'll do my best."

"Well, it's a long story, but it all started few years ago when my neighbor—Old Man Buck—died and one of his wife's relatives—fella named Noland—sued Buck's widow for a piece of property that's right next to mine—actually it's on the other side of river."

"Wow," Delia said. "Suing a widow . . . that's pretty low."

"Don't that beat all? But that's typical Bob Noland for you. Did Eunice or I ever mention him to you?"

Remembering Kevin's request that she not say anything to her grandfather about his association with Noland, Delia chose her words carefully. "No, but Kevin mentioned something about Noland giving his cousin John Ed a job."

Her grandfather looked at her sharply. "Kevin didn't say anything about being mixed up with Noland did he?"

"Why?" Delia asked.

"Noland's bad news. Anyhow, those two—Buck and Noland—were always scrappin' about something. Feudin' like some folks

21

do. I didn't pay much attention to it—just waited to see what would happen. When Buck's widow won the lawsuit, I offered her a fair price for the land and she took it." Hollis smiled slightly. "I think she did it mostly to spite Noland—can you imagine? Kinfolk acting like that?" He shook his head.

"Why'd he want it so bad?"

"I don't know," Hollis admitted. "But whatever it was, you can be sure of one thing: it's not anything good."

"Could there be gas or oil on it?"

"I thought of that. I had it surveyed after I bought it and had a friend of mine, from the extension agency, take some soil samples and such. He even had a geologist do some tests. There's no gas or oil."

"Last night Kevin told me that the land used to belong to Whitakers."

"It did . . . a long time ago," her grandfather told her. "My grand-dad, Samuel, sold it off to pay debts he owed the bank after a couple of bad harvests." He shrugged. "It's not a very big piece of ground, only sixty acres. But every time I looked over there, when I was still farming, I'd think, 'That's Whitaker land'."

"But . . . why now?" Delia asked him. "Kevin told me you don't farm much any more. That you just grow alfalfa for some of your friends and relatives in exchange for beef."

Her grandfather frowned slightly. "What else did that knothead tell you?"

"Nothing much, really," Delia assured him. "On the way up here I asked him if he knew the details of the accident . . . what happened to you . . . more than Eunice had told me, which wasn't much."

Her grandfather stood and awkwardly picked up their plates using his good hand. He went to the sink and rinsed them off. He stood still for a moment, simply looking out the window. Then, he turned to face her, leaning against the sink.

"Well, what he told you is true enough. I lease most of my land now to my brother Bill and his kids. The thing is . . . there's just Bill, Eunice, and me now . . . the rest of my brothers and sisters have passed. My kids . . ." He paused a moment, and Delia thought she saw a shine of tears in his eyes, but when he resumed talking, his voice was strong. "I lost your uncle Wendell in Vietnam. The other two boys, Phillip and Huck, left here a long time ago."

Delia nodded. "I remember them, but I don't know what they've been up to since grandma's funeral."

"Phil's in Detroit. He worked for Ford 'til he retired and Huck's in Seattle. He was in the Navy for twenty years and now he's got some kind of security job for the Port of Seattle. All Phil and Huck's kids are scattered here and there . . . none of them are close by. They're all good kids. I don't get to see them that often, but they keep in touch."

Delia cringed inside and though the words, "Unlike you," were unspoken, she knew her grandfather was thinking them.

"I'm sorry Granddad," she said softly. "I should call more often. . . ."

Her grandfather looked at her with an expression she could not read. "No, Sis. It's not your fault. I can't blame you for something that's on me."

"Granddad," she began. But he held up his hand to stop her.

"I'm not done," her grandfather said. "I made up my mind, when I was draggin' myself back to the house after the accident." He cleared his throat. "I realized, I coulda been killed when that tractor fell in the hole. And the only thing I could think of was, 'If I die I'll go to my grave without . . .' Well, without tellin' you some things. The fact of the matter is—I bought that land from Mizz Buck for you."

"For me?" Delia exclaimed. "Why?"

"Now, just hang on a minute, Sis," Hollis instructed her. "I'm fixin' to explain it to you. My will leaves this farm to Bill's kids. I did that because my own sons and grandkids have never showed any interest in farming; and, when I die, I want to know that

Whitakers will still farm this land. My will says that, as long as there are Whitaker descendents that want to farm, this land will pass to them."

"I think that's fine," Delia said. "It seems fair to me."

"I believe it is. But that sixty acres across the river, well, that's my gift to you. I didn't just buy the land; I bought the whole she-bang—the house, outbuildings, everything. Now, the house is pretty run-down, needs a lot of work before you can actually stay in it. But, it's fixable. This way you can come back here any time you want and have a place to stay. Even after me and Eunice and Bill are gone. I wanted you to have something that means some-thing to me."

"But Granddad, I have a business and my own land to take care of," Delia said gently. "I also help Robert, and in the winters, I go down to Mexican Hat to stay with Ruth."

"I know you're close to your mother's kin," her grandfather said. "That's fine. I'm not givin' it to you to try to get you to come here. I don't want it to be a burden for you. I've already talked to Bill and he'll find someone reliable to look after the house—take care of the mowing and just general maintenance. You don't need to fret about that kinda stuff. Course now, when Bill's gone...well, I'm sure one of my nephews or grandnephews would help you out."

"I don't know what to say," Delia confessed. "I'm over-whelmed...it's such a generous thing for you to do."

"Well, I don't know about that," her grandfather growled. "Anyways, all we gotta do is go on down to the mortgage company and sign some papers, then it's yours."

"Well, I'm grateful, but...what's this got to do with me being an archaeologist?"

"I'm gettin' to that part. I'm an old man. At my age it takes me a while to do most everything. First off, over the past sixty years of farming, I've found my share of arrowheads and pottery pieces." He shrugged. "Most times I'd throw 'em in a cigar box or

24

give 'em to the nephews or nieces. Never found much more than that—just a few arrowheads and a few pieces of pottery."

At her grandfather's mention of pottery and arrowheads, Delia's pulse quickened, and she felt a long forgotten excitement welling up inside of her.

"Did you turn up something when you were clearing out the brush?"

"Something is a good way to describe it," her grandfather said, touching his stitches gingerly. "I've never seen anything like it in my life."

"Tell me," Delia said eagerly.

"Well, I was clearin' brush and saplings with the bush-hog down beside the river. I went up over this mound. It didn't really look like much, but it was steeper than I thought. I reckon the ground is soft from all the rain we've had this fall. Anyhow, I went up over the mound when, all of a sudden, the whole rear end of the trac-tor collapsed into a hole. Darn thing started settling down, and when it started leanin', I jumped off. That's when I busted my wrist and got this cut over my eye."

"Where did the tractor end up?" Delia asked.

"About half in and half out of the hole. It would've sunk more if it hadn't got hung up on some logs sticking up out of the ground."

"What did you see in the hole?"

"Looks like a lot of skeletons down there."

"Could they be recent?"

"Don't think so," he said. "They looked pretty old to me. But I didn't get a real close look. My wrist was hurtin' pretty bad and there was blood runnin' down into my eye."

"What else did you see?"

"Well, like I said, nothing much else right then. Tell you the truth; I was pretty shook up from watchin' my John Deere sink into a hole. But the next day, I went back with Bill, and we took a closer look...the skeletons are wrapped up in bundles. Like little mummies." He shook his head. "And we did pick up some other things that we found. I put 'em in a trunk in the spare room... I'll go get 'em."

He got to his feet slowly and went down the hallway, returning shortly with a circular bundle wrapped in a cloth sack.

Delia watched expectantly as her grandfather gently laid the sack on the table.

She looked up at him. "What's in it?"

"See for yourself."

Delia thought for a moment and then asked, "Do you have any disposable gloves around here?" as she spread the newspaper over the table.

"I think I do, matter of fact," he said, walking over to the sink and opening the cabinet door. "When your grandma was real sick there at the end, I bought some. County nurse said it would be a good idea to wear 'em when I took care of her... Ha! Here they are. I knew I still had some." He returned to the table with a box of disposable latex gloves. Delia took out a pair and slipped them on. "I hope I didn't mess anything up by touching them myself," he said doubtfully.

"No," Delia assured him, as she carefully opened the sack, reached in and removed one of the objects. "It's just that sweat contains salts that, over time, can damage the surface. It didn't hurt anything when you touched them. I just don't want to add my sweat too."

She extracted a thin metal plate covered with a crusty green deposit and pieces of, what appeared to be, very old fabric. She pulled out four more plates and lined them up on the opened section of newspaper.

"You put them in this sack?" she asked.

Her grandfather nodded. "Looks like they were in another sack to begin with, but it was rotted completely away."

Delia turned one of the plates over and examined it, careful not to dislodge the small shreds of cloth that still clung to it.

"Copper," she said. "Fibers from the cloth bag that they were originally in have been preserved by the copper's salts. That's good—the cloth can be dated." She frowned as she continued to examine the strangely etched surface.

"What?" her grandfather prompted.

"Oh, nothing," Delia replied. "It's too early to say. But this design—it looks almost Mayan or Aztec. It'll take some cleaning to reveal the design though."

"What do you reckon we should do?" her grandfather asked.

"Anytime you uncover human remains, even if it's obvious that they're very old, you have to notify the authorities. Where do you keep your phone books?" Delia asked.

Hollis pointed to the kitchen cabinet; Delia removed the phone book and began thumbing through the pages.

"There should be a number listed under the 'State of Arkansas' for the 'State Archaeologist'. Sometimes they'll have other numbers listed. Okay," she said. "Here we are. 'To Learn More about Archaeology', 'To Record a New Archaeological Site', okay. To Report an Unmarked Human Burial. 1-555-542-BONE. Cute." She closed the book.

Hollis looked puzzled. "Aren't you going to call them?"

"First I want to see the site," Delia told him, carefully replacing the copper plates in the sack. "Why don't you put these back in your trunk? Does it have a lock?"

"No. You think I oughta lock this stuff up?"

"Oh, it's probably not important right this minute," Delia said. "Maybe we could padlock the trunk later on though."

"I've probably got one somewhere in the garage," he said. "I'll look for it after we get back."

After returning the plates to the trunk, Delia further questioned her grandfather about the mound. "Can you describe it for me?"

"Well, this particular one, that I ran up over, was rectangular and kind of flat on top."

"You mean, like a Mayan pyramid?"

"That'd be a fair description, sure. It was kind of a gentle slope,

27

though. I didn't realize how soft the ground was though, until the dang thing started collapsing."

"Are there any other mounds?"

"Well, the ground isn't just flat everywhere. I noticed that when I looked it over, before I bought it. I'd say there are maybe twelve to fifteen little rises—small ones. I reckon they might all be mounds. The one I drove up over was about fifteen feet high, the others aren't that tall."

"Okay, so you drove up over this large mound and it collapsed?"

"Right. The log the tractor's resting on looks like it might be part of a roof."

"It sounds like a log tomb, but there's only one sure way for me to know what you've uncovered, Granddad," Delia told him. "We'd better just go take a look."

28

Chapter 3

After washing their breakfast dishes, Delia went upstairs and put on her boots, coat and hat. Her grandfather grinned when she descended wearing her father's white cap with the leather brim and canvas duster. As they walked to the garage, her grandfather asked, "Still wearing your dad's old coat and hat?" Delia noted that her grandfather got in on the passenger side without a word.

"All the time," Delia said, accepting the keys from him. "I'm really glad you saved them for me." She noticed him looking at the coat's repaired rips and faded blood stains that the cleaners hadn't been able to remove completely.

"Looks like you got caught up in some barbed wire," her grandfather remarked casually as she backed out of the shed.

"I had a run-in with drug dealers up in the mountains a couple of years ago." Delia said.

"Drug dealers?"

"It's a long story. I'll tell you some time while I'm here. How do we get to the field?"

"We'll drive along the ditch down to that first field, then cross the bridge."

Delia's grandparents' white frame house was perched atop a gently rising hill. Her great-great-paternal grandfather, Samuel

Joel Whitaker, had built the original house, which had been built on the banks of the Big Right Hand River, in 1874. It had been washed away in a flood during the 1920's. When he rebuilt, he situated his new home on a knoll overlooking his 3,000-acre farm. Surrounded by pin oak trees, the back of the house was nearly flush with the hill. The outbuildings were located in front and down the hill.

The "new" house, as future generations of Whitakers would call it, was larger than the original structure. And in the 1940's, her great grandfather had added a spacious porch that encircled the entire house, from which any Whitaker could see all of the family's land, right down to the river's edge. Delia remembered her father telling her that the screened-in portion of the porch often doubled as a bedroom for him, and his three brothers, during the summer when he was growing up. The summers in northeast Arkansas were long, hot, and humid. And before the advent of air conditioning, sleeping outside to escape the heat was common. Delia believed that her father's boyhood memories of sleeping on the porch, accounted for the one he had built onto his cabin at Half Moon Lake where she now lived.

White oak, hickory, and black gum trees grew along the river and partially shielded from view the property that Delia was finding hard to consider hers. As they drove along the tree line that bordered its fields, Delia questioned him further.

"Granddad, do you know—has this field ever been cultivated?"

"Well, I know that Old Man Buck never planted anything down here. Now, some time back the land was probably cleared—most of the woods in this county were sold off for timber and then replanted with pine trees, mostly. But Buck's land was never cultivated, that I remember anyway. Somebody might've planted something a long time ago, but it hasn't been recent." He looked at Delia. "What're you driving at?"

"I'm just wondering . . . if the land had been plowed, then the mounds might have been reduced in size or shape. Of course, sometimes there are intrusive burials—they bury people in the middle or on top after the tomb is buried under a lot of earth."

"Don't forget about the Big Flood of '27. It carried off a lot of ground." He frowned. "You know, I just remembered something. The flood of '27 killed some folks, mostly along the river. And course it washed away our house. I was just a little boy then, only seven, but I wanted to come down here and see the water." He shook his head remembering.

"Really?" Delia asked. "Before the flood took the farmhouse?"

"Yeah. That was a sad day, like to broke my dad's heart. Anyway, before that happened, us kids were crazy to see the river. My brothers told me there was all kinds of dead animals floating down the river—dead cows, and horses, even buildings, like chicken coops and sheds."

"That must have been scary."

Her grandfather smiled and shook his head. "Naw, we was boys...we wanted to see some excitement. Anyway, my dad told us the river carried diseases...what with all the dead animals floating around. Later on, after we came back to rebuilt, he told us that some folks who lived across the river, on this property, had lost two kids in the flood—a boy and girl. They never found their bodies. That scared me enough to mind my dad."

"It's sad that they never found their children's bodies," Delia commented.

"The river just took 'em." He mused, "My brothers tried to scare me sometimes after that. Told me this land over here was haunted by the boy and girl."

"A local legend," Delia said. "A ghost story."

"Yeah, mostly told by kids and teenagers, young men wantin' to scare their girlfriends. But, it musta died out finally; I haven't heard anyone mention it for years...I'd forgotten all about it myself til just now."

The truck hit a pothole and Delia said, "By the way, how did you get back to the house after the tractor tipped over? It seems like a long way from this field to your house."

"I walked," he told her matter-of-factly. "Took me a while, but I managed."

"Is the tractor still in the hole?"

"Yeah, I had Kevin and my brother Bill run a couple steel cables to it so it wouldn't sink on down into the hole. It's actually wedged in there pretty good, but a John Deere's a mighty expensive piece of machinery to just leave hanging there, you know? We tied it to a big tree on the edge of the field. I'm gonna get Kevin to come down here and winch it out, but I wanted you to get a look at it first. Didn't want to do any more damage to it."

He stopped talking and pointed to the narrow wooden bridge that crossed the river, and Delia drove across the rickety structure. As they crossed over the muddy water, Delia noticed an old but sturdy looking shed at the edge of the tree line along the river.

"What's that shed used for?" Delia asked.

"Just an old fishing shack. Why?"

"No reason," Delia assured him. "Be good to have a shed like that if you were excavating." She paused. "Is there much pot hunting around here?"

"Usual amount, I guess. It's against the law, but folks still do it. Mostly nobody really cares. It's a way some people make extra money."

Delia nodded. "Let's just keep it to ourselves, then, until I look at the site and see what the State Archaeologist has to say."

Following her grandfather's directions, Delia turned onto a road that paralleled the field. From it, she could see the tractor, or at least part of it. The back half was indeed sunk into a hole. As she drove closer, Delia saw large broken timbers sticking out of the hole. She pulled up a few yards away, and she and her grandfather alighted from the truck. The ground underfoot was soggy, and as they climbed the incline to the top of the mound, Delia noted that there were objects near the surface of the pit.

When they reached the tractor, Delia knelt down. Her knee sinking into the wet soil, she picked up a large potsherd. Turning the pottery fragment over in her hand, she noted a distinctive crosshatching around its rim. A few yards further ahead, she saw another mud-encrusted cylindrical object protruding from the ground. She came to it and reached down to pick it up.

"What is it?" her grandfather asked, looking over her shoulder.

"I'm not sure," Delia admitted. She touched her finger to her tongue and cleared a small spot on the object. "It looks like a flute or pipe," she said, putting it gently back into the same spot where she had found it. Next she picked up some arrow points and round stones, flat on one face and convex on the other. Delia examined each one carefully before putting them back down.

"Aren't you going to pick up this stuff and take it back?"

Delia shook her head. "I want to record where things are before I pick anything else up or remove what I've touched. I'd like to take pictures of the tomb, too." She frowned. "I don't like leaving this stuff exposed out here, but I don't have a camera."

"I've got a pretty good Leica up at the house," her grandfather offered. "It's old, but it still takes good pictures. Think it's got film in it, too."

"That'd be great, Granddad. If I could photograph these artifacts, it would help whoever excavates it later. I could use a tarp to cover up the opening." She looked at his arm. "Are you sure you can drive with your arm like that?"

In answer to her question, her grandfather began walking down the slope toward the truck, muttering, "I could drive back to the house with both my legs cut off."

After her grandfather left, Delia walked to the top of the mound and examined the hole that had nearly swallowed his tractor. He was right—if the back end had not become hung up on exposed timber, the whole tractor would have fallen into the hole. Delia suppressed the urge to get down on her hands and knees to look deeper in the hole. The ground around the edges of the opening was wet and probably unstable. However, by leaning at the waist and craning her neck, she could see a little of what her grandfather had described earlier.

Through the broken, crumbling timbers Delia could see wrapped bundles. Some of the wrappings had rotted, or been torn loose, exposing skeletons. Bones protruded from their wrappings. It was clear to her trained eye that her grandfather had unwittingly disinterred a small burial mound; what she was looking at were the long-dead occupants of a tomb.

The realization rekindled an excitement and long-repressed desire to practice the skills she had trained so hard for and which, for years had been taken from her. Since being denied tenure at the eastern university where she had taught for five years, Delia had not picked up trowel or shovel, taught a class or directed an excavation. Her wilderness outfitting business kept her busy through most of the year. But, as she stared down into the burial mound and smelled the wet earth, Delia realized how fiercely she had repressed her love and passion for her profession.

She turned around in a complete circle, looking for the other small rises that her grandfather had told her about. Then she stood up and began descending the mound. When the ground collapsed under her grandfather, it started a chain reaction: to the left side of the hole, a long ragged trench had opened up, exposing more artifacts.

Delia walked carefully, noting small bones, more potsherds, shells and stones. She followed the trench until she found herself at the river's edge. At the place where the ditch intersected the bank of the river, there was another large hole where the bank had totally collapsed. Delia noted that the cave-in of the riverbank had caused a tree to fall into the water, exposing its entire root structure.

Wondering if the collapse of the riverbank might have uncovered more artifacts, Delia clamored down the embankment until she was standing on a narrow sand spit at the water's edge. Peering through earth-clumped and tangled roots, she saw more broken timbers and broken pots. Looking more closely, she made out one large, miraculously unbroken pot hanging precariously from a network of twisted roots. She reached in and carefully pulled it out.

The pot was a deep ocher color, formed in the shape of a human head—"called an effigy pot," Delia recalled. The facial features were delicate, feminine; the ears were tiny and well formed; holes were pierced all along the outside of the ear, from the lobe all the way around. The lips were well formed, the nose small and unbroken; the eyes were closed, mere slits. An unusual design, perhaps indicating a tattoo or scarification, was etched into the strangely dreamy expression on the face: the design covered the entire left cheek and circled both eyes.

As she examined the jar she experienced a feeling of deja vu. Her attempts to recover the memory caused it to slip away. It was a frustrating, yet somehow affirming, sensation—as though the jar was already part of her consciousness and experience. Yet, she asked herself doubtfully, how could this face on this pot—that hadn't seen the light of day for hundreds, maybe even thousands of years—be familiar to her? In all her years of excavating and researching artifacts, she had never had such a feeling.

Reaching in her pants pocket, Delia found her penknife and scraped away some of the dirt to reveal a serpent in the act of uncoiling; its jaws were open and in their clasp was an oval shape. Delia had seen serpent designs before; serpent imagery in combination with a circle, egg, or globe was common symbology among many ancient civilizations and was usually associated with feminine energy or goddess worship. But the feeling of having seen the face and the design was even more immediate and familiar. She turned the jar over in her hands again and again, and finally it struck her. She remembered: It was the face of the woman in her dream! The image became clear to her; and she could see the woman's tattooed face, stained red by the flames from the burning houses: Burning circles under the red sky.

Delia entertained the fanciful notion for a few seconds before rejecting it. Such a thing was unlikely, if not downright ridiculous, and the scientist in her dismissed it out of hand. However, Delia could not dismiss the excitement she felt holding the object. It was a feeling that she had made herself forget—a feeling that she missed and now remembered from childhood as she recalled watching her father excavate the bones of dinosaurs, mastodons and other prehistoric beasts. A feeling she remembered having on her first digs in Turkey and northern Iran. It was a feeling of accomplishment, one that came after hard work and sacrifice, endless hours of back-breaking labor over a small area of dirt with a trowel or brush to expose the history of the human race. The face of the woman with the serpent tattoo from her dream flashed briefly in her mind and then was gone.

Delia felt overwhelmed by emotion. She sat down on a nearby log and tears rolled down her face. Aside from the death of her parents, being denied tenure and then being forced from her job were the most painful experiences that she had endured. Only she, her uncle Robert, and Shawla, knew how close the personal disappointment and professional devastation had come to destroying her life. The process of healing had not yet included a return to the profession she had loved so much, though Beth Collins had taught her to love and trust again. The thought of Beth caused Delia to feel a pang of sadness.

In the end, they were unable to salvage their relationship: unable to negotiate the separation that resulted from Delia's living on an isolated mountaintop and Beth's living in a high-rise apartment in downtown Chicago. Beth was an ambitious, highly motivated stockbroker. The fast-paced world of finance was in her blood and, in the end, she couldn't give it up—not even for Delia's love. Delia stood up and brushed off her pants. The demise of her relationship with Beth had been no one's fault. They were still close and talked to each other at least once a month.

But the pain still lingered.

Delia pushed aside sad thoughts of Beth and turned back to the pot she held in her hand. She knew that many archaeological discoveries were accidental—an ordinary man, or woman, in the course of daily activities, with a shovel or plow, turned up important archaeological finds—she marveled at the series of events that had brought her to this place.

Because one man died and another was stubborn enough to want to clear some land, despite his advanced years, she was sitting on a stump beside a river, engaged once again in the practice of archaeology—an event she had thought would never happen again.

Delia was stirred from her ruminations by the sound of her grandfather's truck returning. She began climbing the embankment. She had work to do.

Chapter 4

That evening, after a much-needed shower, Delia sat at the dinner table and talked to her grandfather while Eunice did the dishes. Delia had cleared the table and offered to help wash, but her aunt had shooed her away.

"We didn't have you come all this way to help with the housework," Eunice told her, pouring two cups of coffee. "Put some milk in your Granddad's coffee and go visit with him."

Following her great aunt's instructions, Delia took the cups over to the kitchen table. She and her grandfather sipped in companionable silence for a while, and then Hollis said: "So, what's next?"

"Did you put the artifacts we picked up today in your trunk?" Delia asked him.

Hollis nodded. "Do you think you got some decent pictures today?"

"I think so," Delia said. "I'm not sure how well I did with the light meter. I haven't used one of them in a long time. We'll see. I'm getting them developed tomorrow morning at a one-hour photo place I found in the Yellow Pages."

"What's the plan?" Eunice asked, joining them at the table with her own cup of coffee.

"Well, I called the State Archaeologist this afternoon and got a recording—apparently the funding for the State Archaeologist's department has been cut, and the guy isn't there very much. Anyway, the recording said to get in touch with the Archaeology Department on the campus of Northeast. I'll go in there tomorrow—hopefully someone will be around. I need to talk to someone who's familiar with this region, get some people out here to look at the site and see what they have to say. They'll probably send out the coroner and the sheriff."

"What for?" Eunice asked. "Those folks have been dead a long time from the way you all describe it."

"In this case it seems pretty obvious, but sometimes it's not," Delia told her. "I have friends who are forensic archaeologists. They get some pretty interesting situations from time to time, especially when it's not obvious that the remains are recent." She shrugged. "At any rate, it doesn't matter what we think—it's the law. We have to notify the authorities and go from there based on what they say."

"If the remains are pretty old, will there be an excavation?" Hollis asked.

She spread her hands. "It's possible the state, or maybe even the university, may have funds to conduct an excavation—if they think the site is important. It's hard to say at this point because I'm not sure what the law is in Arkansas. Each state is different."

"Seems to me you're doing okay by yourself so far," Eunice said.

Delia shook her head. "I don't know very much about the archaeology of this area. Most of my work has been in the Middle East. There will be people at Northeast who are experts though." Delia looked at her grandfather and wondered whether to share her apprehension about visiting the archaeology department at the university. Studying his tired face, pale against the dark stitches, she decided against it. "You look exhausted, Granddad. Maybe you should turn in."

"I'm all right," he countered. "A little tired, but not bad."

"When do you get your stitches out?"

"Couple days," he answered. "Glad you're here to take care of this—appreciate you coming all this way."

Delia looked at her grandfather and decided to ask him the question that had troubled her ever since he had shown her the tomb.

"Granddad, I'm more than happy to come and help you with this. But, why did you ask me to come here when you could easily have handled this yourself?"

At first Delia was worried that she might have offended him; it was the last thing she wanted to do. But as she studied his expression, she recognized it as one that her father had often worn—one of surprise that she had asked such an obvious question. He stood up and said, "Let's you and me go into the front room and talk."

Delia looked over at Eunice.

"Go on, Dee," she said lightly. "Lord knows, he's talked more since you got here than he has in the last ten years."

"You talk enough for both us," her grandfather growled at Eunice as he left the kitchen. Delia picked up her coffee cup and followed him. He sat down in his recliner with a sigh, and Delia took the armchair next to him.

"Okay," she said. "You could have looked up that number in the phone book as easily as I did. Why did you want me to come here?"

"Your father was one of the top paleontologists in the world," he told her. "He didn't get to be the best by thinking the same as everyone else. I was as proud of him as a father could be. Do you think if your father was still around and I found a dinosaur skeleton in my field I would call anyone else?"

"This is different," Delia said. "Dad didn't have to leave his job in disgrace."

"Well, I . . ." Her grandfather began. "I admit when I first heard about what happened to you . . . I didn't know what to think. But I've had some time to turn all that over in my mind now." He

40

paused. "I'm not getting any younger, you know."

"Granddad, you don't have to explain..." Delia said.

"No, now I'm talking, let me finish. I haven't done right by you. After that mess with your job happened, I should have called. That's what family does during hard times...they stick together and support each other. I just...well, I didn't know what to say to you. And by the time I figured it out, you were gone and nobody knew where you'd got off to...I was pretty worried. I finally found one of your mother's kin—Robert—and...well, you know what next."

Delia was stunned. "Robert never said anything about you looking for me," she told him. "Not that I remember."

"I told Eunice to tell Robert not to tell you," he admitted. "I know that sounds crazy, but by that time...hell, I didn't know what to say to you. 'I'm sorry' just didn't seem good enough."

"I thought the reason you didn't call me is because you were embarrassed...even ashamed of me," Delia said. "Granddad, I didn't do the things they accused me of. You know that, don't you? I would never salt a dig. It's a stupid thing to do and people who do it always get caught eventually."

"Good Lord, no. I didn't think anything like that. My son didn't raise a daughter who would try to lie about finding artifacts. It never once crossed my mind that you did what those bastards said you did. It was...all the other stuff."

Delia opened her mouth to speak but her grandfather continued to speak. "Hear me now, Dee." He shook his head in disgust. "It just beats all how some folks think they have the right to poke their noses into other people's personal business. That's why I can't abide politics anymore. Used to be, your personal life was private. People might gossip and say things about you, but decent folks kept their dang mouths shut." He made a sound of disgust and Delia's heart sank. She should have known that her grandfather would have these feelings, but it hurt nonetheless. However, his next words surprised her.

"This country is going to hell in a hand basket and all that the politicians want to do is try to get people to not look at the facts. It's all a diversion. When you're doing something wrong, that you don't want people to know about, you create a diversion to keep people's attention away from your own evil actions. And I figure, that's what happened to you at that college."

"I don't know what they were doing, Granddad," Delia told him. "But one thing was pretty clear to me . . . they wanted to get rid of me. When people like that want to get rid of someone, they'll find a way to do it. But I appreciate what you said . . . it means a lot to me."

"Well, I figured what I turned up with the bush-hog might be important. Way I see it, might as well be you that digs it up as anybody else." He smiled. "After all—it's your land."

Eunice came into the room, drying her hands on her apron and looked at the two of them. "Well, will wonders never cease? That's the first time I've seen him with anything other than a scowl on his face in weeks."

"Oh, be quiet, old woman. Nobody asked your opinion," Hollis grumbled.

Eunice raised her eyebrows. "You don't scare me, brother. You're all bark and no bite." She turned to Delia. "I have to agree with him, though, Dee. No reason why you shouldn't do it. Surely nobody else around here is half as qualified."

Delia finally began to understand. "I really appreciate your confidence in me—both of you—but even if the archaeology department has funds, which they usually don't, it takes more than one person to excavate a site. I couldn't do it alone."

"I know that," Hollis said. "Your father's life insurance policy—you remember when he died, I told you that you were the beneficiary."

"I remember," Delia said. "I told you I didn't want the money that came from his death."

"I know," her grandfather said. "That's why I put it in a mutual fund in your name. It's been there for a while now. Called the bank the other day—it's worth a good bit of money now. I know that your dad would want you to use it for something like this. If you decide you want to stick around and look into this, all you've got do is go down to the bank and get the money. Far as you getting around while you're here, I've got an ATV that I haven't used in a couple years out in the shed. Might need new spark plugs and a change of oil, but otherwise it'll get you back and forth to the site."

"And we thought if you're going to be staying you'd probably want to be closer to the excavation than this house," Eunice added eagerly. "Your great grandma lived in a trailer house and after she died, nobody wanted it; so Bill and your granddad pulled it out here. It's nice enough, a little dusty inside, but I can fix that."

"We figured we'd pump up the tires and haul it down to the field for you," Hollis told her. "That way you don't have to spend all your time runnin' back and forth twixt here and there."

"That's not to say we don't want you here at the house," Eunice assured her. "I'm cooking for Hollis and cooking for three isn't any more trouble than cooking for two. So at night we expect you for dinner at six. You can bring your dirty clothes up here too, and I'll throw them in with Hollis's things."

"I don't know what to say," Delia said hoarsely.

Now it was Hollis's turn to be embarrassed; he stood up and awkwardly patted Delia's shoulder. "No need to say anything," he assured her. "Guess I better be gettin' on to bed now." He looked around for Wally, who was under the table, and said: "Come on, boy." He turned to Delia. "You better get some sleep too, Sis, if you're going to town tomorrow."

After Hollis had gone to bed, Delia sat with her great aunt.

"I'm not kidding, Dee," Eunice said. "He's been in a funk—even before he fell in that hole. He's perked up since you're here." She patted Delia's hand. "If you can stay, we'd sure like having you."

43

After Eunice had gone home and Delia went up to bed, she considered her earlier apprehensions about going back to the university. She told herself that her nervousness was understandable; the male-dominated archaeological community had never welcomed her theories about women's roles in warrior cultures. That her publications were popular and drew the praise of the women's community, put her picture on the cover of magazines, and landed her spots on talk-shows, had made her even more suspect in the narrowly prescribed academic field of archaeology—a field presided over by mostly white men whose primary interest was the perpetuation of a patriarchal view of history and culture.

As a woman with a Native-American heritage, Delia's theories were scorned by male colleagues as "untenable;" her excavation sites decried as "a three-ring circus with Ironfoot as the ring-master." She was called a "publicity-hound," accused of "self-promotion," and once, a sympathetic male colleague had sheepishly told her that the men in her field had coined a new term for her feminist approach: "pussy-archaeology." Finally, there had been the stunning charge of falsifying artifactual evidence. The accusation prompted the university's denial of her promotion and tenure and her career was shattered. Since then, Delia hadn't set foot on a college campus, had not granted interviews, or answered the letters and phone calls that occasionally came from universities or museums interested in either hiring her or inviting her to lecture.

Now, going over the memories that she had tried so hard to forget, Delia wondered if her grandfather understood how tempting it was for her to become involved in her profession again or how painful involvement might be.

Delia awakened in the night, her sleep again interrupted by the dream of the Tattooed Serpent woman standing on the earthen mound—the burning city below and the red sky above. Heart pounding, Delia lay quietly as the images of the dream again faded rapidly now that she was fully awake. However, she was more familiar with the dream now, and Delia found herself recalling additional details. The woman with the serpent tattoo was hurrying down a narrow, dark street. As she ran, she looked back over her shoulder and saw the flames staining the night sky red. In her hand the women grasped a wooden staff topped with an elaborate copper ferrule in the shape of a hawk with spread wings and an open beak posed in a silent scream. Emerging from the narrow street, the woman came to a cluster of nine or ten houses, similar to the others in the city but larger, the wood painted in bright colors. Over and down the sides of their doorways, carved into the wood, was the same uncoiling serpent design that the young woman wore tattooed on her face. The woman stood over the young chief, shaking him awake and pulling him from his sleep mat. Then, they were both running through the city. And finally, the young people stood on a large mound overlooking the searing flames. The man wore a copper armband on his left bicep, again the uncoiled serpent with an oval in its open jaws, a reflection of the design on the woman's face. The two stood close together, their shoulders nearly touching—their expressions a study in contrasts. The woman watched the destruction of the city with the same dreamy, almost peaceful expression, as that on the head pot that Delia had recovered from the roots of the tree.

The young man's boyish features were twisted in agony as he watched his people, their hair and clothing aflame, running through the streets like macabre torches. Suddenly, the dream shifted again and Delia saw the young warrior, his face contorted by rage, running toward the burning houses. In one hand he carried a polished stone mace, which he swung over his head as he waded into the battle, screaming. Crushing the skulls of the invading warriors, the young man threw himself into the blood fight with uncontrolled fury.

When he lost his stone mace, he grabbed two copper axes that lay amidst the broken and bloodied bodies of his fallen people and took up the defense of his city again. Hacking at the enemy with both axes, he cleared a path for himself and the few young men he had rallied to his side. They fought their way toward the central plaza and the temple. It was here that the enemy had herded the women, and some children, of the city.

As she woke, she tried to shake off the effects of what had become a disturbing, even horrifying dream; Delia got out of bed and walked to the small round window that overlooked her grandfather's land. The empty fields were bathed in light from the huge melon-colored moon. Standing by the sill, her feet grew cold on the bare planks, and Delia pondered the dream's possible meaning.

Perhaps she had seen a pot like the one she had uncovered today in a book or exhibit sometime before. The rational scientist part of her nature struggled with the disquieting certainty that she felt earlier in the afternoon as she held the head-pot in her hands. That she had seen the face of the woman before. Not in a book, not in a museum, but in her dream. Delia pushed this notion from her mind firmly. Turning away from the window, she shuffled across the cold floor and crawled back into bed. Her dream of the woman, the burning city, and the red sky did not return, and she slept soundly.

Chapter 5

The next morning, Delia dressed in khaki pants, a flannel shirt, and her well-worn Red Wing boots. Eager to be on her way to the university, she nearly tripped over Wally who lay in a block of sunlight outside her bedroom door. Delia bent down and briefly dug her hand into his fur, missing her own dog, Neji. Images from her dream and the nervous apprehension that she felt the previous night had faded. She was now anxious to get on with her new work. She thought that perhaps her high spirits were based on the knowledge that if she decided to excavate the burial site, she would not be dependent on anyone, especially not on an archaeology department or university for funds. And therefore, she would be under no pressure. She could reveal truth with her findings, whatever that truth might be. This thought made her feel even more anxious to get underway.

She and Wally joined her grandfather in the kitchen and while Delia again fixed breakfast for them, she told him of her decisions and immediate plans.

"I was thinking last night after we talked, I should call my lawyer in Utah and ask about the possibility of setting up a non-profit foundation with the money Dad left. Even if I don't personally direct the excavation, you could hire a contract archaeology firm to do it. Anyway, I'll tell her to look into the logistics of the whole thing and let me know. Is that okay with you?"

"Sounds fine to me," Hollis said. He dug into his pants pocket and pulled out a set of keys. "Your grandmother's Taurus is out there in the garage. I just haven't gotten around to selling it yet. I keep up with it pretty regularly. It's ready to drive. Figured you'd need your own transportation while you're here." He handed her the keys and said, "I know you're busy and all. You have your own life, but—well, I wouldn't mind having you around for a while."

Delia put her arm around her grandfather's shoulder. "I know what you mean, Granddad. I'd like to see more of you, too."

"Got the film you took yesterday?" he asked.

"Got it," she replied.

After cleaning up the breakfast dishes, Delia donned her duster and cap, carefully put the various artifacts into a canvas duffel, and set off for Crowley's Ridge and the campus of Northeast Arkansas State University.

The drive from her grandfather's farm to Crowley's Ridge was a brief twenty minutes, and she was happy to see that the one-hour photo store was next door to a small coffeehouse. After handing over her film to the clerk, she went next door and had a surprisingly good cup of cappuccino while waiting for her photos. An hour later, she drove to the university and looked for a parking place in the visitor's lot. It was a few minutes before the hour; many students were leaving, and she easily located one.

As she walked toward the Earth Science building that housed the departments of Archaeology and Anthropology, Delia remembered the only other time she had ever visited the campus of Northeast. Her father, Jack, an alumnus of the university, had distinguished himself as one of the world's foremost dinosaur bone hunters. Because of that distinction, after his death, his alma mater had announced that the new Paleontology wing of the Earth Science building would be named after him. Delia had been invited to the ceremony, along with her grandparents and Eunice. She remembered how proud they had been of the honor bestowed on her father.

Northeast Arkansas State University was located in the far northeast corner of Arkansas. Surrounded by flat delta country, the university was a land grant college founded in 1887. Its primary mission was to educate the sons and daughters of the cotton, soybean and rice farmers from the surrounding countryside. This legacy was reflected in the old cement arch at the center of the campus. It still bore the original name of the university—Northeast A and M College. As Delia walked along the pine and magnolia tree lined sidewalks, she noted that the majority of students wore the faded jeans, baseball caps, fraternity or sorority sweatshirts, and athletic shoes typical of their young and carefree, not yet professionally obligated, generation.

Delia entered the Earth Science building and consulted the directory. The Archaeology Department and Archaeological Survey were both located on the third floor. When she reached the top of the stairs Delia looked to the right and saw a long dimly lit corridor lined with cardboard and clear plastic boxes. She had found the department she was looking for. Every archaeology department in the world was short on storage space, and artifacts ended up being stored in any available nook and cranny—usually in hallways, basements and empty offices.

Delia smiled slightly and walked down the hallway until she reached a door that read: DEPARTMENT OF ANTHROPOLOGY & ARCHAEOLOGY. She opened it and walked into a large empty room with cement floors. Once painted an institutional gray, it was now largely bare of any color. Long wooden tables filled the center of the room and ramshackle shelving lined the ugly, yellow walls. A few fly-speckled signs asked people to "PRESERVE ARKANSAS'S HERITAGE" and "REPORT ILLEGAL EXCAVATIONS". Though the room was empty, Delia could hear voices from another room off to the left and walked in their direction. Unlike the room she had been in previously, this one was brightly lit and contained two desks with phones and computers. A man was seated at one of the desks, talking on the phone. He was a large man, going a little soft in the middle, with unruly gray hair that fell onto his forehead. A pair of muddy work boots rested on a piece of newspaper atop the desk in front of him.

"No, see that just isn't gonna happen, Bob." Pausing to listen to the voice on the other end, he hesitated before adding, "Well, I'd hate that, but it could, you know? Let me know what you decide. I'll be up at the site in Parkin. Okay."

He hung up the phone and glanced up at Delia. "Help you?" He opened his desk drawer and began rummaging through the contents.

Delia took off her hat and ran her hand through her hair. "I hope so. I need to report a burial site."

The man smiled condescendingly, not looking up at her. Then, he removed a pair of reading half-glasses from his shirt pocket and placed them on the bridge of his nose. With a pencil from the drawer, he began making notations on a piece of paper. "Find some bones did you?" he asked. His tone of voice was that usually reserved for asking children if they'd found money the tooth fairy left under their pillow.

Delia repressed her irritation at his tone. He would be more likely to help her if they didn't start on the wrong foot. Yet, his attitude toward her was reminiscent of the way males in her field had treated her during her career that she felt a long repressed anger well up inside her. She pushed it down, paused for a moment, then said mildly, "Well, not me. My grandfather found them."

The man continued making notes on his paper and glanced up at her again. "They're most likely animal bones," he said flatly, flipping over the piece of paper and continuing to write. "Most folks see animal bones, and they think they're human, but it's not true."

Delia fought an urge to grab the pencil out of his hand. Instead she merely said, "I know these aren't animal bones. My grandfather was clearing some land and collapsed a log tomb."

"Well, I can take a look at them for you, but I'm telling you, ninety-nine percent of the time? They're..."

"Animal bones," Delia completed his sentence. She was beginning to lose the battle with her slowly building anger, and she heard some of it in her voice when she spoke. "I called the State Archaeologist in Fayetteville and the recording told me to report the remains here." She pulled the recently developed photographs from of her duffel bag and spread them on top of the papers he had been writing on where he couldn't ignore them. It was childish, she admitted, but it was either that or lose her temper, something she had learned not to do. "I think this might be a pan pipe, and my grandfather also uncovered five copper plates. Unfortunately, the exact spot in the stratigraphy can't be determined but that couldn't be helped."

Now, the man looked up at her, studying her face and frowning. Delia could tell by his expression that he wasn't used to having his judgment questioned, and she wondered if he might simply order her out of his office. Instead, he finally looked down at the photographs, albeit distractedly. "You seem to know something about archaeology. Take a few courses through the extension, did you?"

"I know a little something about archaeology," Delia said simply.

Now, the man studied her more intently, and Delia saw the look of belated recognition. "Hey, I recognize you...you're..."

Delia extended her hand. "Delia Ironfoot, Jack Whittaker's daughter."

He took her hand reluctantly and said, "Jim Kincaid. Your father was a good man. I was sorry to hear about his death. So, you say it's a log tomb, huh? How do you figure that?"

Delia shrugged. "I've excavated log tombs before. Though not around here." She pointed to the photographs. "What about the burial site?"

"You say your grandfather was clearing some land. Whereabouts is this property?"

Delia sat down, though he had not invited her to do so. "This is land my granddad bought just recently. It's adjacent to his property, which is along the Big Right Hand."

Kincaid looked up sharply. "What's that? Where?"

"It's a sixty acre parcel across the river from my granddad's farm. From what he's told me, the land hasn't been cultivated, at least not in recent times."

"The *Buck* property?" Kincaid asked.

"Yes," Delia answered him. "Why? What's the problem with that?"

"Nothing, per se," Kincaid said curtly. "It's just that . . . there's an Arkansas law that protects human remains. House Bill 1479, passed in 1991. Says you can't excavate unmarked burial sites—even on private land. It's been pretty hard to enforce though. People can pretty much do whatever they want if the authorities don't know about it." He paused, gathering himself. "I hope you did nothing to compromise the site."

"Of course not," Delia replied defensively. She had been about to show him the copper plates, but decided against it. "I'm not an amateur archaeologist. There were some surface objects that were exposed when the roof collapsed. I photographed them and then picked them up. My grandfather has them stored in a trunk."

She explained what had happened when her grandfather had uncovered the tomb. When she finished, she said, "I assumed Arkansas had an antiquities law that stipulates certain conditions before you can excavate."

Kincaid shook his head and glared up at her. "You should have known better than to go tramping around the site."

Now Delia's anger bubbled to the surface. "Hey, Granddad's bush-hog and tractor collapsed the top of the tomb. I followed conventional procedures. I took pictures of them before I picked them up. I couldn't just leave them on the surface." She paused and pushed her anger down. More calmly she asked, "What procedure do I need to go through if I want to excavate the site?"

"There's a board—the American Indian Cultural Center in Little

Rock. Kate Treadaway, down the hall, handles all those requests. She can give you the information you'll need to contact them and outline the steps they require."

"Thanks," Delia said. "My grandfather will be relieved to know it's taken care of properly." Delia paused. "I was also hoping to get your opinion about the site—have you look at it. Perhaps you could give me some advice about getting interested amateurs and a few graduate students to help. It would be a good field school opportunity for the summer, for the grad students—give them some experience, and give me some help."

Kincaid pushed back his chair. "Look, Miss Ironfoot," Kincaid said, deliberately omitting the "Dr." or "Professor" to which Delia was entitled. "I don't have time to help you or lend you any grad students. We're excavating a site in Parkin right now...my plate is full already."

Delia felt her face getting red and knew it was time to go. "I wasn't asking you to drop everything and *help* me. I simply thought as a professional favor..."

Kincaid glowered at her. "You don't have any professional standing," he snarled. "I certainly don't consider you a professional colleague. The charges brought against you were serious enough for your university to dismiss you. So, I can't imagine why you think I would allow any of my graduate students to work with you." He tossed the photographs across his desk. "For all I know, you planted these artifacts. Maybe you think you can revive your tarnished career by salting another site." He sneered. "Take my advice: go on back to wherever you came from and leave the excavating to reputable professionals."

"What?" she exclaimed angrily, jumping to her feet. Old rage swirled inside her like a whirlpool as she swept the photos from his desk, shoving them back into her duffel. "That's crazy and you know it." Delia picked up her hat and jammed it on her head. "I've directed over twenty excavations during my career. I have a net-work of friends and colleagues. I can have all the materials and volunteers I need here, on site, within forty-eight hours."

Picking up her duffel bag, she strode angrily out of Kincaid's office, slamming the door behind her. She tried to calm herself, but she was so angry and intent on getting far away from Jim Kincaid that she didn't see the woman coming down the hallway until they collided. The woman was carrying a file folder, which flew into the air, scattering papers all over the floor. Mumbling apologies, Delia bent down to help her pick them up. When she straightened, she found herself face to face with a beautiful young woman.

The woman looked at Delia with brown eyes fringed with thick amber lashes. Her face was deeply tanned, an obvious testament to her outdoor profession. While she was not what most people would call beautiful, her lips were beautifully full. But it was the tawny mane of unruly hair that was her glory. A rich coppery profusion of curls and waves, it spilled onto her shoulders and back. Delia imagined that the woman's hair had never known a rubber band or barrette or anything that could possibly contain its waywardness. She stared at the woman, her anger at Kincaid forgotten, and imagined what her hair would look like in sunlight.

"God, I'm sorry," Delia said. "I wasn't paying attention."

"Not a problem," the woman replied in a slow Southern drawl. She looked in the direction of Jim Kincaid's office. "Lots of people come running out of his office like that lately. It's a damn trend." She took the papers from Delia, and Delia looked at her hands.

Though she was a small-boned woman, her hands were large; Delia noticed that her nails were chipped and broken, her skin chapped and cut in places. An archaeologist's hands, Delia thought. Dressed in a pair of well-worn, blue painter's pants, she also wore a red sweatshirt that had UNIVERSITY OF ARKANSAS RAZORBACKS emblazoned across the front. Finally Delia took off her hat and offered the woman her hand.

"Hi, I'm—"

The woman broke into a huge grin and pumped her hand

vigorously. "I know who you are, Dr. Ironfoot. I recognize you from your pictures. Wow! What are you doing here in Arkansas?"

Delia motioned in the direction of Jim Kincaid's office. "Well, I was trying to report a burial site and get information about possibly excavating, but..."

The young woman—Delia guessed she was in her mid-twenties—shook her head ruefully. "But you ran into a brick wall." She hooked her arm through Delia's, a friendly gesture that Delia appreciated. "How about a cup of coffee?"

Delia motioned at the papers the woman was holding. "I wouldn't want to keep you from your work."

The woman—Delia still didn't know her name—started walking in the direction of the office. "Nah, don't sweat it. It's not a problem. I was just on my way to the copier. It's probably broken down again anyway, just like everything else around here."

The woman stopped at the doorway of an office and Delia noted that the sign overhead read: ARKANSAS ARCHAEOLOGICAL SURVEY. Below that was the name: Katherine Treadaway, Survey Officer.

Inside, Delia sat down on a wooden chair by the door and watched as the young woman poured two cups of coffee into ceramic mugs. She handed one to Delia, who declined her offer of cream and sugar, preoccupied by the artifacts she saw around Kate's office. In one corner was a long table covered with plastic sacks containing pieces of pottery. Disorganized mounds of papers, folders, and books covered her desk. In one clear spot, however, was a photograph in a silver frame. Inside was the photo of a young man with short reddish-brown hair and wire-rimmed glasses wearing a naval officer's dress uniform. His brown eyes were serious, but a puckish smile turned up the corners of his lips. Something about his face seemed familiar to Delia, but she couldn't put her finger on it.

Delia nodded toward the picture. "Nice looking guy." Then she realized who he reminded her of. "He looks like Ron Howard," she said. "Opie grown up."

Kate face clouded. "That's my brother—Buddy." She turned the photo toward herself. "He was the county prosecutor here until he disappeared ten years ago."

"*He* was your *brother*?" Delia blurted, remembering the story that Kevin had told her the night he drove her from the airport.

Kate stared at her in disbelief. "You know? About what happened? How do you know? You just got here."

"My...oh, I don't know what to call him...he's my great uncle's grandson. Something like that, Kevin...Kevin Whittaker. He told me a story about a bad business deal on the ride to my grandfather's house from the airport the other night."

"He told you about Buddy?" Kate asked puzzled.

"No. He didn't mention Buddy's name," Delia replied. "The story he told me was about Bob..."

"Noland?" Kate's voice had grown cold and flat.

Delia cursed inwardly and wished she hadn't mentioned Kevin's story. It was clearly a very painful subject. "I'm so sorry. I didn't mean to..."

Kate waved her hand impatiently. "It's okay. I need to stop getting all choked up every time someone mentions him. It's just that...Buddy was a really good guy." She looked at his picture wistfully. "I was just sixteen when he disappeared. And everybody knew Noland killed him." She paused. "My parents...they grew up here, but after Buddy disappeared, they...we moved to Louisiana...my dad's parents lived there. They just couldn't stay here...where everything reminded them of him...it almost killed my father."

"I'm so sorry," Delia repeated softly. "Sorry I brought it up."

Kate turned the photo back toward Delia. "He did look like Opie...had that goofy grin and reddish brown hair...like me. Everybody liked him. He did all kinds of funny things—corny things."

Delia smiled too, seeing that Kate now wanted to talk about her brother. "Like what?" she asked.

"Oh, you know—nothing big," Kate said, smiling. "He just liked everybody, you know? He was kind and generous. People just liked him. You'd see him walking down Church Street in the morning, blowing on his coffee cup. He'd have his tie draped around his neck, untied . . . he always looked like he'd forgotten where he was going." She smiled wistfully. "He coached kid's basketball at the Y. He loved kids. He loved to play basketball." She brushed tears from her eyes. "Everyone assumes he's dead. I keep telling myself that he's not, but realistically . . . if he was alive, he'd have contacted me by now. He wouldn't put me through this torture of not knowing."

Delia wanted to comfort her, but she didn't know what to say.

"Well, enough of that," Kate said briskly. "In case you haven't figured it out—I'm the Survey Officer, Kate Treadaway." She shook her head and smiled. "Yeah, it says that on the door." She put her hand on her forehead. "I'm kind of nervous. I never met anybody famous before. Especially someone I've respected for so long. I remember, I read about you in *National Geographic* when I was fifteen. I cut out all the pictures of you and taped them all over my bedroom wall." She motioned to the shelves behind her desk. "See? I have all your books." She pointed to another shelf behind her desk. Along with framed photographs of what appeared to be Kate and her colleagues on digs, there were books on archaeology, many of them Delia's. Delia smiled ruefully.

"Well, Professor Kincaid just reminded me how long ago all that was," she said softly. "Like you, I need to remember to live in the present."

"Did he say something to you?" Kate demanded. "He's such a jerk."

Delia waved her hand, dismissing the subject. Then she smiled. "Fifteen, huh? I guess that makes me pretty old. Well, forty-five must seem pretty ancient to you."

"I'm twenty-six," Kate protested. "Anyway, you look great for forty-five." She closed her eyes and sighed. "I should just shut up, shouldn't I?" Using both hands, she gathered her unruly hair and pulled it back into an impromptu ponytail. As she did, Delia was startled to see the profusion of earrings adorning Kate's ears. The piercings started at the top of her ears with small gold studs and continued down the curve of her ears where the studs were replaced by longer, dangling earrings.

"Wow!" Delia said. "You're really serious about earrings."

Kate stuck out her tongue and revealed a tongue stud. Delia winced.

"Doesn't it hurt?" she asked.

Kate shook her head. "No. I mean, it did at first, but it doesn't now." She touched her ears and laughed a little. She grinned. "Kincaid hates them and that makes them worth having."

Delia laughed, pleased by Kate's delight in flustering Kincaid. "Well, I agree it's worth it then. As to my age, I don't think any-one's ever told me I'm old quite so charmingly." She held up her hand to stem any further protest from the young woman. "No, really. I was excavating when you were in junior high school. You know, that was the best part of being famous, even if was just for fifteen minutes. I liked knowing that I inspired younger women in some way." She sipped her coffee.

"So what *did* Kincaid say to you? I guess he told you to come see me about reporting the human remains, huh? Get out of his hair and don't bother him?" Kate asked.

"Basically. I called the State Archaeologist yesterday, got a recording telling me to report the remains here. I could have sworn I heard 'Archaeology Department' but maybe it did say Arkansas Archaeological Survey. I don't know. At any rate, Kincaid accused me of compromising the site by removing surface arti-facts." Delia paused. "He even suggested that I had planted them in order to 'revive my tarnished career'. When I asked about grad students and interested amateurs for a possible excavation, he told me he didn't have time to help me."

Kate Treadaway looked aghast. "I can't *believe* he said that to you. God, that's so over the top. It's nuts . . . the only reason I can think of why he acted like that is he's been under a lot of stress lately. He and most of the graduate students are involved in an emergency salvage excavation over by Parkin. They've found remains of a camp that Kincaid thinks is part of the Desoto expedition."

"So you're telling me he's really a nice fellow most of the time?"

Kate appeared to think for a moment. "Not really, he's pretty much an asshole the rest of the time, too." They both laughed, and Delia noted that Kate Treadaway had a wonderful, throaty laugh.

"He doesn't have anything to do with this situation anyway," Kate assured her. "He's a professor in the archaeology department. I'm the Survey Officer and taking care of this kind of thing is my job. Are the remains on private property?"

"Yes," Delia said and gave her a brief account of her grandfather's accidental discovery of the log tomb. "I've looked at the site briefly—picked up a few surface artifacts, took pictures. But my grandfather is anxious for me to excavate the site. He has funds to pay for an excavation, so I told him I'd look into it. See what could be done."

Kate turned to a metal shelf in the corner behind her desk, pulled a number of forms from it and stapled them together. "The first thing we have to do is assign you an AAS site number and have you fill out a site form. I'm sure you've done all this kind of stuff before." She handed Delia the forms. "The only thing that may be unfamiliar to you is that we use the U.T.M. Coordinate Grid System." She flipped through the forms and pointed to a page. "The instructions are right here, and it's a lot easier than the Geographic Coordinate System. All you need is a straight-edge, a sharp pencil, and a UTM coordinate counter plus a USGS map."

Delia nodded. "Okay. You know, I don't even know if I'm going to excavate yet."

"Doesn't matter," Kate told her. "You still need to record the site and be assigned a number. Did Kincaid tell you about notifying the coroner and sheriff?"

"No. He didn't mention it. He was so angry. It was like I'd insulted him personally or something."

"Okay, well, we need to do that. It's just a formality, but the sooner we do it, the sooner they'll release the site. It'll take them a day or so to sort it out, but there are some things we can do in the meantime. Most important, we need to notify Harriet Richardson in Little Rock. She's the director of the Native American Cultural Center."

"I'd like to talk to her myself, if you don't mind," Delia said.

"No, of course I don't mind. I'll just call and tell her a little bit of the background situation. Kind of smooth the way for you. Harriet and I work together a lot."

"Sure. That's fine. I just want to make sure she understands: if the Board has any objection at all to me disinterring these remains, I'll step aside," Delia said. "I'll do whatever makes her feel comfortable. If she wants the remains reburied or turned over to the Board, that's fine with me too. I also want to donate any found artifacts to a local or regional museum. I'll ask her if the Board has a preference in that matter."

Kate looked at Delia approvingly. "That's a good idea. She won't believe someone actually took the time to get permission...a lot of people don't."

"Well, contrary to what Kincaid thinks, I am a professional," Delia said. "I've been through this before. And, I've taken part in a number of reburials."

"There aren't really any direct descendants of the tribes whose remains would be uncovered. Harriet's Cherokee; but, the Cherokee left this area around 1890: Which brings us to the mound."

She settled down in her swivel chair and looked at Delia eagerly. "Tell me more about the site."

Chapter 6

After Kate refilled their coffee cups, Delia told her more details about the site. She lifted her canvas duffel bag onto Kate's desk. "I brought some of the surface artifacts—just stuff that got turned up by the plow. I thought you might recognize some of them. Maybe give me an idea of what we're looking at in terms of time or culture." She reached into the bag, carefully removed the objects and set them on the desk. As she did, she explained her grandfather's accident to Kate.

"So, he took them back to his house, but I got him to show me where he found them. I took pictures of the approximate location where he turned them up—so at least we'll know the 'find spot'." She touched the effigy pot gently. "This head pot was in the roots of an old tree overhanging the river bank. Normally I'd have left it where it was, but I was afraid it would drop into the river and be washed away."

She watched as Kate picked it up and studied it. "Hmmm...looks like this woman liked her ears pierced too." She frowned thoughtfully. "I don't think I've seen one like this before. Her expression is so..."

"Dreamy?" Delia asked.

Kate shrugged. "I guess. She looks like she's either asleep or stoned."

"She does at that. Take a look at the copper plates for me."

Kate did as Delia asked, picking up the one closest to her. "Wow! Copper plates." She touched the fibers still clinging to the surface. "Hmmm. Must have been inside a sack. Copper salts preserved some of the original fibers."

She wet her forefinger and rubbed a small spot clean. "You know, I've seen plates like these before. Do you know about the Malden plates?"

"Sounds vaguely familiar."

"Sometimes they're called the 'Wulfing plates'. They're probably the most widely known artifacts from the Central Valley. Eight embossed copper plates plowed up by a farmer in southeast Missouri. I remember reading an account by someone—Stephen Williams, I think—about interviewing the widow of the guy who plowed them up. Anyway, the plates were associated with the Southeastern Ceremonial Complex."

"Southeastern Ceremonial Complex? The mound culture where? Ohio, Illinois?"

"Yeah, basically the Central Mississippi Valley."

"What were the dates of these plates?"

"They were Middle Mississippian period. I think the radiocarbon dates were something like 800 AD."

"Okay, go ahead," Delia said.

"Well, what's interesting to me, and probably to you, is that these plates, or at least some of them, were found on the forehead of a female burial. The plates depict female warriors wearing hawk regalia beheading male captives. With your interest in women warrior cultures..." For a brief, but intense moment, Delia flashed on her dream of the lone woman holding a wooden staff topped by a hawk. She pushed the image from her mind and told herself to pay attention.

"Hmmm," Delia murmured. "They look almost Mesoamerican."

"Yeah, you can see why the Mexican diffusionist theory had a lot of proponents for a long time."

"It doesn't anymore?" Delia asked. "Why not? A Mexican connection seems logical to me. I mean, the mounds are similar to the Mayan and Aztec pyramids. These engravings look like something from Mayan stelae."

"For a long time archaeologists thought that Mexican colonization was fairly obvious in the Central Valley. The mounds, the artistic motifs, the inhabitants' physical similarities, even the staple crops of beans and maize originated in Mexico."

"Sounds like a neat diffusionist theory to me," Delia asserted. "Mexicans bring staple crops, artistry, and mound building into the Central Valley woodlands and voila—Moundbuilder Culture."

"It sounds logical," Kate agreed. "The problem is that the Ohio mounds are older than the ones in the Central Valley. If the diffusionist theory was true, the farther away from Mexico you get, the newer the sites would be. Plus, there've been some excavations in northeastern Mexico. But there's no evidence of mound builders. The final nail in the diffusionist coffin is that the Hopewell and Adena sites in Ohio and Illinois haven't shown much maize growing."

"But if I remember correctly—don't the grave goods associated with Hopewell and Adena burials include obsidian knives—probably used in sacrificial ritual? Like Aztecs?"

"Exactly. Nobody's saying there aren't a lot of similarities. There's just no hard evidence for a direct connection."

Delia motioned to the other objects. "What about these things? I recognize the objects—the gorgets, panpipes, and the effigy pot. Any ideas about time period?"

"Oh, these are pretty characteristic Mississippian artifacts." Kate picked up the arrow points and turned them over. "This could be Scalloran or Madison, maybe Sequoah."She picked up the flat round stone. "I bet this is a chunky stone. The Indians played a game called chunky with stones and sticks, like the Mayan and their ball courts. So if you do excavate you want to be on the lookout for a chunky ball court. The time period depends or whether we're talking Early, Middle or Late Mississippian culture—it's a span of about six hundred and fifty years. This kind of stone—it's called a discoidal—is characteristic of late Mississippian. The chunky game got more complex over time. That may be why there's two different kinds of designs on either side of the stone."

"Of course the problem is these things were exposed when the log tomb collapsed," Delia said. "We don't know where they were stratigraphically. So they could all be from different time periods. Until the mound is excavated we don't know how many periods we're dealing with."

"Absolutely," Kate agreed. "Until you expose the stratigraphy of the mound, these artifacts are meaningless." She stopped and looked at Delia in embarrassment. "I'm sure I'm giving Delia Ironfoot a lesson in stratigraphy. The point is: this stuff is typical Central Valley Mississippian stuff."

Delia nodded, unoffended. "That's what—500 AD?"

"The Mississippian runs from around 700 AD to about 1500—the peak was around 1200 to 1500," Kate said, turning the pot over in her hands. "Lord Almighty, this is a beautiful head pot. Did you wash it?"

"Yeah, I washed the points and the pots. How much would a pot like that bring on the black market?" she asked.

"Oh, the pot hunter would probably only get a couple thousand or so—tops maybe three. But for the collector ultimately buying the pot in New York or Tokyo? An unbroken pot like this could cost twenty thousand dollars, depending on the year. Depends on what's hot. Sometimes it's polychrome pots, sometimes hand axes. You never know." Kate ran her fingers over the pattern. "Interesting. It's an effigy pot for sure, but the marking isn't any

64

kind of Mississippian type I recognize. How much do you know about ceramic typology of this region?"

"Nothing," Delia admitted.

"Okay, the ceramic sequence in the Central Valley starts with Tchula which is about 500 BC. I won't list them all: there are seven. Then there are about a million different decoration types. A typical diagnostic decoration for this time period—late Mississippian—is that O'Byam Incised is replaced by Matthews Incised. And of course, there are about a billion different paste types. Bell Plain, for example, became an established paste during late Mississippian." She stopped, looking embarrassed again. "Ceramics are my specialty, in case you haven't guessed."

Delia laughed, charmed by Kate's embarrassment. "It's okay, you ought to hear me go on and on about the distribution of obsidian in Early Neolithic sites in central Turkey."

Kate handed the pot to Delia. "I don't want you to think I'm just trying to show off. But based simply on its appearance, this appears to be a Mississippian head effigy pot. These pots are more typical of Late Mississippian—1350 or thereabouts. Could be earlier though. But this design—do you recognize it?"

"Well, the serpent-globe—or egg, or oval—symbol isn't unusual," Delia said. "It's prevalent in Egypt, Greece, and other ancient civilizations. I've seen it on pots, cave walls, medallions, tablets—you name it."

Kate turned to the bookcase behind her and pulled a book from the stacks. Flipping quickly through the pages, she found what she was looking for and handed the book over to Delia. "Look at that picture."

Delia accepted it and looked at the image Kate's finger was touching. "The Serpent Mound. I've seen pictures of it." She studied the image and then the pot. "Wow! It's an exact replica. Have you ever seen this design on pots from this area before?"

Remembering her dream of the previous night again, Delia

wondered about copper armbands, but she kept silent.

Kate shook her head. "No," she said firmly. "Never."

"Tell me about the Serpent Mound. Isn't it in Ohio?" Delia asked.

"It's near Chillicothe, Ohio." Kate glanced at the picture again. "I think Squier discovered it." She consulted the book again. "It says Putnam wrote about it first in 1883. He got a campaign going to buy the Mound before it was plowed up or excavated by slaphappy tourists and amateurs. It's the largest Adena object, and probably the most famous of all American effigy mounds. Measures 1,254 feet from its tail to the tip of its upper jaw. The average width of the body is about twenty feet, height four or five feet. It's a state park now."

"Adena? That's pre-Hopewell, right? BC?" Delia smiled. "I'm not real good with dates."

"Like it matters! You're an expert in everything else." Kate smiled, then continued, "Yeah, Adena is pre-Hopewell. It's the local name for a culture in the Central Ohio Valley."

"Any artifacts associated with the Serpent Mound?"

"Nope, no human artifacts ever found there. Strictly ceremonial. But I think there have been some excavations of burial mounds nearby that turned up some characteristic Adena stuff—copper plates, animal effigy pipes, and pots, panpipes, shell beads—lots of exotic ritual grave goods. That's typical Adena-Hopewell. They were into death."

"And you've never seen this design on any pots from excavations around here?" Delia asked again.

Kate shook her head. "Absolutely not. See, the Serpent Mound represents a different time period and a different cultural phase. The spread of Mississippian culture into Arkansas is the result of down-river drift—from Illinois and Ohio."

"Ah," Delia said. "Yeah, I remember—Cahokia. That's east of St. Louis." She frowned, trying to remember. "Largest ceremonial center in North America, lots of mounds, right?" The image of the woman standing atop the earthen mound above the burning city flashed into Delia's mind again.

"Yes," Kate said. "Cahokia was huge—some estimates run as high as 30,000 people. But the Serpent Mound is in Ohio. And it's also Adena, so we're talking 1000 BC until around 400 BC—the beginning of Hopewell. Cahokia is something like 1050-1250 AD. That's a long, long time for this design to be around and not show up on anything."

"Trade?" Delia postulated. "Surely there was a lot of trading among settlements along the Mississippi."

"Yeah, but I don't know if the Cahokian trade route included Ohio or not. I know they got as far west as Montana and as far north as Michigan—but I don't know about Ohio. I guess they could have. I'll have to look into that. But this is weird. I've never seen this design on any pottery in North America, anywhere. I mean, like you said, the serpent and globe are common designs—but that's the Serpent Mound in Ohio. I can't imagine why an effigy pot with this type of design would be present at a middle or late Mississippian burial site in Arkansas. I mean—how did it get here?" She turned the pot over in her hands. "We'll know more about its origins when we do some tests on the composition of the clay. But it really doesn't fit."

Delia and Kate exchanged a meaningful look. Kate had just uttered the magic words to any archaeologist. Although amateur archaeologists excavate for treasure, or to satisfy their curiosity, modern-day archaeologists only excavate to establish a sequence of cultures in a region and to fill in gaps relative to regional information already collected. The problem that Kate had just delineated was reason enough to justify an excavation, and they both knew it.

"You know, this assemblage you've found on the surface is pretty intriguing," Kate said. "Are there any other mounds in this field?"

"Yes, I didn't take anything more than a brief look at the whole parcel—it's sixty acres, but yes, there are other mounds. I was mostly concerned with the log tomb. Are you thinking that the mounds may be part of a settlement?"

"Absolutely," Kate said. "This chunky stone is a good indication of that. Have you looked at aerial photos of the land yet—looked for features?"

"No," Delia said. "I've only been here a couple of days."

"Have ever you used the National Archaeological Data Base?" Kate asked.

"A few times," Delia said. "It didn't have that many sites on-line when I . . . before I got fired."

"Well, it's got over a million entries now, and it's really useful. All you need is a laptop and a modem to see if there've been any excavations near that field . . . there're a lot of new gadgets now that make our jobs easier."

"I've used the GIS before," Delia told her, referring the Geographic Information System.

"Good. After we survey the site, we can download all our measurements, and generate a topo map. Then, we can call up aerial photos of the site. See if there is one. I use my laptop more than paper anymore. It's got statistical packages that are so slick—it can analyze data in seconds. Data that it used to take days or weeks to analyze by hand."

They both looked at the objects on Kate's desk, and then their eyes met.

"You need to excavate," Kate told Delia.

Delia nodded slowly. "I think you're right," she said. "But you don't know what that means. I haven't excavated in a long time."

"I'll help you," Kate offered eagerly. "Not just with the paperwork. You'll need a field supervisor. Someone who knows the archaeology around here. Someone familiar with procedures and people. I can get you volunteers."

Delia frowned. "What about your job here?"

"This *is* my job—to facilitate significant excavations. I might even be able to round up a few graduate students to help."

"I thought most of them were helping Kincaid."

"They are. But there are a couple who aren't—Paula Jeffries, for one. Adam Bernstein, too. He was working on Kincaid's excavation in Parkin, but for some reason he quit. Or Kincaid didn't want him . . . I don't know the details, but I know Adam would be grateful to be involved in another excavation. Paula's been around for a couple of years; she started as a volunteer but got so interested that she enrolled in the master's program. Adam just started in the program last fall. Both of them are interested in Mississippian culture. They'll jump at the chance to work on this project."

"You mentioned volunteers?"

"I've got a list of trained amateurs who have been through our summer field schools. Most of them are experienced. We're going to need a bone person." She snapped her fingers. "Wait a minute. I know somebody. She's a physical anthropologist. She knows more about bones than anybody in this region. Hell, she knows bones better than anybody I've ever met."

"Great," Delia said. "Does she teach here?"

"No. This is wild. Her name is Colleen Redfield. She owns an herb store in Jericho Mill. It's about two hours northwest of here. It's a resort town. College kids and tourists go canoeing and camping there. Very artsy-craftsy place. Lots of bed and breakfasts, antique stores."

"An herb store?" Delia asked, puzzled. "Why would an expert on bones own an herb store?"

"Good question," Kate assured her with a smile. "A lot of people wonder that. Colleen's quite a character. She used to do volunteer work for the Survey until she had a run-in with Kincaid."

"Her name sounds familiar," Delia said. "Wait a minute. I remember hearing her read a paper at a conference in London years ago. Something on Middle Paleolithic tools and mandible development. It was a brilliant paper, best one I heard during that conference. She's British, isn't she? What's she doing here in Arkansas growing herbs?"

"I think her son goes to school in Fayetteville," Kate said.

Delia chuckled. "Why would some kid from England want to go to school in Arkansas?"

Kate frowned. "I'm trying to remember what she told me. If I remember right she married an American professor who taught at UCA in Conway. University of Central Arkansas. They eventually got a divorce, but I think her son wanted to stay with his dad—something like that. I don't remember exactly what she told me, but she ended up staying too. She used to work as a consultant for the state of Arkansas, but she retired and moved up to Jericho Mill." Kate paused. "I've worked with her a couple of times. She came down to help us out on a salvage project. Highway construction uncovered a camp we thought might be Archaic near Marked Tree. She was there a few weeks, and we got to know each other a little. She's very cool. Her accent really got to me. She's attractive, too. Anyway, she told me about her herb garden. She has a couple greenhouses and a store. Lots of hill-people don't trust doctors. And a lot of them don't have access to doctors. Colleen is their granny-woman."

"What? Like a folk healer?"

"Yeah," Kate said. "It's a very old tradition in the Ozarks. Most granny-women I remember my Mama talking about were midwives." Kate's eyes locked on Delia's. "She is really hot. I had a pretty bad crush on her during that dig. I made what I'm sure were clumsy attempts to woo her. No doubt she thought I was a pathetic, love-sick kid."

"And were you?" Delia asked, bolder now that Kate had openly declared her preference.

Kate put her chin in her hands and smiled sweetly at Delia. "Yeah, I was. See, I have this thing for older women."

"Do you now? Is Colleen old?"

"Oh, yeah," Kate said. "She's way older than you."

Her face flushed red again, and Delia laughed.

"Well, if you reminded her of how old she was as much as

you've reminded me in the past hour, I'll bet you weren't very successful in your wooing," Delia teased.

Kate put her head down on her desk in mock defeat. Then she looked up. "Some people around Black Rock and Jericho Mill say that she's a witch."

"Well, good," Delia said. "Maybe she can conjure up a spell to keep the looters away."

"Other people say she knows things before they happen. What people in the hills call 'the Vision'."

"Even better. She can tell us when the looters are coming."

"I'm sure the 'witch' stuff is just talk, but I saw her do something on that dig near Marked Tree that . . ." Kate saw Delia's skeptical expression and stopped.

"What?" Delia said. "What did she do?"

"Never mind," Kate replied cryptically. "You'll see when you meet her."

"Should I call her or write her?"

"If you really want her to help us out, you should go up there and either do some fast talking or charm her."

"Maybe I'll do both," Delia said with a smile.

Kate grinned. "Hey, it worked with me."

As Delia got up to leave, Kate suddenly turned serious. "You know if this is a late Mississippian site we'll have more problems with looters than usual."

"Why?"

"Because late Mississippian burials usually have a lot of unbroken ceramics in good condition."

"Do you have any place to secure these things?" Delia asked, motioning to the plates, pot and other artifacts.

"Absolutely," Kate said. She reached down and unclipped a set of keys from her belt loop. "We have a caged room where we keep some of the really valuable artifacts. Ones that haven't been catalogued yet or that somebody might be tempted to lift." Kate motioned for Delia to follow her and led her down a short dimly lit hallway. At the end of the hallway, Kate inserted her key into the padlock of a large steel door, which opened into a room containing a large caged in space.

"It's not really that secure," Kate said, as she unlocked the door to the cage. "It's just that not that many people know about this room or that we keep valuable stuff in here."

"Has anything ever gone missing from here?" Delia asked.

"No," Kate assured her. "From time to time we can't find something, but it's not because someone has stolen it. It's just, well, look around ... it's kind of a mess."

Right inside the door was a battered metal desk covered with file folders, sheets of paper, scissors, rubber bands, and other office supplies. Rows of iron shelves were stacked with more of the plastic and cardboard boxes that Delia had seen in the hallways of the archaeology department. Kate unlocked the cage door and rummaged around until she found an empty white cardboard box.

"There should be a black Magic Marker on that desk," Kate said, as she gently lifted the items from inside Delia's canvas duffel bag. "Would you get it for me?"

Delia did as Kate asked and, after labeling the box with the date, Kate wrote in large block letters; **WHITTAKER EXCAVATION**. She looked up at Delia then and grinned. "How's it feel?" She asked.

Delia shook her head. "It's been a long time," she said. "It's a little bit ... scary."

Kate nodded. "But you can handle it, right?"

"Oh, yeah," Delia said. "Now if I can just handle Colleen Redfield, we're in business."

That night the "burning city and red sky" dream again haunted Delia's dreams. The woman with the serpent tattooed on her face stood atop the earthen mound once more, holding her wooden staff with the copper hawk ferrule. This time she was bare-breasted and wore a calf-length skirt belted with grizzly bear canines.

Below her, a stockade of upright wooden posts surrounded the city, but the invaders who now ran through the streets setting fire to the houses had broken down huge sections of the wall.

In the distance, a river reflected the flames of the burning city and illuminated hundreds of people: some of whom were on fire and were throwing themselves into the water, trying to escape. Others clamored aboard canoes and desperately paddled into the river's current. The open plaza, in the center of the city was swarming with men in loincloths wielding copper axes.

Suddenly the scene shifted, and once again, Delia could see the woman standing atop the earthen mound. Her expression still seemed preternaturally calm as she watched the slaughter of her people, but Delia also saw the tears that flowed down her face, tears that glistened red in the reflection of the flames.

When she awoke from the horrific dream, Delia flung off the sweat-soaked sheets and sat up on the edge of the bed. She ground the heels of her hands into her eyes trying to erase the gruesome scene, and when this failed, she rose and walked to the window. As she had the previous night, she looked over the moonlit fields, the harsh light etching sharp shadows of trees and buildings across the landscape. Continuing to look out the window, she spotted two lights bobbing on the river. Night fisherman, she thought sleepily as she turned away from the window and stumbled back to bed. No red sky or burning people. Just night fishermen on the river.

Chapter 7

After a quick shower, breakfast, and directions from her grand-father, Delia started off toward the town of Jericho Mill. It was a pleasant drive through the Ozarks; the trees were still ablaze in their fall colors, and the dark green pines provided a beautiful contrast to the red, yellow, and gold foliage. Despite such gor-geous colors against the bright blue sky, Delia's thoughts were dominated by her recurring dream. For the first time she admitted to herself how unusual and even frightening they had become.

Unusual because it was unlike any dream she'd ever had before—or even heard of; it was like watching a movie, or more accurately, a mini-series. Each night the dream picked up where it had left off the night before. And each night, as Delia watched, the story of the burning city unfolded. As she drove she tried to account for the strangeness of the dream.

She wondered if she could simply be remembering a movie that she had seen. Once she had gone to the movies fairly regularly. But since moving to Half Moon Lake, she had no television and had gone to the movies only three times in the last five years. It was true that her uncle Robert and aunt Lilah had both a television and a VCR, as did her relatives in Mexican Hat, and when she was with them sometimes she watched television or rented a video.

But as she searched her memory, Delia could not remember a movie that even vaguely reminded her of the dreams she had experienced since arriving in Arkansas.

Certainly she had not ever seen a movie that incorporated her current archaeological finds.

Thinking about her dreams now, in the hard light of day, Delia knew they were more than unusual. They were inexplicable. During long excavations she had often dreamed about artifacts she had found. Dreaming about them wasn't that unusual. The difference was in the order—find the artifact, then dream about it. Not dream the artifact, and then find it. That was why she had shared her dreams with no one. She had thought of telling her friend, Shawla, the other night when she talked to her on the phone, but even that thought had made her uneasy. Her friend and business partner Shawla was a down-to-earth, no-nonsense woman. In addition, Delia could imagine the silence that would have greeted her had she told Shawla about the burning city of circles and the killing of women and children. Delia had no desire to remind her friend of the tragedy of losing her own children in a fire. Therefore, she had said nothing to the one person she would have felt comfortable telling.

After two hours of fruitless pondering and speculation, Delia arrived in Jericho Mill and drove down the narrow main street lined with ice-cream parlors, T-shirt shops, and antique stores catering to tourists. However, now that fall had arrived, few people walked along the sidewalks to window-shop, and Delia had no trouble locating a parking place.

A short walk down a weathered boardwalk led her to the front door of a shop housed in a brick building with a gray slate roof. The antique sign on the door read: Blessed Thistle Herbal Apothecary Store, and announced: Colleen Redfield, Proprietor.

Delia pushed open one of the double screen doors and stepped inside. It was dark in the store; the air was redolent with the scent of herbs. To her left a long wooden counter ran the length of the store. At the far end of the counter, Delia saw a woman she recognized as Colleen Redfield engaged in a conversation with a man. They both turned as Delia moved closer, and Colleen nodded in her direction.

"Feel free to browse while you wait," she said, in a friendly voice.

"Thanks," Delia said, backing off a few feet and gazing around. An old-fashioned scale with a large scoop hung from the ceiling, while on the counter below, there were other scales of varying sizes. A roll of white butcher paper in an old metal dispenser sat beside a roll of scotch tape on the counter. Behind the counter were shelves lined with books about herb gardens, herbal cures, folk remedies, and homeopathic medicine. To the right, Plexusglass covers that contained herbs. Herbs indeed were everywhere, in plastic sacks lying on the counter, in glass jars, and hanging in clusters from the ceiling.

A potbellied stove perched on a brick hearth; rag rugs and rocking chairs were scattered around the stove. Mismatched chairs to the left of the stove surrounded a battered pine table. An assortment of teacups sat with coffee mugs on the table's top, along with metal tea balls, cups, and saucers. A large teakettle steamed on a hot plate in the middle of the table.

Even though she had moved a polite distance away, Delia could still hear the conversation between Colleen and the man.

"All right, Eldon, here's what you must do . . ." Colleen said, her accent as entrancing as Delia remembered when she listened to her deliver a conference paper in London years before. She spoke to a gaunt, middle-aged man with a patchy gray beard and a haunted look in his eyes. His overalls were palest blue, almost white from innumerable washings. He wore a white dress shirt with frayed sleeves and an equally frayed collar, and knee high rubber boots caked with mud. As she talked to the man, Colleen tore strips of the butcher paper from a large roll and expertly wrapped clumps of herbs, her hands moving gracefully without a single wasted motion.

"The main thing to watch for with ringworm is infection. Be certain she drinks at least eight cups of Echinacea tea every day." Colleen pushed one package toward him and made a notation on the butcher paper with a grease pencil on another. "Sprinkle this goldenseal on the open sores and use the extract of comfrey for itching."

The man nodded his head slowly.

"How's the swine business this year?" Colleen asked as she finished wrapping the herbs. "Did you get a good price for those shoats?"

"Naw, it don't hardly pay a man to raise pigs these days. Cost more to feed 'em than I can make at auction. I butchered the yearlings. We got us a garden, though—tomatoes was good this year. Sarah canned a mess of okra and corn. What with the pork and all, I reckon we'll make out." He reached into his pocket. "How much do I owe you?"

Colleen touched each package on the counter slowly, adding mentally.

"Three dollars ought to cover it," she said briskly. Delia watched as the man pulled three crumpled dollar bills from the front pocket of his overalls and handed them to Colleen.

"What Mother really wants is a visit from you," Eldon confided shyly. "She does so love it when you call on her."

Colleen nodded and smiled. "More than likely I'll get up that way next week. You tell your mother to be careful with that ring-worm, and when I come I'll bring some of my poppy seed cake that she likes. Do you need a bag for those?" she asked.

"Naw, I'll just stuff 'em in my pockets here," he said. "Thank ye, Colleen. Be seein' you."

"Good day to you, Eldon. By the way, it won't hurt any of you to drink the tea as well. It's good for whatever ails you."

"I'll be mindful of that," Eldon said and opening the door, he was gone.

As Delia watched Colleen tidy up the counter, she heard a faint scratching sound coming from the floor and was surprised to see two fat raccoons, each with an apple core in its mouth. One was missing its rear left leg, causing it to walk with a curious hopping limp. When the other, able-bodied raccoon spied Delia, it rose up on its hind legs and held up its apple core, as if offering it to her.

"Thanks, but I already ate," Delia laughed. She looked over at Colleen who shook her head.

"If you tried to actually take it, you'd find out how insincere an offer it is," she told Delia wryly.

"What are their names?" Delia asked as she watched the raccoons waddle over to a shallow pan of water in the corner and began washing their apple cores in a fastidious manner.

"I call them Rocky and Prudence," Colleen said, smiling at Delia's laugh. "I have a fondness for the Beatles. I admit it."

"So what's their story?" Delia asked.

"I found Prudence in my vegetable garden early last fall. She'd obviously been caught in a trap. Her back leg was badly mangled—it was gangrenous and eventually had to be amputated. Two days later, Rocky appeared. I assume he's her mate." She sighed. "Prudence can hardly survive in the wild now that she's lame, and I don't have the heart to separate them. I don't relish having wild animals as pets, but I don't know what else to do. So they stay and—for the most part—are a bloody nuisance."

She leaned over the counter, looked down at the animals and pointed toward the back room. "Rocky, Prudence—exit please," she said sternly.

Delia watched with amusement as the raccoons, ignoring Colleen's instructions, waddled into the next room and curled up next to the potbelly stove on the brick hearth.

"Disobedient beasts," Colleen muttered. "I'll be glad when they go into hibernation." She turned back to Delia and offered her hand. "I'm honored that Delia Ironfoot would trouble herself to pay me a visit—even if it is to offer me a job that I have to refuse." She looked at Delia curiously. "This burial mound must be an interesting one indeed."

Delia stared at Colleen open-mouthed and then smiled weakly. "Kate Treadaway called you."

Colleen began putting away the herbs that remained on the counter. "Lovely woman, Kate. But no, I haven't seen nor heard from her lately."

"Then how..." Delia stopped. "Is this the fortune telling ability Kate told me about?"

"I don't know what Kate told you, Dr. Ironfoot," Colleen said, sweeping up some loose herbs into her hand and putting them into a small trashcan. "But one doesn't have to be psychically gifted to know who you are and what you're doing here." She motioned to the table. "Would you fancy a cup of tea?"

Delia took off her cap and ruffled her short dark hair in an uncharacteristically puzzled manner. "Sure, whatever you've got."

Colleen walked over to the table, peered into the pot and inhaled deeply. "This is a special blend of mine—hibiscus flowers, cranberry, chicory, cinnamon, rosehips, chamomile flowers, and a little licorice root. Very delicious and excellent for the complexion...." She looked up at Delia with a mischievous twinkle in her eyes. "Though your complexion doesn't seem to need any help." She poured two cups of tea and gestured for Delia to sit down.

Delia felt herself blush at the unaccustomed compliment and mumbled, "Thank you." Then she sipped the tea and nodded. "Delicious." As Delia drank, she studied Colleen appreciatively.

Kate had been right in her appraisal—Colleen Redfield was indeed an attractive woman. Her strong face, with prominent cheekbones and broad forehead, made her striking rather than simply pretty or handsome. At six feet, Colleen was a commanding presence. She wore her light brown hair, generously sprinkled with silver, in a braid. Though the store was dimly lit, Delia sat close enough to Colleen that she could appreciate the depth of blue in her eyes. Eyes that missed nothing, she was sure. Though her face was brown from the sun, she had a healthy rosy color in her cheeks. Her skin was smooth and unlined, except for the crow's feet around eyes.

Colleen wore a collarless blue shirt with rolled up sleeves and baggy khaki trousers. A short, green, canvas apron with pockets across its front protected her clothes. A roll of twine and a pair of scissors protruded from one of its many pockets. Delia thought it unsurprising that Colleen had the reputation of being a witch. Her angular features and self-possessed demeanor gave away nothing of her thoughts, yet, her demeanor was not at all forbidding. And there was no denying the charm of her accent, uniquely British expressions and manner.

Delia sensed something else too—a rough but genuine kindness shone from Colleen's face. She chose her words carefully and spoke with precision in a gravelly voice that was deep but not unpleasant. Her demeanor reminded Delia of her Navajo grandmother, Ruth Manysheep—a calm, deliberateness that bespoke great wisdom and strength. Delia imagined that Colleen Redfield's manner inspired the trust of the cautious mountain people she cared for and served.

She was, Delia decided, an attractive, compelling woman; she could understand why Kate had been so entranced with her since she was beginning to feel the same.

"You were going to tell me how you knew who I was and why I'm here," Delia prompted, unable to take her eyes away Colleen's face. She found herself watching Colleen's full, generous mouth as she talked.

"It's simple, really," Colleen demurred. "You are a well-known person in a field closely related to my own—it's not surprising that I would have seen your picture. As to what you're doing here—that was a little more difficult. However, Arkansas is rich in archaeological sites; you're still an archaeologist, albeit a retired one. It doesn't require a big jump to deduce that someone has hired you to direct an excavation, and since I'm a physical anthropologist, I'll wager that someone who knows me, Kate Treadaway I presume, has recommended you come and see if I will help with the excavation of a burial mound. I assume it's a provocative problem you've run across, or you wouldn't have been persuaded to abandon your retirement."

"It wasn't exactly retirement," Delia interjected. "I was fired."

"They fired you because you were lesbian," Colleen said bluntly. "It's happened to a lot of people I know."

Delia found her eyes straying to Colleen's generous figure and then realized that the woman was aware of her stare. Delia blushed with embarrassment. "So, uh, how did you know it was a burial mound?"

"A lucky guess," Colleen admitted, smiling. Delia wondered if she was smiling at Delia's obvious interest in her or at her own ability to guess. "But an educated one. Why else would you need a bone person?" Colleen asked.

"Well, you're right on all counts." Delia briefly explained the events that had led to her coming to Arkansas and becoming involved in the excavation. She described the mound and the artifacts that she and her grandfather had uncovered so far—particularly the effigy pot with the tattooed serpent. As Delia spoke, Colleen looked around the room, absently rubbed Prudence's ears, and fiddled with the teapot. Remembering her patience with the slow-talking Eldon, Delia stopped and spread her hands, puzzled by Colleen's distracted manner.

"Did I catch you at a bad time?" she asked. "I guess it was pretty presumptuous of me to simply show up here and expect you to make time for me." She paused, waiting for Colleen to respond. When she said nothing, the silence became awkward, and Delia began to feel irritated. "I could come back later, if you'd like. Or even write you an e-mail."

"I'm just wondering—where are you going with this? What's your point?" Though her words were blunt, her tone was not rude or abrupt.

"My point?" Delia asked, her irritation evident. "I'm putting together a team to excavate a burial mound, perhaps an entire settlement. I need a bone person. You're the best one available."

Colleen shook her head. "No, thank you."

"Jim Kincaid isn't involved in the excavation—not even marginally," Delia said, trying to anticipate her objection.

"Kincaid doesn't enter into my decision in the slightest."

"I can offer you a small salary," Delia said, looking around at the store. "To offset any financial loss by you not being here during that time."

"Money isn't the issue," Colleen said.

Delia held her gaze and said politely, "Perhaps it's my theories? Some people have found them too far-fetched or radical."

"Really?" Colleen arched her eyebrows and smiled. "I find that aspect of your work to be its greatest strength." Delia noticed that her dark eyebrows were perfectly formed; yet clearly Colleen did not have the vanity of a woman who would pluck them.

Delia couldn't stifle the exasperated tone that had crept into her voice. "Well, if it's not the money, the personnel and it's not me...what is it?"

Before Colleen could answer, a phone started ringing and she arose to answer it. Delia sat watching the two raccoons tumble playfully in an old armchair. A few minutes later Colleen came back into the room.

"I'm sorry. It was one of my customers," she said. "You were saying?"

"I wasn't saying anything," Delia said. "I was trying to get you to tell me why you aren't interested in excavating."

Colleen shook her head and picked up one of the raccoons that had been playing with her apron strings. "It's simple, really" she said. "Excavating doesn't interest me anymore."

"Oh? What does interest you?" Delia asked.

To her surprise, Colleen smiled at her. "I'm interested in a lot of things." She gestured around the store. "I think it's rather obvious what those other interests are. I have people depending on me—on my knowledge and my availability."

"Why did you say you thought that the far-fetched, radical part of my work was what you liked the most?"

Colleen shrugged. "Dr. Ironfoot," she began.

"Please don't call me that," Delia said. "Only my students call—called me that. Dee is fine."

"Alright. Dee. I always found your vision much more fascinating than your findings."

"Vision?" Delia said, suddenly reminded of her frightening dreams. "I don't know what you're talking about."

Delia found that, despite her attraction to Colleen Redfield, she was suddenly tired of their frustrating conversation. She stood up abruptly and began buttoning her duster. "Well, I'm sorry that you won't be joining us for the excavation. I'd better be getting back. I've got a lot of work to do. It was nice to have met you."

Colleen stood up but made no response to Delia's good-bye, and Delia felt a surge of annoyance at her blatant lack of interest and also at the strong attraction she felt for the woman. Disgusted with Colleen and with herself, she jammed her hat down on her head and strode toward the door. Her hand was on the door, ready to push it open, when Colleen's voice stopped her.

"Are you really going to leave without telling me about your dreams?"

Delia froze, her hand firmly grasping the door handle. She

didn't speak for a few moments, and when she did, her voice was flat. "I don't know what you're talking about."

She heard Colleen's footsteps behind her and then felt the warmth of Colleen's hand on her shoulder.

"Why don't you tell me about them? You want to tell someone, I'm sure."

Colleen's hand tightened on Delia's shoulder, and Delia sagged in defeat as she turned to face Colleen. Later, Delia decided that the look on her own face must have been alarming because Colleen gathered her into her arms, an event that she objected to not at all.

Chapter 8

"So," Delia said, looking down at the remains of her salad. "What do you think?" After Colleen's embrace, her earlier irritation had disappeared. She decided she had merely been upset that Colleen seemed indifferent to her request. Once the subject of her dreams was raised, however, Colleen's interest had obviously been piqued.

"I don't think the question should be directed to me," Colleen said, standing up and clearing their lunch dishes. She held the plates shoulder high, out of the reach of the two raccoons that followed her progress to the sink on their back legs. She had changed into a pair of cut off khaki shorts before preparing lunch, and Delia was enjoying the sight of her tanned, muscular legs. "I think you're the only one who can decide the significance of the dreams."

Delia leaned back on her chair and regarded Colleen as she worked. Her impatience—an emotion she was beginning to associate strongly with Colleen Redfield—returned. Impatience with herself because she was regarding Colleen's shapely rear end with far more interest than she had for their discussion. She was also remembering how good it had felt to be held in Colleen's arms. It was an experience, Delia decided, that she would like to repeat.

Up close, Colleen had smelled of soap and rosemary.

They were sitting in Colleen's apartment, a large airy loft over the store. The room was flooded as sunlight poured in through three large windows that formed an alcove with a padded window seat. Rocky and Prudence had given up their quest for food and were curled up together, napping on the window seat cushions. The room was comfortably furnished with overstuffed chairs, a small blue-tiled kitchen table with two wooden chairs, and a worn red sofa.

A small bathroom and conveniently arranged kitchen were at one end of the loft, and Delia noted a large brass bed with a beautiful fan quilt, each block a different shade of green. Brightly colored throw rugs covered polished wood floors and bookcases lined whitewashed walls. A long rectangular table dominated the center of the room. Colleen had cleared books, papers, and seed catalogs from one end of the table, stacking them on the floor.

While she had fixed them a lunch of homemade bread and salad, Delia had examined the apartment and its contents, particularly the books. One large section was devoted to forensic anthropology and archaeology, and it was here that Delia found her own books. She had taken one of them down from the shelf and flipped through the pages, finding many passages underlined and annotations written in the margins. She smiled at one particular passage that Colleen had written the word "Yes!" next to, and frowned at "Rubbish!" next to another.

As she watched Colleen prepare their lunch, mixing the green salad with fresh produce from her garden and slicing the home-made bread, she decided that Colleen's apartment, and indeed lifestyle, was very similar to her own at Half Moon Lake. Colleen's obvious love for books, her bemused tolerance of the raccoons, her apparent affinity for living alone, and her devotion to a way of life that afforded her distance from her education and professional training—all these things reminded Delia of herself. She, too, had rejected her field and had isolated herself from her former friends and colleagues, choosing a solitary existence with only Shawla and her animals for company.

After lunch, Delia watched Colleen rinse their lunch dishes and realized that her attraction, which was admittedly physical, was also the result of feeling that she and Colleen were somehow kindred spirits. Indeed Colleen's refusal to assist her in the excavation reminded Delia of her own initial refusal to help Beth Collins a few years ago. Beth had appeared one evening in search for her missing friend, Jill Davis. Delia remembered the resentment that she had experienced when Beth had shown up in the restaurant in Bitter Creek and her frustration at Beth's persistent pursuit of her. She shook her head at the perfidies of life. Until she became aware of the similarities between her own rejection of Beth and Colleen's apparent reluctance to join the excavation, Delia had been puzzled by Colleen's behavior. Particularly puzzled by her seemingly indifferent response to Delia's obvious attraction to her. Perhaps, she thought, Colleen was merely *feigning* indifference—hoping that Delia would go away and leave her in peace. With some difficulty she turned her attention back to the matter at hand.

"But you said you wanted to hear about them," Delia reminded her as Colleen finished cleaning up.

Colleen sat down, reached across the table and took one of Delia's hands in hers. Her own hands were large but not ungainly. Her fingers were long and her nails were cut short. Warm and slightly damp from the dishwater, the touch of Colleen's hand once again reminded Delia of her attraction for the woman sitting across from her. Delia squeezed Colleen's hand and felt Colleen return the pressure.

"I *did* want to hear about them," Colleen assured her. "And you wanted to talk about them."

Delia thought a moment and nodded. "I guess I did. I didn't think I wanted to, but when you asked me I just—caved."

Colleen smiled, the lines in the corners of her eyes deepening.

"You have a nice smile," Delia told her. "What did I say to make you do that? I'd like to know so I can do it again."

Colleen chuckled, a deep throaty sound that Delia liked. "I just keep waiting for you to ask me how I knew about your dreams."

"I wondered, but I figured you'd have another answer that would make me look like Dr. Watson, so I decided to wait and see if you volunteered an answer." Delia moved her fingers cautiously across the top of the hand that held hers, but this time Colleen did not return the gesture. "I am pretty curious though."

Colleen smiled. "You look tired; like you haven't had much sleep lately or that your sleep has been troubled. It's not a big jump to think that you might be having bad dreams." She smiled. "Other than that, Dr. Watson, I'm afraid I don't have a logical explanation. I simply know some things—I don't know how I know them, I just do."

"It's funny," Delia said. "I don't usually dream—or at least if I do, I don't remember them very often." She released herself from Colleen's grasp and stood up, beginning to pace. "I guess that's why these dreams have disturbed me—they're so real."

"Vivid?"

"Vivid, yes," Delia agreed. "But also—you know how some dreams don't make sense. I mean, in some dreams people change or you find yourself in one place and then the place changes? There's not always continuity or a progression, you know?"

Colleen nodded.

"But these dreams...I was thinking this morning on the way up here, it's almost like watching a movie. Like each dream is an episode."

"And you really dreamed about the head pot before finding it?"

Delia nodded. "I know it sounds crazy—irrational, but I really did."

"I don't think it sounds crazy all," Colleen assured her. "Irrational, maybe. But who says 'irrational' is a bad thing?"

"Well, it's not scientific."

Colleen made a disgusted sound. "As if science has the corner on truth."

"I've never had anything like this happen to me before," Delia said. She stood up and went over to the window. Rocky and Prudence stirred as Delia stood and looked out toward the street. "You know, I can handle physical danger fine. I've been in a lot of tight spots in my life—and I have the scars to prove it. But I don't do well with things I can't explain. And these dreams just don't make any sense."

A few moments passed, and then Delia felt Colleen's hand on her shoulder.

Delia automatically leaned back into Colleen's touch and wound up with her head resting on Colleen's shoulder, next to her cheek.

"Are you frightened by the dreams?" Colleen asked softly.

Delia shrugged. "They're frightening dreams," she admitted. "But I wouldn't say I'm frightened by them."

She turned around and looked at Colleen directly, their faces only inches apart. Delia looked steadily into Colleen's deep-ocean blue eyes, trying to read something of her thoughts. Finally, she sat down on the edge of the window seat. One of the raccoons made a groaning sound, and Delia reached back to pet it. "It's just—I don't know. I feel so disoriented since I got here. Maybe it's being away from home or being with my granddad."

"Maybe it's being faced with your profession again," Colleen said.

Delia smiled at her. "Are you a shrink in addition to your other talents?"

Colleen smiled back. "Actually, yes. I do have a degree in psychology."

"I always seem to be putting my foot in my mouth with you."

"Well, in terms of the dreams—there are a lot of possible explanations. I'm not sure any of them will satisfy you, but we can look at them if you want to."

"If it means I can keep sitting here with you, I'd listen to you recite the multiplication tables," Delia said.

Colleen shook her head. "I don't do multiplication tables," she said solemnly and then smiled at Delia. "Would you care for some more tea?"

Delia nodded and watched as Colleen went to the stove and poured them each a cup. "Well, there is the psychological explanation. The dreams are a manifestation of some psychological need—or maybe some Jungian symbol rising to the subconscious level of a dream. Or maybe you really are simply dreaming about archaeology because you haven't practiced or thought about it much for a few years. Or . . ." She held out the cup of tea.

"What?" Delia asked, taking the cup from her.

"I think the dreams might be spiritual."

"Spiritual?" Delia asked. "In what way?

"Perhaps your dreams are trying to teach you something."

"Such as? Not to drink coffee after seven?"

Colleen resumed her seat beside Delia and sipped her tea. "I don't know. They're not my dreams. But sometimes if we can't or won't learn things in our physical lives, the spirit world tries to reach us through our dreams."

Delia was struck again by how much Colleen reminded her of her Navajo grandmother, Ruth, the way they both spoke of spiritual matters in a calm, matter-of-fact tone.

"And just what do you think the spiritual lesson is?" Delia asked her. But spiritual wasn't calm and matter-of-fact for her, indeed it was something that her scientific mind looked at skeptically. Spiritual matters and religion were something she studied, how they affected the cultures she unearthed. That was all. Delia changed the subject to what really interested her, "And is it just me, or do you feel a remarkable attraction for me?"

"You have a remarkably short attention span," Colleen remarked, but her laugh took any sting away from the remark.

"Back to the subject—I told you already. You're the only one who can answer that question."

"Well, I can't imagine what spiritual lesson I'm supposed to learn from the destruction of a city or from wholesale slaughter."

"That's because you're not open to the spirit world," Colleen told her gently. "You think about everything in terms of science, things that are tangible."

"The head pot and the other artifacts I dreamed about are real," Delia pointed out.

"True," Colleen assented. "And it may help you to know that the dreams you're describing do have a basis in reality—it's mere speculation of course, but there was a historically known chiefdom, who may have adapted the organization for their culture from the Cahokians—the Natchez. The Natchez were presumably the final phase of a cultural tradition called the Plaquemine."

"What's the time period?"

"I believe..." Colleen went to her bookshelf, pulled down a book and began flipping through the pages. "I think it's described briefly here in Fiedel...ah, yes. Here it is." She read for a moment and then said, "Around 1150 AD He says that the 'traits were derived from the Coles Creek culture'...which I know nothing about...'The Natchez were ruled by the Great Sun; he was a priest, and his younger brother, the Tattooed Serpent, the war chief.'"

"That's him!" Delia exclaimed. "The man in my dream...he had a tattoo of a serpent on his face, so did the woman."

"Fiedel doesn't say anything about a woman," Colleen said. "Nor does he describe the tattoo or say where the tattoo was."

"That's what Kate and I were puzzling over," Delia explained. "This serpent design on the head pot is exactly like the shape of the mound in Ohio—you know, the Serpent Mound."

Colleen frowned. "But that makes no sense. The times are wrong—the Serpent Mound is Adena—500 BC. And it's a

Woodlands culture, Ohio Valley . . . West Virginia and Illinois."

"I know, I know," Delia said excitedly. "Kate says the Great Serpent design has never shown up anywhere on pottery or other artifacts, not even in the burial mounds around the Serpent Mound itself."

"Yes, well, it's all very interesting," Colleen said.

Delia sighed. "I've never had anything like this happen before. Dreaming about artifacts and then finding them. That's definitely strange."

"Yes. I agree." Colleen reached back behind her and moved the raccoons, striking up a sleepy protest. She leaned back against the cushions, her bare knee touching Delia's pant leg. "Maybe you'll just have to wait and see what happens next. Perhaps the meaning will become clearer as you have more dreams."

"Assuming I have more dreams," Delia said, reaching over and lifting Colleen's legs so they lay across her own. Colleen smiled and didn't object.

"Oh, I think you'll keep having the dreams until you somehow resolve the meaning behind them."

"I see," Delia said dubiously. "Any particular reason for thinking so or just your famous intuition?"

"Well, from what you've told me, it doesn't sound like the dream is over—there's much to be seen yet, so it would seem."

"Great," Delia said glumly. "So I'm stuck with them?"

"You said it was like a movie—with each segment picking up where the last one ended. Have the words 'The End' appeared yet?"

Delia looked at her to see if she was joking. Colleen waggled her eyebrows, and Delia chuckled. Colleen joined her, and soon they were holding onto each other's arms and laughing uncontrollably. The raccoons looked up at the two women with quizzical expressions that caused Delia and Colleen to break into fresh peals of laughter.

"Would you answer my question now?" Delia asked.

"What question do you mean?" Colleen teased.

"About the attraction we feel? I mean you can't deny that we feel remarkably comfortable with each other. It wasn't a half an hour after I got here that you were holding me in your arms." She stroked Colleen's bare calf. "We can't seem to keep our hands off each other, and I bet you're like me—not the touchy-feely type with just anyone."

Colleen reached over and touched Delia's cheek with the back of her hand. "I agree with that assessment. But physical attraction is a small part of what I feel for you."

"Why don't you tell me about that?" Delia said, capturing Colleen's hand.

The moment was interrupted by the sound of Colleen's phone ringing in the background. She smiled suddenly and said, "Saved by the bell." She removed her warm hand from Delia's and walked across the room to answer the call.

Colleen spoke a moment and then beckoned to Delia with her hand. "It's Kate Treadaway," she mouthed. Delia walked over to Colleen and took the phone from her.

"Kate, what's up?" Delia asked.

"Well, basically all hell's broken loose this morning."

"What's the matter?"

"First off, somebody took a shot at your Granddad and Kevin this morning."

"What?" Delia exclaimed.

"He and Kevin went down to the site after you left. They were going to winch the tractor out of the hole but, when they got down there, they saw someone had disturbed the site. So they started looking around and that's when somebody shot at them."

Delia suddenly remembered the two lights she had seen down by the river from her window the previous night. Not night fishermen after all, she thought. Looters? But how had they learned of site so quickly?

"How's Granddad? Are either of them hurt?"

"No, Kevin pushed your granddad to the ground when he heard the first shot. When I was out there, your granddad said that his shoulder hurt."

"But he's okay?"

"He's okay. Mad as hell, of course."

"You said you were out there?"

"Yeah, your granddad called me after he phoned the sheriff. Wanted me to be there to keep them from messing anything up."

"How much disturbance of the site was there?"

"I don't know," Kate admitted. "We don't know what all was inside the tomb—but if the contents of the grave, some of the bundled skeletons, were crushed by the logs that collapsed...it's hard to say what's damaged from the collapse or from someone climbing down in there. Anyway, it's a good thing you picked up the ones that were on the surface because they'd be gone for sure now."

"We'll look at the photos I took and compare them to the site now," Delia said.

"Good idea," Kate said. "But that's not all. There were some wooden poles—sticks, actually, with feathers stuck in the ground—all around the burial mound. One of the poles had a note taped to it that said: 'Let our ancestors rest in peace'."

"*What?*"

"I know...it's ridiculous."

"But how did...who knew about the site?"

"You, your grandfather, Kevin, your great aunt, and now the cops and the coroner."

"*Before* someone shot at Granddad and left the notes on the pole—who knew about it before then?"

"Well, I would imagine lots of people *could* know," Kate said. "The people in the emergency room, your great uncle—your grandfather mentioned it was your great uncle who took him to the emergency room—Kevin, Eunice—and they could have mentioned to other people."

"You forgot to mention Kincaid," Delia said.

"Oh, I can't imagine he would say anything to anyone," Kate told her. "Like I said, he may be an asshole, but he'd know better than to tell people about a site. Why? What are you thinking?"

"Nothing," Delia said. "If you say he wouldn't tell anyone, that's good enough for me."

"Oh, before I forget, I called Harriet Richardson this morning, and she's coming up to look at the site later this week. There won't be any problem getting approval to excavate. Harriet says it's really a formality anyway—I'm betting these remains are over six hundred years old. There aren't any tribes in Arkansas today who would try to exercise any claims on them."

"Did you tell Harriet about the note and the poles?"

"Yeah," Kate said. "She thinks it's bogus. And I agree ... totally. No legitimate group with valid concerns would send an unsigned letter like that. The Indian Cultural Board in Little Rock has never had a problem with excavations. So, the issue is moot."

"Well, who do you think did it?"

Kate was quiet and then said, "Someone who doesn't want us to excavate, I guess."

"Why would someone not want us to excavate? That doesn't make sense."

Kate didn't answer, and finally Delia spoke, "Did you call the authorities?"

"Kincaid beat me to it. He told them you'd uncovered human remains and hadn't notified them. Got you off on the wrong foot with Sheriff Pettit. He's an asshole anyway, even without this bad start. He called me. I gave him the true story. Anyway, he's going out there to take statements from Kevin and your granddad."

Delia turned her head to look at Colleen, who was cleaning up the kitchen from their lunch. Again, she noticed the way Colleen held herself. The line of her back and butt, elegant curves that somehow bespoke beauty and a calm grace. Colleen must have felt Delia's eyes on her and turned to look at her questioningly.

Delia blushed, much to her chagrin, and tried to concentrate on what Kate was saying to her.

"Anyway, I just thought you should know about all this. It's going to be like a three-ring circus out there."

"It sounds like every other dig I've ever been involved with," Delia said. "Speaking of circuses, I wonder how long it'll be before the media finds out about it. They'll be all over this."

"They'll find out after the coroner examines the remains. The coroner might send a sample of the remains to the State Crime Lab for examination. But the newspapers will find out about it. The local paper gets a report from the police blotter every day. I can see the headlines now: 'DELIA IRONFOOT DIGS AGAIN'."

"Don't say that," Delia moaned. "I might change my mind before I start. Okay, I'll come back, and we'll get this straightened out. You're sure Granddad's okay?"

"He's fine. Just sore and probably tired. How's it going with the beautiful Colleen? Did you charm her into helping us?"

"Not in the least. She's totally unimpressed with me," Delia answered, ducking her head as Colleen threw a potholder at her. She grinned at Colleen and told Kate, "I'll be headed home soon."

"We'll figure it out when you get back," Kate said warmly. "Are you coming back today?"

"Sure," Delia said. "Why wouldn't I?"

"Well, I thought if you and Colleen got along *really* well—"

Delia laughed. "I told you she was totally unimpressed by my meager charms. Anyway, even if we did get along really well, I'm not that kind of person."

"I'm sorry to hear that," Kate chuckled. "If I don't see you when you get back, I'll catch you tomorrow."

"Okay," Delia said and hung up. She went into the kitchen.

"Trouble?" Colleen asked.

Delia nodded and told her of the shooting, the poles, and the note. She also mentioned the lights she had seen from her window.

"How much disturbance of the site?" Colleen asked.

"Kate didn't think that much, just the silliness with the poles. She didn't think anyone had gotten down into the tomb, but I won't know for sure until I get there," Delia answered "I took pictures of the tomb though before I went to the university. We'll have to compare the photos with the site when I get back." She went into the other room and picked up her duster. "I appreciate the lunch and the company." She tried a crooked grin on Colleen. "Are you sure I can't talk you into helping out? I'm going to need as much help as I can get."

"I have a lot of faith in Kate; she's an experienced excavator," Colleen assured her. "She's intelligent. Best of all, she's young and she has lots of energy. You're in good hands."

"I'd rather be in your hands," Delia said ruefully.

Colleen smiled. "A pleasant thought, but one I must decline."

"Well, you know where we'll be if you change your mind," Delia said, kissing Colleen's lips quickly and walking out the door. She looked back once to see if Colleen was still standing there.

She was. Delia was pleased to see that she was smiling.

Chapter 9

It was late afternoon by the time Delia arrived back at her grandfather's farm. A white Crown Victoria with the Sheriff's Department logo was on one side of her grandfather's driveway, and her aunt's Buick was parked in the yard on the other. She entered the house to find the sheriff, a tall man with a blond crew cut, leaning against the kitchen counter taking off his coat as if he had just arrived. He greeted her great aunt and her grandfather, nodded to her and began his questioning. Her aunt Eunice stood nearby listening, her arms folded over her chest.

"So Hollis, heard you had a little trouble out here today. Any idea who might have shot at you?" the sheriff drawled.

"No," Hollis said wearily. "I told you that already on the phone."

"I'd bet my hat that it's Bob Noland who's behind all these shenanigans," Eunice injected. "Mark my words, Jackson Pettit."

Delia stepped between her great aunt and the sheriff. "I'm Delia—Hollis's granddaughter."

The sheriff nodded curtly to her and then turned to her great aunt. "Miss Eunice, just because the man tried to sue his relative to get the property doesn't mean..."

Delia tuned out both Eunice and the sheriff and turned to her grandfather who was sitting with his head bowed at the kitchen table. Wally sat beside him, his head resting on her grandfather's leg. When Delia put her hand on his grandfather's shoulder, he raised his head and she read weariness on his face.

"Are you all right, Granddad?"

"I'm okay," Hollis said. "Tell the truth, I didn't even hear the shot. Kevin heard it and he pushed me down and lay down on top of me." He rolled his shoulder and winced. "I think he broke my dang neck. He's a load."

"Does Kevin know which direction the shot came from?"

"He said it came from the woods that border the west side of the field," her grandfather replied. He turned to the sheriff. "Kevin had to leave before you got here, Jack. He had to be somewhere."

"That's okay," the sheriff told him. "I'll catch up with him tomorrow. See what he has to say."

Delia turned to her great aunt and said, "Eunice, I could use some coffee. Would you mind making on a pot?"

Eunice broke off her bickering with the Sheriff and looked surprised. "Well, good Lord, where are my manners?"

Sheriff Pettit closed the notebook he was holding and directed his remark to Eunice's back. "That's what I was wondering."

Eunice stopped her preparations long enough to turn and glare at him. "You just button it up mister, or you'll be leaving without a cup."

Delia hid a smile when the sheriff held up his hands in surrender.

"So, Miss Eunice, why do you think Bob Noland had something to do with this?" the sheriff asked.

"Because that no-good snake called this morning right after I got here. Delia hadn't been gone but a few minutes." She looked at her brother. "Tell Jackson what he said to you. Go on."

Hollis shrugged. "He offered to buy the property I bought from Arlene Buck. I turned him down. That's the extent of it."

"Well, if that isn't the understatement of the century!" Eunice was at the sink peeling potatoes furiously.

"Why?" the sheriff asked mildly. "What happened?"

"Noland pitched a fit when Hollis turned him down," Eunice replied.

"That true, Hollis?" Sheriff Pettit asked.

"I wouldn't call it a fit," Hollis countered. "He was a little upset when I told him no, but..."

"Oh, for pity sake!" Eunice exploded. "I could hear him squalling clear across the kitchen. I couldn't believe it, a grown man acting like that on the phone. If you ask me, it's too much of a coincidence—Noland calling up here to ask if he can buy the property and when Hollis said, 'No,' just a little while later...somebody shoots at him."

"Did he threaten you or in any way try to intimidate you?" the sheriff asked.

"What do you call shooting at him?" Delia asked. "Threatening? Or intimidating him?"

"We don't have any evidence yet that anyone shot at him," Pettit said calmly.

"Granddad said Kevin heard the shot..." Delia started.

"He said Kevin heard 'a shot'," Pettit countered. "Your granddad didn't hear anything."

"What are you saying, Jack?" Eunice countered. "Are you saying Kevin doesn't know what a gunshot sounds like? The boy's hunted all his life. I think he knows a gunshot when he hears it."

"Have you searched the scene yet?" Delia asked.

Before the sheriff could answer, Hollis pushed his chair away from the table. "Noland didn't say anything threatening on the phone, Jack. Now, if it's all right with everyone, I'm going upstairs to rest before dinner." He snapped his fingers at Wally, and the dog followed him out of the kitchen.

"Did you search the scene?" Delia repeated.

"I looked around before I came up here," he said. "I didn't find anything...no shell casings, no footprints...but I'm not surprised. The leaf cover on the ground out there is pretty thick."

He sighed. "I'll have our crime scene techs come and check around tomorrow, but I don't think they'll find anything."

Eunice stared hard at Pettit. "So you're just going to wait around until whoever shot him tries it again." She made a disgusted sound.

Pettit shook his head and turned to Delia. "I don't have any other questions for your granddad, but I got a feeling *you* could shed some light on this situation."

"Me?" Delia asked in surprise. "I just got here a few days ago."

"Well, you sure have been busy in that few days," the sheriff observed sourly. He flipped open his notebook again. "You went to the college and ruffled old Jim Kincaid's feathers pretty good, got Katie Treadaway stirred up about her brother again—and while all the commotion is taking place down here, you take off to Jericho Mill trying to get that witch woman, Redfield, to come down here and get people riled up too. Not to mention tampering with a crime scene and not reporting human remains."

"What are you talking about?" Delia said, truly puzzled. "I called the State Archaeologist in Fayetteville and couldn't get an answer. So I went to the university and told Kincaid about the site and then I went down the hall and told Kate Treadaway. Who else did you *want* me to call?"

"Seems to me anyone with common sense would know when you find dead bodies, first thing you do is call the police." The sheriff looked at her quizzically. "Kincaid said that you'd tampered with human remains, which is against the law no matter how old they are ... that you'd been down at the scene, moving things around, removing evidence and maybe even planting evidence ... that it wouldn't be the first time you'd done something like this. Told me you'd been fired from some college because of it ... he was pretty irate."

Delia took a deep breath and tried to relax. "I don't know what Kincaid's problem is, but he's totally misrepresented what I've done since I've been here. I took photographs of the scene when Granddad showed it to me. That was the first and last time that I was at the site. You're welcome to look at them. I've documented everything I've done. I've followed proper archaeological procedures... at any rate, I've seen enough dead bodies to know these weren't recent deaths. Based on my professional experience, I *did* notify the proper authorities."

"I'd like to take a look at those photos, since you offered," Pettit said. He waited while Delia went up to her room and retrieved them. Jackson took the pictures and then said: "I notified the coroner myself. He'll be out here first thing tomorrow. It's too late to do anything more today." He tapped the photo envelope against the kitchen counter. "I'll look at these tonight and if everything seems all right, you can get them back tomorrow."

He began putting on his coat.

"You said Kate was stirred up about her brother... what's she upset about?"

Sheriff Pettit made a face. "Oh, she's got this notion that the police didn't investigate his disappearance vigorously enough."

"Maybe she's right," Delia countered. "I've only been in a town a short while and already two separate people have told me the story of Noland's involvement with the disappearances of his partner, the gaming commissioner, and Buddy. Of course I don't know everything about the case but..."

The sheriff glared at Delia. "You don't know *anything* about it... and neither does Katie, as far as that goes. Let me fill you in on something—if Buddy Treadaway had kept his goddamn mouth shut, we might have actually been able to find out what happened to those people. But no, he went off half-cocked and..."

Aunt Eunice, who had been preparing dinner, slammed a lid down on a pan and turned to face them. "Now you listen to me, Jackson Pettit. As long as you're in my kitchen, you'll not take the Lord's name in vain."

To Delia's surprise the sheriff flushed. "I didn't intend any disrespect, Miss Eunice...ma'am. It's just that every time Katie Treadaway sees me, she hounds me about her missing brother. I mean it's been *ten years*. He's legally dead. I haven't had to talk to her for six months until this happened—so in my book, that makes your niece here responsible."

"Whatever," Delia said impatiently. "Let's get back to Buddy being responsible for his own disappearance. What do you mean if he'd kept his mouth shut?"

Sheriff Pettit sighed. "After Noland's business partner and the gaming commissioner disappeared, we had a few leads. Buddy interfered with that and as a result, he probably got himself killed."

"So it was Buddy's fault...interesting. So...why are you calling the site a crime scene?" Delia asked him.

"Anywhere there's dead bodies, that's a crime scene in my book...so until the coroner is done, you stay away from it...now; let's talk about your friend, Colleen Redfield."

"What about her?" Delia asked.

"I was hoping you could tell me that," the sheriff said. "Kate said you were up at Jericho Mill today, trying to get Redfield to come down here. What do you want her to do, cast a spell or something?"

Delia looked around with disbelief and in confusion. "Am I missing something here? Do you know Colleen?"

"Whole town knows about her," the sheriff informed her. "Knows she's a foreigner and a witch, probably a devil worshipper. People don't want her around here."

"I think you'd be better off actually investigating who took a shot at my grandfather and Kevin...and who left that silly warning...instead of worrying about 'spells' and 'witchcraft'."

"Listen up, missy, I might not have fancy letters after my name," Pettit said sarcastically. "But you don't need a lot of education to see that things were fairly quiet until you got here. Now we got bodies everywhere, people hearing shots, Kate Treadaway in a tizzy. Next thing you know, they'll be radical Indian groups marchin' around here—claimin' we're disturbin' their burial grounds or something."

"I thought there were no indigenous Indians in this area."

The sheriff shrugged. "Weren't till you got here." He eyed her suspiciously. "You've got an Indian sounding last name. That stuff down there's worth a lot of money to pot hunters—willing to pay top dollar for pottery and such."

"So now you think *I* had something to do with the disturbance of the site? Maybe you think I took a shot at my Granddad and Kevin, too."

"You said it. Not me."

"That's brilliant detective work," Delia replied. "Never mind that I wasn't here when they got shot at." She paused to gain control of her temper, and then asked. "Do you think there's some connection between the site and the shooting?"

"Won't know that until I finish interviewing Kevin," the sheriff said, looking warily at Eunice. "My feeling right now is, no. What I think is some duck hunters on the river are mighty poor shots."

"What about the looting?" Delia asked.

"What looting?" the sheriff returned. "Far as I know, nobody's decided anything's missing. Even if you could prove that there had been looting, I got more important things to do than chase some laid-off construction workers who're only tryin' to make a little extra money to feed their families after the rice harvest is over. So there's a few less pots—so what?" He paused and eyed Delia. "Far as the bodies go, I'm satisfied they're not recent. But like I said, I got to get the official word from the coroner."

The sheriff's shoulder microphone crackled. He walked to the back door and turned his back to them. Delia couldn't hear what he was saying, but shortly he said, "Ten-four. I'm on my way."

"I got other things to do now," Pettit said, opening the back door. "I'll send the coroner out tomorrow with the crime scene techs." He pointed to Delia and said, "You stay out of their way." He nodded to Eunice and stepped out the door. When Delia heard his car start up, she turned to her aunt.

"He sure is contrary, isn't he?" Delia asked. "How long have you known him, Aunt Eunice?"

Eunice snorted disdainfully. "He was in my Sunday School class when he was six and he hasn't changed a bit since then."

Delia walked over to the stove where her aunt was cooking and sniffed appreciatively. "Sure smells good—what is it?"

Eunice opened the oven door and slid a pan of rolls onto the top rack. "It's pot roast with potatoes and carrots. There's things for a tossed salad in the refrigerator...these rolls'll take about five minutes. Don't let 'em burn."

Eunice took off her apron and hung it over a kitchen chair. "Oh, and before I forget, an overnight package came for you today from Shawla."

"Oh, good," Delia said. "I asked her to mail my laptop and a few other things that I can't live without." She looked at her great aunt who was putting on her coat. "Are you leaving?"

"I've got a Missionary Society meeting tonight at the church. I fixed Hollis a late lunch; I could see he was getting tired and thought he might go lie down—he probably won't wake up for dinner."

"But why did you fix all this food...just for me?"

"It's not just for you," Eunice declared, picking up her purse. "It's for you and your friend."

Delia heard a vehicle pull up in the driveway and then the sound of a car door slam. "My friend?"

"Yep, that should be her right now," Eunice said opening the back door to the porch. "I invited her out for dinner. Didn't want you to have to eat alone. Bye now."

Just then, Kate Treadaway walked up onto the porch and grinned at Delia. "I smell pot roast. Let's eat."

◆◆◆◆◆

After dinner Delia and Kate sat at the kitchen table drinking coffee and eating peach cobbler. Delia recounted the day's events in Jericho Mill with Colleen and then said, "I wonder if Kevin would help out with the excavation. I could afford pay him." She paused and took a bite of the cobbler. "He seems like a pretty good kid."

Kate looked up from her plate with a frown. "I heard he hangs out with that no-good cousin of his, John Ed. Doesn't John Ed work for Bob Noland?"

"That's what Kevin told me . . . he's unloading cars and detailing them."

Kate's expression darkened. "Kevin needs to stay away from John Ed then. Noland's a criminal."

Delia stood up and began clearing off the table. Kate rose to help her, and they worked in silence, but Bob Noland's name hung in the air. A sudden thought occurred to Delia.

"Kate, do you know—is Noland a collector?" Delia asked curiously.

"Kincaid told me once that Noland has one of the biggest private collections of Mississippian grave goods in the county. He knows people who have seen it."

"Does Kincaid know Bob Noland?"

Kate shook her head. "I don't think so. I can't see him hanging around with known criminals like Noland. Anyway, Noland's not the only one around here with illegal artifacts. I hear rumors all the time about people who have incredible collections and who are holding onto them until their prices increase." She paused. "Are you thinking that's why Noland wants to buy the land now?"

"The thought occurred to me," Delia confessed. "But I wasn't sure how interested he'd be if he wasn't a collector."

"You don't have to be a collector to be interested in artifacts. You just have to be interested in money."

"But how would Noland have known about the tomb?" Delia asked.

"We already decided that a lot of people could have found out about it. Maybe Jack Pettit told somebody. If I had to pick some-one, it'd be him. He blames Buddy for his own disappearance."

"Yeah, he was talking about it this afternoon."

"He's a jerk," Kate said flatly. "He just didn't do his job, and he had to have someone to blame. It's always easier to blame the victim."

After they finished in the kitchen, Delia and Kate went into the living room and sat on the couch.

"You know," Kate said. "This whole situation is weird. The note, the fact that someone may or may not have shot at your grand-father, Noland's involvement..."

"We don't know for sure that he was involved," Delia objected.

"Look, if Noland wanted to buy that land from your grand-father, there's a reason behind it," Kate said firmly. "And if he's involved in anything, it's illegal. Everybody in town knows he killed his business partner and the Gaming Commissioner; and, I *know* he had something to do with Buddy's disappearance."

"Was there anyone else you can think of who might have had a problem with Buddy? One of his other cases, maybe?"

"Well, he sent bad guys to prison; I guess it's possible one of them might have wanted to hurt him. But like I said before, he was well liked—the basketball team he played on, in high school, went to the State Championship every year. That counts for a lot around here. He was a good person and a good prosecutor." She shook her head. "I know I brought this up, but could we talk about something else for a while?"

Delia reached over and took her hand. "Absolutely. Want me to tell you about how I came up empty with Colleen?"

"Sure. That would definitely cheer me up," Kate said with a renewed smile on her face.

Delia leaned back and told Kate what happened between her-self and Colleen, leaving out the part about her "burning city" dreams and its mysterious connection to the head pot. That just didn't seem real enough to share with anyone else. She now wondered why she had so easily told Colleen. Delia also didn't share the physical attraction she had felt for Colleen. When she finished Kate shook her head.

"Well, you tried. Too bad she won't help, though I'm not surprised. Kincaid made her pretty mad the last time she volunteered for a dig, and she swore she'd never work for us again."

"Yes," Delia said. "I was disappointed; we'll need a good bone person."

Kate slid across the couch and, with a mischievous grin, playfully poked Delia's kneecap.

"Why do you want to go looking out-of-town for? I'm a pretty good judge of bones myself."

Delia laughed, falling into Kate's mood.

"Are you flirting with me?"

"Absolutely," Kate said, touching Delia's cheek with her fingertips.

Delia turned her face and gently kissed Kate's palm. "I thought so."

Kate slid her hand down to Delia's neck. "I want to kiss you," and began to slowly pull Delia's face towards her own.

"I don't think this is a good idea," Delia murmured. "It could lead to . . . complications."

Kate, her lips inches from Delia, drew back a fraction and grinned lazily. "I like to think that there's a better word describing what it could lead to."

"Oh? Like what?"

Kate pressed her lips gently but insistently against Delia's. "Hmm, like maybe pleasure?"

Delia felt herself responding to Kate's kiss, having secretly wanted to kiss her since seeing Kate for the first time, and she buried her hand in Kate's wild coppery hair.

"Right here, on the couch in my Granddad's living room?"

"It would be kind of outrageous," Kate admitted, planting a small, soft kiss at the edge of Delia's mouth.

Kate slid her hand over Delia's shoulder and let it rest lightly on her breast. "Dee, I'm not proposing marriage...just...sex. Nothing wrong with a little old-fashioned fun." She rubbed her thumb gently across Delia's nipple through her shirt.

Delia closed her eyes and tried not to enjoy Kate's hand on her breast. "You're awfully young, you know."

"Oh, yes, I'm sure I'm must seem young to someone of your advanced years," Kate said sarcastically. "Get real. You're only as old as you feel."

Delia laughed softly. "Spoken like a twenty-five year old."

"Twenty-six, I told you before," Kate corrected her. She leaned over and kissed Delia again, this time slowly and more deeply. Though she had reservations, Delia returned Kate's kiss, leaning into her and then resting her head on the back of the couch. Kate took this as encouragement; she stroked Delia's face with her left hand and kissed her neck, her other hand still softly caressing Delia's breast. Delia shuddered with pleasure and finally pushed her away.

"Not here, Kate," Delia said firmly. "Not with Granddad upstairs...I just can't."

"Listen," Kate stood and began putting on her coat, "If we're going to be sleep together, you need to stop harping on how young I am. It'll get really old after while." She grinned.

Delia laughed out loud. "That's a very big 'if', kiddo. You better go home. I think you've overheated your engine."

"See, there you go again, being so negative." She kissed Delia lightly before being pushed out the back door. "Call me tomorrow when the coroner and sheriff get here. Then, we can figure out what we're going to do—about the bones."

After Kate had gone, Delia leaned back and rested against the door. As she mounted the stairs, she had the feeling that her dreams might not be about the woman with the tattooed face but about a different woman; which, Delia admitted, would be a welcome change.

In the background, the burning city backlit the aftermath of the slaughter. Blood from the raging battle had pooled on the stones of the courtyard and began to run down through the streets in a crimson stream. Some invaders ran into the square; they slipped and fell in the bloody pools.

The battle came to its conclusion in the courtyard, in the center of the burning city, and the invaders gathered to witness the act that they had come to see. The Tattooed Serpent, who had fought so bravely, was dragged before them. And though he struggled to keep his face expressionless at the sight of the senseless slaughter, his countenance twisted with grief and pain as his eyes scanned the bodies of the dead. The two men who held his arms behind his back dragged him toward a man dressed in a bearskin head-dress and forced him to his knees.

Suddenly, the Serpent Woman ran into the courtyard, screaming and fighting her way toward her brother. The dreamlike expression on her face was gone, replaced by fear and rage. The Tattooed Serpent twisted in the grip of his captors and managed to raise his head as two invaders grabbed his sister and held her. Just for a moment, they looked into each other's eyes.

The end was swift. The man in the bearskin headdress lifted a stone club with hands already slippery with blood and crushed the young man's head with one powerful, brutal blow. Contemptuously, the executioner then spit on his lifeless body and the invaders screamed victory cries.

The same stone club that had killed her brother came for her. One blow, and now her blood mixed with his.

This time when Delia awoke from the gruesome dream, she was more frightened and distressed than she had been about any of the previous dreams. Not only was this one more grisly but it was more disturbing because she now knew the young man in the dream looked like someone who was familiar. She had first seen his face in the photograph on Kate's desk. The Tattooed Serpent looked like Buddy Treadaway.

Delia sat up in bed and ran her fingers through her hair, remembering the distinctive tattoo on the woman's face and her many earrings. Though they did not share facial features and though she had never seen a look of peace on Kate's face, Delia knew that the there was a connection between Tattooed Serpent woman and Kate. Was this what Colleen had talked about with her? Could there be a connection between her dream world and reality? Or had exhaustion and nights of fitfully interrupted sleep finally caught up with her? She lay back down on the bed and drew the covers back over her.

She would think about it tomorrow when her mind was clearer.

Chapter 10

"Hey, don't walk over there! What's the matter with you?"

Delia grinned as Kate harangued two deputies, and then she turned back to the scene around the hole. A gaggle of law enforcement professionals had collected by her grandfather's tractor and the hollow space exposed by the collapse of the log tomb ceiling. Footprints covered the ground and the area around the cavity was trampled down.

The coroner and sheriff's deputies had arrived earlier that morning. When she saw them go by, Delia made a quick phone call to Kate, alerting her to their arrival. Then she dressed hurriedly and drove down to the site on the ATV. It was a beautiful fall morning. Dressed in a pair of khaki work pants and a blue flannel shirt, Delia had also taken her fleece vest to wear in case the air was chillier by the river.

Delia had parked the ATV well away from the crowd, and then stood aside it to survey the scene. Her grandfather's tractor was still half-in, half-out of the hole; the deputies had added two more steel cables to secure it. One of the deputies had approached her, a tall, heavyset man with coarse red hair that stood in corkscrews all over his head. With a protruding belly and a waddling gait, the deputy looked remarkably like a clown without make-up.

"Howdy," he said in a friendly tone. "You must be Hollis's granddaughter." He stuck out an oversized hand. "Name's Henry Williams."

Delia took his hand. "The sheriff didn't come?"

"Naw, he's up in Faraday...bad trailer-truck accident. Said he'll be down later in the morning."

"Did he send the crime scene techs to check out the woods?"

Williams shook his head. "No, they had to go to a convenience store break-in that happened last night. Sheriff said to tell you that they'll be here when they can get away and...uh, well, for you to stay out of the possible crime scene."

Delia nodded. "Is the coroner here?"

"He's down inside the hole," Williams told her. "Been down for about thirty minutes maybe." He grinned. "He ain't exactly happy about that tractor hanging over him, but he's down there."

"Well, if I can't be of any help here, I think I'll go back up to the house and get some breakfast," Delia had said agreeably. "Kate Treadaway is on her way and..."

Williams's face flushed. "Kate's coming here?"

"Yes, I called her before I came down."

"Well, that's great," Williams said. "Just great. She'll be all over our butts." He shook his head. "That woman...she's..." He stopped, turned on his heel, and walked away.

After she had returned to the house, Delia cooked breakfast for herself and her grandfather, and when Kate arrived she ate with them. Following a last cup of coffee, Delia and Kate had gotten on the ATV and headed down to the site. As they had neared the scene, Kate had pointed to the coroner's white van, and Delia pulled the ATV up next to it. Then, Kate leapt off and ran over to the tomb.

Now, to Delia's delight, Kate had turned her attention to Henry Williams and another deputy who were walking aimlessly around

113

the site, looking at the ground. Each carried a plastic bag. Delia waited patiently by the coroner's van until Kate came back, shaking her head in disgust. "Those two idiots are worse than useless. Come on; let's see what damage the coroner's doing."

Delia followed Kate, and they approached the mound carefully. Delia noted that the coroner had used an extension ladder to get down inside the tomb. Kate pushed two people dressed in jump suits with CORONER'S OFFICE on the back out of the way. "Don't you two have something constructive to do?" she asked them, turning on her flashlight and pointing it down into the dimness of the tomb. "Is that you, Doc?" Kate asked. "It's Kate Treadaway."

"Yeah, it's me," came a deep, bass voice from the tomb. "And you stop harassing my people...they *are* doing something constructive. They're going to pull me out of this hole if that damn tractor decides to fall the rest of the way."

"Did you crush anything with that damn ladder getting down there? You might wanna think about retiring if you're too old to hop down in a hole now," Kate called to him jokingly.

In the beam of the flashlight, Delia could see a short, stocky, African-American man wearing a fisherman's hat. He was kneeling among the bundled skeletons, many of which had been broken open and whose errant bones were scattered around. Delia noticed too that one side of the tomb had collapsed, reburying some of the skeletons.

"You find me someone to take over, and I'll be glad to go to fishin' full time," he told her. "Give me another half hour or so, and I'll be done," he said. "Do you mind gettin' that damn flashlight outta my eyes?"

Kate turned off the flashlight and then knelt down by the opening. "C'mon, Doc. You know as well I do that those are archaeological remains—when's the last time you saw a dead body like any of these? With knees drawn up to its chest and a copper axe buried its head?"

"Go away, Katie," he growled. "I already have a tractor hanging over my head; I don't need you up there bitchin' at me. Now git."

Kate sighed, stood up and brushed the mud from her insulated pants. She had tried unsuccessfully to capture her wild coppery mane by tying it into a ponytail, finally giving up and pushing a baseball cap down on top of it. Delia smiled as she read the words on the cap: "ARCHAEOLOGISTS DO IT IN THE DIRT."

"Who are these people?" Delia asked Kate. "The only one I've met so far is Deputy Williams. He introduced himself to me before you got here." She commented, "He got annoyed when I told him you were coming out here."

Kate smiled at Delia's mention of Williams's discomfort with her presence, then said, "That's Doc Rogers, the coroner, down in the hole." Then, raising her voice loudly, she added "Tramping all over the skeletons!"

"I am *not* tramping anything," came his rough voice from the hole.

"And these two are his techs." Then, she motioned to the two deputies who were still walking around with their plastic bags. "And those clueless idiots are the 'Clown Brain Trust'—'Bozo and Clarabelle'. They're supposed to be looking for a bullet."

"The sheriff seems to think that the shot came from duck hunters on the river," Delia said.

Kate shrugged. "It's possible, I guess. But, if that's the case, then it was a shotgun. And I doubt if the 'clowns' are going to find any pellets. Forget about that." She slipped her arm through Delia's, a repeat of the gesture that endeared her to Delia the day they first met.

"This is just a little part of the field," she said. "You told me your granddad said there were more mounds . . . let's go for a walk and see what we can find."

"Okay. I can show you the trench that opened up too . . . it leads down to the river, where I found the head pot."

Kate followed Delia away from the others until they reached the line of trees that bordered the south side of the field; then she walked beside her as they cut back up field until they encountered the trench. Stepping carefully, they approached it and peered down inside.

"Too dark," Kate grumbled, pulling out her flashlight and shining it down into the chasm. Bits of pottery and arrow points stuck out from the sides and, as Kate moved the beam of her flashlight down, they could see the stratigraphy of the trench exposed to a depth of perhaps five feet.

"Can I use the flashlight for a minute?" Delia asked, holding out her hand. Kate handed her the flashlight, and Delia dropped down to the ground. Lying on her stomach, with her head positioned over the opening, playing the beam over the exposed dirt, Delia said, "Look at that, Kate."

Kate joined her on the ground and squinted. "What is that?" she asked.

Delia moved the flashlight a few inches closer. "It looks like a layer of ash."

"What?" Kate asked.

"Just a minute," Delia said, and moving herself around, lowered her legs carefully into the bottom of the ditch. Standing firmly on its floor, squatting down to bring her eyes level with the line of ash, Delia followed the layer along the length of the trench with her light.

"Kate," she said. "It is a layer of ash." Delia continued to move the beam of light, following the gray layer.

Delia came up out of the trench and motioned for Kate to follow her. "Let's see how far it goes," she said. Training her light on the ash, Delia continued to walk along the edge. Finally, they reached the river's edge where the trench had collapsed the riverbank.

"That's a long layer," Kate said. "Not from a fire pit or even a funeral pyre."

The dream of the burning city washed over Delia—the burning circles, the people running to the river to escape the flames, people and canoes and round houses ablaze.

"A whole city," Delia whispered. The image was like a blow to her solar plexus. But her dreams couldn't be real. Maybe she had noticed the ash when she first saw the tomb and the trench. Maybe it hadn't really registered consciously; maybe she carried it home with her that night, unaware.

"Wow, this could really be something," Kate said, her voice full of wonder and excitement. "We need to photograph this and then cover it with a tarp or something." She watched as Delia got to her feet unsteadily. "You okay?" she asked. Delia brushed off the seat of her pants and nodded.

"Yeah, I'm fine. It was just a . . . surprise."

"Right," Kate replied. "Well, let's look around a little more," and she began walking away from the trench, examining the ground. Delia followed her, still shaken by the layer of ash and thoughts of the burning village from her dream. Suddenly, she wished Colleen were with her; she wanted to talk to her, have her examine the layer. She considered telling Kate about her dreams, but decided against it. Kate seemed excited by their discovery, eager to explore the rest of the site. For the first time since they met, their conversation had not touched on her missing brother and, as a result, her mood was ebullient. Delia was reluctant to spoil Kate's enthusiasm, so she said nothing. She continued to follow Kate as she walked farther away from the trench, letting Kate get ahead of her.

"Hey, Dee, look at this," Kate shouted, beckoning to her. "Holes."

Delia caught up with her and looked at what Kate was pointing too. "Ah, pothunters, right?"

"Yeah," Kate confirmed. "They use car radio antennae. Put a metal ball on the end and probe around till they hit something."

"But why would anyone be probing for pots when there's a hole

117

with artifacts already exposed?" Delia asked.

"I don't know," Kate admitted. "Most pot hunters around here would grab whatever was easiest to reach and get out before somebody noticed them."

"Maybe this particular pot hunter was looking for a particular kind of pot...or something unbroken." Then Delia added, "You know, I saw lights down here, by the river, the third night I was here. Did I tell you that? I thought the lights were night fishermen."

Kate shrugged. "Could've been. Let's get back and talk to the 'clowns' and the coroner. After they leave we can take pictures of the trench and some of these other mounds. Then we should find something to cover the trench with."

When they were standing over the hole again, Kate yelled down into the hole. "Hey, doc? You done yet?"

"Get off my rear, Katie. When I'm done, you'll be the first to know."

Kate frowned and walked over to the deputies. "What's with the plastic bags?"

The tall, red haired deputy shrugged. "The Sheriff told us to pick up anything that looked like it might be part of a crime scene."

"The only thing that's a crime at this scene is you two pretending to be cops," Kate scoffed. To Delia she said, "Come and look at this." Kate motioned her over and pointed to numerous small holes in the ground.

"More probes?" Delia asked.

Kate nodded. "Yeah, I was afraid this might be a problem."

"On some of the excavations I've been involved with, we had to hire armed guards to keep the looters away—and then it was mostly a losing battle," Delia told her. "In Turkey, looters broke into the 'finds shed' at night and stole the artifacts we'd unearthed during the day."

Both Delia and Kate knew all too well the damage that looters could do to a site before an excavation even began. Like most archaeologists, they had different priorities than those of pothunters and collectors. While looters wanted only undamaged and unbroken artifacts for black market sales, reputable archaeologists cared about recording the provenance, or exact location, of each object. Broken or not, each artifact, feature, or skeleton, revealed the story of people who lived and died hundreds, even thousands, of years ago. Here, on the land where her grandfather and his ancestors had lived and farmed for mere generations, the story of an entire civilization might be uncovered in the strata below. Each looter's disturbance made Kate and Delia's ability to reconstruct the stories of these long-dead people much harder. Delia remembered the words of one university professor from a long-ago lecture: "Every excavation is destruction so you better do it right the first time." They were words she never let herself forget.

"Okay, I'm done," Doc Rogers called. Climbing the metal ladder, he emerged from the tomb as they watched.

"Well?" Kate asked, her arms on her hips.

"It'll take a forensic specialist to pinpoint it," he said, unzipping his coveralls as he walked to his van. "But you're right, they're not recent. Probably Mississippian from the looks of the grave goods."

"I could have told you that before you started," Kate said.

He began pulling off his dusty rubber boots and dirt stained insulated coveralls. "If you excavate, I'd get Colleen Redfield down here to help you with the bones. She's the best." He winked. "Even if she is a witch." He opened the back of his van and threw his boots and coveralls inside. "I'll write up my report and give it to the sheriff. Site should be released to the owner in a couple of days, less if the paperwork doesn't get hung up."

"What about the 'dummies' over there?" Kate asked.

Doc Rogers shrugged. "They're Jack's 'dummies'. Talk to him."

"But as far as you're concerned, this isn't a crime scene?" Kate asked.

119

"Well, I'm sure the poor guy with the axe in his head thought it was a crime," Rogers chuckled. "But it's too late to press charges." He laughed heartily at his joke and was still laughing as he drove away.

"He's kind of weird, but he's not an asshole like Pettit," Kate observed. Then she turned to Delia and grabbed her shoulder. "Come on," she said, suddenly eager. "I've got a camera in the truck, and tarps too. Let's do our thing, baby."

Chapter 11

The next day was overcast and cold. As Delia drove down to the site in the early morning, she saw mist rising off the Big Right Hand, a sure sign the water temperature was warmer than the air. A wind in the night had blow away the dying leaves, and the tree limbs were stark black against the gray-white sky. Delia hoped it wouldn't rain. She had dressed more warmly this morning in her moleskin pants and a red plaid flannel shirt. Just in case it did rain, she threw her yellow rain slicker and an extra pair of rubber boots into the basket on the back of the ATV.

Kate and the two graduate students, Paula Jeffries and Adam Bernstein, were already setting up at the site. Adam seemed especially enthusiastic about excavating the mound. He was a dark-haired young man with an unruly moustache, deep-set brown eyes and a stocky build. He reminded Delia of a young Harvey Keitel. In her brief interaction with him, as they unloaded the truck, Delia observed that he was quiet and almost quaintly polite.

"Thank you so much, Dr. Ironfoot, for this opportunity." He looked shyly at the ground when he addressed her and then said, "I assure you, my problems with Professor Kincaid had nothing at all to do with my competence or energy level. It's just that he..." His voice trailed off, and Delia put a hand on his shoulder.

"It's okay, Adam," she assured him. "I met the guy myself. I don't know if I could work with him either."

Adam nodded, thanked her again and resumed unloading the truck.

Paula Jeffries, on the other hand, was a large, blond-haired woman with an abrupt, borderline bossy manner who, Delia surmised, would try to have her hand in every aspect of the dig. She would have to outline responsibilities and establish her leadership early with Paula.

Kevin had promised Delia that he would help her pull her grandfather's tractor out of the hole, but he had yet to arrive, and while Delia waited for him, she helped Adam and Paula unload Paula's truck.

Both young people had obviously participated in excavations before; they quickly set up a large tent, folding chairs with tables, boxes of equipment, and a battered Honda gasoline generator. When they had completely unloaded the truck, Delia suggested that they assist Kate, who was taking pictures of some of the smaller mounds.

Shortly after Adam and Paula left with Kate, Kevin arrived. He and Delia then spent the next few hours pulling her grandfather's tractor from the hole. Delia was surprised and gratified to find that Kevin expressed a genuine interest in the mound. As they worked to free the tractor—a muddy, frustrating task that took them much longer than she thought it would, Kevin asked knowledgeable questions which Delia gladly answered. She found that talking to him and responding to his questions helped her to clarify her own thoughts.

"How old do you think the tomb is?" Kevin asked, as he wrapped the chain and hook around the axle of the tractor.

Delia shook her head. "It's impossible to tell at this point. Kate thinks the pot I found is probably middle or late Mississippian—which would be around 1050 to 1350 AD. Of course, we won't know for sure until we conduct dating tests. This site could represent just one time period, or it could be the site of multiple burials and occupations. There's no way to tell until we begin excavating."

"Do they still use radiocarbon dating to find out how old stuff is?" he asked.

"Only for organic material suspected of being younger than about 30,000 years old." Delia said, again surprised at how knowledgeable Kevin was. "Actually, C-14 range is accurate to over 75,000 years now. But there are a lot of ways to date a site." She stopped and chuckled. "You have to stop me when I start lecturing 'Intro to Archaeology'."

"No," Kevin assured her. "I'm interested."

"Well, there's dendrochronology—or tree-ring dating—we could use that on the timbers of the log tomb. There are all kinds of new technology too. Thermoluminescence, archaeomagnetism, potassium-argon dating—to mention just a few. Of course, you can use some or all of them to cross-check and confirm each other." She eyed him. "You seem pretty interested in all this. Have you ever taken an archaeology course?"

"Nope, I was a business major—went to U of A in Fayetteville, but I flunked out last semester." He shrugged. "Too much partyin', not enough studyin'." Kevin shook his head as he jerked on the chain to make sure it was secure. "Archaeology sounds real complicated to me, Dee. I don't know how you keep it all straight."

"I don't," Delia admitted. "I excavate, record the data, enter the data into a software program, and send samples to a lab. Archaeology is specialized like every other field now. It's impossible to be an expert in every sub-specialization."

"Well, it sure is something to think about . . . those people living here on the land and farming and hunting—just like we do."

Delia nodded her agreement. "That's always been the fascination for me too. Not the technical aspects of excavation . . . but imagining people going about their daily lives—growing their food, raising their children, tending their animals, and making beautiful things like pots and the copper plates we found. To me, archaeology is a way of remembering the dead."

"Yeah, I guess so," Kevin said dubiously. "But why should we remember the dead? They're . . . dead."

Delia stopped what she was doing and said, "Kevin, can you tell me your grandparents' names?"

"Sure," he said.

"How about your great grandparents?"

"Uh, yeah, I think so . . . at least on my dad's side. My grandma's parents . . . they died when she was just a baby."

"So I guess it goes without saying that you don't know your great-great grandparents names? Where they came from . . . where they lived?"

"Nope. But why is that so important?"

"Well, the obvious reason is—without them . . . you wouldn't be here."

"Uh-huh."

"But a more important reason is—well, what does that say about *your* descendents?"

He was quiet for a few seconds, and then an expression appeared on his face that Delia couldn't read. "What about you, Dee?"

"What do you mean?"

"You told me, the first night you got here, that you couldn't name all your granddad's brothers and sisters and wouldn't know your cousins if they passed you on street."

Delia looked at the mud-covered teenager she was slowly beginning to know. Everything he had done since she arrived had made her feel more a part of her family and a special place. He had put her at ease; he had been a good host. And now, he reminded her of how her sometimes pedantic, professorial manner blinded her to her own shortcomings. She hung her head briefly and then looked up at him . . . this uncertain, yet intense relative of hers.

Looking, into his eyes and it was like looking into her own. She saw that his dark hair was the same texture as hers. His ears were small and flat against his head like hers. They shared a common genetic heritage ... he was a Whittaker and so was she.

She smiled and dropped the steel cable she had been holding. "This land?" she said, gesturing around her. "Grandpa gave me this ... he bought it for me, so I would feel part of ... you all."

Kevin smiled slightly. "Do you?"

"Yes. I do."

"Good," he said. Then the moment passed, like a cloud moving over the sun. He gestured at the mound. "We won't be able to find out what their names were."

"Nope," Delia turned her attention back to the cables. "We won't. But at least we can try to figure out how they lived, what they ate, what they wore."

"How can you tell what they ate?"

"Well, hard as it may be to believe, some archaeologists study shit—if they can find a preserved latrine or privy."

Kevin laughed. "I've never heard of that specialty before," he said.

"There will be other indications too. If we find fishhooks, arrowheads, axes—other hunting and fishing implements, all that will tell us that they ate fish and deer, small game."

"In a museum, in Little Rock, I saw the neatest fishhooks made from deer antlers—they were so perfect and tiny. I didn't think primitive people could make things so perfect using crude tools."

"You know ... a lot of tools and implements that prehistoric people made were pretty effective. Take obsidian knives, for example."

"Isn't that what the Aztecs used to cut out people's hearts?" Kevin asked.

"Yep," Delia said. "But obsidian blades are as sharp as new diamond blades, and they're three hundred times sharper than steel scalpels." She paused. She pulled on the steel cable that connected the two tractors and added, "I think we're ready to go here. Give it a try."

"Cool," Kevin said, climbing into the tractor seat and turning on the engine. "I'm glad we have another tractor, instead of a horse, to help us pull this sucker out of the hole."

Delia laughed. "Me, too."

After they finished pulling her grandfather's tractor up and out of the mound, they determined that, other than a thick coating of red muddy clay, it seemed undamaged. As Delia and Kevin were unhooking the winch and steel cables from the pulling tractor, Adam and Paula arrived at the site tent. They sat down on the ground in a rough semicircle and were talking when Eunice unexpectedly drove up with lunch.

She waved as she emerged from the car. "Yoo-ho, can I get some help over here? This fried chicken is getting cold."

Kevin and Delia grinned and high-fived at Eunice's appearance with her specialty meal.

"You all are in for the best fried chicken you've ever tasted," Kevin told the others.

As they laid out the chicken and the potato salad and poured the iced tea into cups on the folding table under the tent, Delia invited Eunice to stay and eat with them.

"No, child. I'm cleaning up the trailer so's we can get it down here this afternoon." She turned to Kevin, who was already halfway through his second chicken leg and asked, "You able to stay and help with that, Kevin?"

Kevin looked embarrassed as he wiped his mouth on his muddy sleeve. "Ah, no, I'm sorry, Eunice. I've got something important I have to do this afternoon."

"We'll help," Kate said, gesturing to Paula and Adam, and the two chorused their agreement.

"I'm sorry, Dee," Kevin said, brushing off his pants. "I really need to get going or I'm gonna be late."

"No problem," Delia said. She stood and walked Kevin to his battered pickup truck.

"I appreciate your help...pulling that tractor out. I'd never have been able to manage it myself."

When Kevin was sitting in the truck, Delia leaned against the driver's side door. "Listen, I don't know your situation—whether you have a job or not—but we could use some help here on the dig."

"But I don't know anything about it," Kevin told her.

"You don't have to know anything," Delia assured him. "Digs always need volunteers. You know how to use a shovel, measure things, and take notes, don't you?"

"Sure."

"Okay then. You can work on the dig. I can pay you an hourly wage, if that's what you're worried about. We have enough money."

"The thing is..." Kevin began. "The thing is I might have a job. That's what I'm going to see about now."

"Oh," Delia said. "What kind of job?"

Kevin gestured vaguely. "Oh, it's not a big deal, Dee. I might not get it, you know?" He started the truck and put it in gear. "I *really* need to get going...I gotta get cleaned up and stuff."

"Will you be back for dinner?" Delia asked.

"I'm not sure," Kevin said. "Maybe. Just depends on how things shake out."

"Okay, well I hope everything goes okay," Delia said, patting his arm. "Thanks again. And, my offer stands."

"No problem," Kevin replied and waved at her as he drove away.

Delia and Kate were cleaning up their litter from lunch and making lists of things to do and buy, when they heard the sound of a truck laboring along the road on the opposite side of the river. Eunice was driving and Hollis was in the passenger's seat. They were

127

pulling a blue trailer of ancient vintage.

"I hope that thing isn't too wide for the bridge," Kate said.

"I hope it doesn't fall apart before they get here," Delia replied.

As the truck approached the wooden bridge, Hollis stopped and leaned out the passenger window. "Where do you want this, Sis?" he called.

Delia walked over to the truck. Eunice had her hair tied up in a handkerchief and her cheeks were flushed. Delia eyed the bridge and the trailer. "Granddad, Eunice...why didn't you let us do this?"

"Are you saying that we're too decrepit to pull a trailer?" Eunice asked, eyeing her sternly.

"Of course not," Delia assured her. "I just...you've done so much already." She paused. "Are you going to try to pull it across the bridge?" she asked skeptically.

Hollis shook his head. "We may be old, Sis, but we aren't crazy. I don't know if that old bridge would hold us. It held up for the tractor, but this trailer weighs a lot more. I thought we might pull it up under those trees over there by the electric pole." He pointed to a spot a few hundred feet away from the bridge and that shielded the view of the site.

"I guess that's okay," Delia said. "But I'd really like it to be where I could look out the window and see the site...or at least the mound."

"We can do that," Hollis told her. "It'll just take a little more wire to reach the trailer."

"Whoa!" Delia exclaimed. "I'm going to have electricity?"

"Yep," Hollis answered. "I called the electric company; they'll be out day after tomorrow to connect you up. I got a propane tank, too. We have to get it filled up, but that's no big deal. I called the propane folks, and they're coming out tomorrow to fill her up. That'll give you hot water."

"That's great, Granddad. You've thought of everything. You'd make a great field supervisor."

Hollis smiled. "Well, I'll leave all that up to you. We just figured you might want some privacy since you're going to be staying for a while. Person likes some privacy at night. Your father always worked late. Figure you would too...and speakin' of your dad..." Her grandfather gestured with his thumb to the gun rack behind him. To it was secured an old, but well-preserved, Winchester lever-action rifle. "This was your great grandfather's rifle. It's a Model 94. Best selling civilian rifle ever made. My dad gave it to me when I was a youngster; I gave it to your Dad, and he used it when he was home. I want you to have it now—keep it down here with you, in case those looters come back and want some trouble."

"Dad told me about this gun—I wondered what happened to it," she said softly. Then she said, "Granddad, I don't really need a weapon. Even though looters may be a nuisance, even destructive, I don't have any right to shoot at them."

Nevertheless, she reached out and took the rifle from the gun rack. She stroked its beautiful walnut stock with the kind of reverence that some people reserve for guns, pickups, and dogs.

"I appreciate this...truly. I have Dad's other gun, the .30-.30 at home. But this...this is beautiful."

Her grandfather cleared his throat and said, "Well, we best be getting this done. Your aunt Eunice's got a class tonight, and we're burnin' daylight here." He squeezed Delia's hand and took the rifle from her. "I'll put this in the closet of the trailer. You can lock it up, if you want. There's a padlock on the broom closet in the front room."

"Dee, I gotta a few more things to do before you're set up," Eunice told her. "I brought you some pillows and blankets, towels, and the like." She shook her finger at Delia. "Now, I don't want you to think that just because we're settin' you up down here that it means you aren't welcome up at the house. And don't forget to bring your laundry up regular, too. Don't wait til it piles up."

Delia laughed. "I won't. I sure appreciate the work you all have done. I don't know how to thank you."

Kate had finished the clean-up of the tent and sauntered over to the truck. "That sure was some good fried chicken you made, Miss Eunice. It hit the spot. So did the pot roast you made Dee and me last night."

"Hello, Kate." Eunice smiled at her compliments. "I'm glad you enjoyed it."

Kate turned to Delia. "You and I should go into town and get the things on this list. Paula and Adam can set up the trailer while we're gone."

Delia thought her grandfather looked a little relieved. "That okay with you, Granddad? Eunice?" She smiled mischievously at her great aunt. "I wouldn't want to insult you by suggesting you couldn't finish this job by yourself."

Eunice sniffed disdainfully. "As your grandfather said, Dee...we're old, but we're not crazy. Anytime young folks want to help me out...I'm more than willing." Then she smiled and patted Dee's cheek. "It sure is good to have you here. It put the spunk back in your granddad, that's for sure."

"I'm glad to be here," Delia said, and then realized with surprise that she *was* glad. Despite her uneasiness before she arrived, she felt closer to her grandfather and Eunice than she ever had. Her relationship was Kevin was growing, and she looked forward to knowing him better. She was enjoying her venture back into her chosen field, and she was enjoying the chance to get to know Kate better. She still wasn't sure what she was going to *do* about Kate, and her feelings for Colleen were still free-floating around in her head. But since Colleen had refused to participate in the excavation, Delia's attraction to her seemed futile. Even considering all the strange events that occurred since her arrival, she had to admit that the trip was worthwhile, despite her initial uncertainty. It truly gave her an opportunity to connect with her father's family—her family—again.

"Well, then, we'll be on our way," Eunice said, grinding the gears of the truck, as Hollis winced.

"I'll go fill in the kids and meet you at the truck," Kate told Delia. "Nice to see you both again. Hollis. Miss Eunice."

As Eunice began maneuvering the trailer into position, Delia turned around and watched Kate walking away from her and felt a surge of warmth and affection. Then, letting Kate slip out of focus, she turned her gaze to the field beyond. It was so different from her beloved mountain home in Utah on Half Moon Lake.

But it was beautiful just the same. And, now it was hers.

Chapter 12

In the end Kate and Delia took separate vehicles to town, knowing that it might be late when they finished their errands. Kate had suggested that they go to the university first and see how much equipment the Survey had available for their use before Delia bought anything new for the dig.

"I'm sure we don't have everything, but we can save some money by using what we can find here."

"Hey, anything that can save us money, I'm for," Delia told her.

As she and Kate drove past the courthouse, Delia was surprised to see Kevin standing beside a black Cadillac Escalade. As she slowed to wave at him, she saw that the vanity plate on the Escalade read: GMBLER and remembered Kevin's story about Bob Noland's casino. She slowed as she passed Kevin and noticed that he was talking to a man inside the vehicle. A few hours ago, he had sat in front of her, covered in mud, his dark, curly hair poking out from his Red Birds ball cap, in need of a shave. Now he was dressed in pressed chinos, a white shirt and tie; he was clean-shaven, and his hair was freshly cut.

She slowed down even more and stuck her hand out the window, calling out his name and waving. Kevin turned from his conversation with the man in the car, looked directly at her, and then looked away without a single sign of acknowledgement. Delia was confused; she was driving her grandmother's car and knew that he was familiar with it. She was sure she saw recognition in his face when he turned to look at her when she waved at him.

As she drove on to the university behind Kate, Delia at first felt puzzled by Kevin's reaction, and then angry. She had grown fond of him, and now she felt that he had deceived both her and Hollis. Everyone she had talked to, even Kevin himself, had expressed the strong opinion that Bob Noland was bad. That he would put off her job offer, for what she presumed was a possible job with Noland, hurt and worried her.

She continued to think over the scene by the courthouse, and finally realized that Kevin could have simply run into Noland on his way to see about the job he mentioned to her. She figured it was possible that Kevin wanted to thank Noland for giving Spaz to him and perhaps for giving his cousin, John Ed, a job. She decided that there was nothing sinister about Kevin talking to Noland. If, indeed, the man in the Escalade was Noland. Sometimes, Delia thought, she jumped to hasty conclusions that she later lived to regret. She wondered if, knowing Kate's distaste for Noland, she should even mention that she thought she saw Kevin with him. She still hadn't decided when they arrived at the university.

It was getting dark when she and Kate parked their vehicles in the parking lot behind the Earth Science building. The night had turned cold and windy, and Delia was glad she had worn her father's duster. They hurried down the sidewalk, as fallen leaves skittered across the path in front of them, moving like small, frightened animals running from the cold. The sodium vapor lights glowed a gaseous orange, a vaguely unsettling contrast to the dark mass of institutional buildings around them. As she waited for Kate to unlock the side door to the building, Delia shivered and thrust her hands deeper into her coat.

"Damn, it's cold," she muttered to Kate.

"Cold?" Kate mocked her tone. "I thought you came from the snowy mountains of Utah. Surely it gets colder than this there?"

"It's a different kind of cold," Delia grumbled. "Hurry up; I'm freezing my butt off."

"Now that would be a tragedy," Kate told her. "I haven't even seen it naked yet."

"You're assuming you're going to see my naked rear end?" Delia teased her.

Kate pushed the door open and welcome warm air washed over them. The hallway appeared the same as the first time Delia had entered. Dark, musty corridors were lined with metal shelving and filled with boxes. As they made their way to her office, Kate began switching on lights, dispelling some of the gloominess and uneasiness Delia felt. The wind rattled the windows along the corridor to Kate's office, and Delia thought she heard a low rumble of thunder.

"Damn, it might rain tonight. Good thing we covered up the trench," Kate said, pushing open the door to her office and then stopping so quickly that Delia ran into her from behind. "What the hell!" Kate exclaimed, looking around her office.

"What?" Delia asked, making her way around Kate. Then she saw what Kate saw, and she understood.

Someone had thoroughly ransacked Kate's office. File folders, papers, photographs, and artifacts were strewn around the room. Everything on the shelves and on her desk had been swept off; the contents of her desk drawers had all been dumped on the floor. Even the telephone had been ripped out of the wall. Kate walked over to the mess and squatted down amidst the storm of paper. She picked up the silver-framed photograph of Buddy and, after removing the broken glass, set it gently on her empty desk.

"Okay," she said in a strangely calm voice. "Now, I'm pissed." She pulled out her cell phone and dialed a number: "Hi, Ralph?

134

This is Kate, at the Archaeological Survey Office? Yeah, we're in the Earth Science Building. Uh-huh. Right. That's the one. Listen, I'd like to report a break-in. . . . I don't know, Ralph. That's why I'm calling you. Somebody broke in here and trashed my office. No, I don't teach here so, I don't give tests. . . . No, I don't. Look, Ralph, just come on, okay? And listen, call Jack Pettit too, would you? See if he can come over here. I'll explain later. Uh-huh. See you soon."

She hung up the phone and looked at Delia.

"I assume that was Campus Security?" Delia asked.

"Yeah. Ralph. He's on by himself at night. There's usually not that much for him to do. Mostly he drives around at night, shining his spotlight into the girls' dormitories."

"He sounds like a winner."

"Right. Well, that's why I had him call Pettit too."

"Oh, I thought you were dragging Pettit here because you think this is related to the stuff that happened at the excavation. You do, don't you?"

"Of course I do," Kate said vehemently. "And speaking of being related to stuff at the excavation, did you happen to see your whatever-he-is to you, Kevin, cozying up to Bob Noland in his Escalade by the courthouse?"

"Yeah," Delia confessed. "But I didn't know he was talking to Noland."

"Didn't you see the vanity plate on the Escalade? Gambler?" Kate snorted. "That asshole . . . I thought you said Kevin told you he wasn't hooked up with him."

"I think you're jumping to conclusions," Delia said defensively. "Just because Kevin was talking to him, doesn't mean he's hooked up or whatever."

Kate kicked at a toppled potted plant and dirt scattered. "You're right. I'm sorry. I didn't mean to cast any aspersions on Kevin. He seems like a nice guy. I've never heard of him being in any trouble. I just think it was weird . . . a little suspicious even. If Noland is behind all this, shooting at your granddad and putting all the fake Indian crap down there, then . . ."

"Maybe Kevin's his pipeline of information?" Delia said.

"Hey, I never said anything like that," Kate objected.

"Well, you're certainly implying it," Delia countered. "And I don't appreciate it. Kevin has been nothing but good and helpful to me . . . hell, to *us*, since I got here. Just because he was talking to Noland doesn't mean he's a bad guy."

Kate's tone softened, and she took Delia's hand. "I'm sorry. Really. I am. I just . . . Noland pushes my buttons."

Delia pulled Kate to her and held her a moment. "I know. It's all right. . . . Hey, can we have some coffee while we wait for the cops to show up?"

"Sure," Kate said absently, looking around for the coffeepot and finding it, miraculously; unbroken in a corner. "Now if I can just find the filters and . . ." Suddenly she stopped and stared at Delia.

"What?" Delia asked, alarmed by the look in Kate's eyes. "What's the matter?"

"Whoever did this was obviously looking for something, right?"

"Seems so," Delia said. "Unless some kind of insane 'Trading Spaces' terrorists broke in here."

"So . . . what would whoever did this be looking for?"

"I don't know," Delia said and then, "Oh, shit! You don't think they were looking for the copper plates and the other stuff I brought in, do you?"

Kate pulled out her key ring and said, "There's only one way to find out. Let's go look before the 'clowns' get here."

The steel door that led to the storeroom had been pried open—probably with a crow bar. The doorframe was deeply gouged by the force required to open the door. The padlock that secured the door to the caged room had merely been cut off with bolt cutters. Inside, a few of the containers and boxes had been opened, their contents scattered around, but nothing was broken, and nothing seemed damaged—except the door and the door-frame.

Delia stood looking at the boxes. "Where was it?"

"It was right there," Kate said, pointing to the bottom of the first shelf in line. "It wasn't hidden or anything. And...now it's not there."

Delia and Kate were on their third cup of coffee with Officer Ralph when Sheriff Jack Pettit showed up.

Pettit was not happy about being summoned from wherever he had been.

"What's this got to do with me?" he demanded.

"Well, Sherlock," Kate began until Delia laid a hand on her arm. She took over, telling the sheriff what they'd found.

"We thought it might be connected to the disturbance of the site," Delia said evenly. "The missing artifacts are from my excavation site."

"Were they valuable?" Pettit wanted to know.

"Hell, yes they were valuable!" Kate exploded. "Goddamnit, Jack..."

Pettit looked at her dispassionately. "Shut up, Kate."

Kate jumped up from her chair and went nose to nose with Pettit. Delia had never seen her so angry. "You big, overgrown jerk. You never do anything unless someone lights a fire under you."

"Kate," Delia warned. She took Kate's arm and made her sit down.

"I repeat—were the things that were taken valuable?" Pettit asked.

"That all depends on what you mean by 'valuable'," Delia told him. "They were certainly valuable to our excavation of the site...would they be 'valuable' to a collector? I suspect they

137

would be. I'd say they were 'rare' artifacts, wouldn't you, Kate?"

Kate nodded, obviously not trusting herself to speak to Pettit.

"You gave the campus security officer a list of people who have access to this building?" he asked.

"Anybody can get in this building," Kate said through clenched teeth.

"Unless the University Police ask for our assistance in this matter, I don't see that I can help here," Pettit said. "Certainly not tonight." He turned to Ralph. "I would suggest that you get a list of people with keys to this building, talk to them, see if anyone saw anything unusual. . . . I'm sure there have been other break-ins around here. The University Police are perfectly capable of handling something of this kind." And with that, he turned around to leave.

Officer Ralph drained his cup of coffee and rearranged his leather belt, all of his police paraphernalia shifted with his adjustment. "Well, ladies, that about covers it. I'll give my report to the Chief when he comes in on Monday and I'm sure we'll get back to you when we learn something." He seemed to run out of police clichés and began backing up. "Thanks for the coffee. Be seeing you."

"I'm gonna go home and take a hot shower and hit the hay," Kate declared as they stood by their vehicles behind the building.

"What happened to your overwhelming desire to sleep with me?" Delia joked, as they stood close to each other between Kate's truck and Delia's car. Kate leaned over and gently kissed her on the lips. Then she laughed and got into her truck.

"Let me know when you get electricity and hot water," she said as she drove away.

Delia laughed too and was relieved that Kate still had a sense of humor. When she got to the farm, Delia thought about how much more at home she felt here than she did just a few nights ago. The porch light was on and, as she walked up the steps, she heard

Wally's soft "woof" and knew when she opened the door he would be sitting just inside the door.

She scratched his ears and said: "Hush, Wally. You'll wake granddad." And, at that, Wally retreated to his spot under the kitchen table. A note rested on the table, written in her grandfather's hand: *Dee. Maybe your Aunt Eunice and I are old and crazy. HA! Eunice was too tuckered out to go to her class. She's sleeping in the guest room. She said to tell you there's some leftover pot roast and fried chicken in the fridge. Trailer's ready for habitation. We moved your gear for you. Granddad.*

After a quick meal and a shower in the small bathroom off the kitchen, Delia dressed in clean clothes. Though she was tired, she was anxious to see her new digs. Stepping onto the back porch, she stood and watched as clouds swept in front of the moon. Then, she pulled the collar of her duster close and put on her gloves. The ATV was parked down by the shed, and Delia popped it into neutral so it would roll down the driveway before starting the engine, so as not to disturb her great aunt or grandfather.

The wind was cold but bracing as she drove down the road toward the wooden bridge. Her earlier weariness had receded since she ate and showered. Driving carefully along the road that bordered her grandfather's field, she watched as clouds temporarily revealed the full moon. Delia saw the rounded bulk of the trailer ahead of her. Set up on an angle with both the road and the bridge in plain view, it was a perfect checkpoint. It was the ideal location to allow anyone in the trailer to keep track of site visitors—welcome and unwelcome. The only other ways on to the land were through the Buck's property or by way of a river landing. Both were possible, but Delia knew that the main access to the Buck's property was gated and locked while the banks of the Big Right Hand were particularly unstable and steep. If she could talk Adam and Paula into setting up their tents on the other side of the field, they would have a decent chance of limiting access to the site.

As she parked the ATV next to the trailer, Delia wondered if she might have more dreams of the burning city . She wondered idly how Colleen and the raccoons were faring and if she would ever see the three of them again. She saw the someone had opened the windows of the trailer, and knew its mustiness would be mostly gone now, replaced by the smell of the pine cleanser Aunt Eunice used.

As she unlocked the trailer's door, Delia heard a small noise from the back of the trailer and tensed. She wished, not for the first time, that Neji was with her instead of back in Utah. As quietly as she could, she opened the closet door beside the small refrigerator and reached inside for her father's rifle. She pushed the safety off and began to walk down the hallway. The moonlight shining through the small back window of the bedroom provided enough light for her to see. Someone was sitting on the edge of the bed.

Delia cleared her throat. "I'm armed . . . who's there?"

Laughter came from the figure on the bed and Delia asked, "Colleen?"

Something soft hit Delia in the chest.

"*Colleen*? Is that who you hope is in your bed?"

Kate's voice sounded pouty and, Delia admitted, sexy. She picked up the pillow Kate had thrown at her and threw it back. "I was just kidding, I knew it was you." She laughed. "How did you get here?"

A match struck, and Delia saw Kate's beautiful red hair shining as she lit a candle on a narrow shelf above the bed. Delia also noted a pile of clothes on the floor beside the bed, which she assumed were Kate's, and that the sheet she had wrapped around her covered her nakedness.

"I parked at Buck's, climbed a couple fences and walked over. I wanted to surprise you."

"I thought you were tired."

Kate laughed, a low, throaty sound. "I got my second wind and

140

I figured that after the break-in you wouldn't be anywhere but here. You're not going to get out of this, Dee. I drove all the way out here after I did nothing but work for you all day. I'm naked under this sheet, and I don't get naked for just anyone."

"I'm sure you don't," Delia said. "And believe me, it is taking every ounce of willpower to keep from ripping that sheet right off you, but Kate, we have to *work* together." Delia stood up and put the safety back on the rifle. As she leaned the rifle in the corner of the small room, she hesitated for a moment, and then she made her decision.

Delia sat down beside Kate and pushed the hair from her face. "You're very, very beautiful," she whispered; running her hand over the smooth, bare skin of Kate's shoulder.

Kate frowned. "You're not turning me down, are you?" She put her arms around Delia's neck and pulled her into a long, deep kiss, afterward murmuring into her ear. "I want you so much. Come on. Kiss me. You know you want to." Then she pulled Delia back to her, and this time the kiss grew deeper as Kate pushed her tongue slightly into Delia's mouth Delia pulled away the sheet that covered Kate and, in the candlelight, her pale body was glorious. Her breasts were small, high and perfectly shaped. At that moment, Delia wanted to feel Kate's skin against her own. She reached out and touched Kate's left breast gently, letting her palm rest softly on the nipple.

"Aw, Dee, come on," Kate breathed in her ear, sending a shudder down Delia's legs. "Take off those clothes and get in here with me."

Delia stood up and began taking off her clothes. She watched Kate as she unbuttoned her shirt, swept it over her shoulders and pushed it to the floor. As she discarded her pants, she smiled as Kate's eyes traveled down her body. She grinned at her and purred with amusement, "Looking at my scarred, grizzled old carcass?"

"You're beautiful," Kate said, lifting the covers and shifting to make space beside herself as Delia crawled toward her.

Once under the blanket, with Kate in her arms, Delia gave herself up to desire. Kate was a passionate lover; she held nothing back. The intensity that Delia had observed earlier was now directed in a passionate sexual outpouring. Delia had always considered herself a quiet lover, but she could not keep herself from responding to Kate's frenzied lovemaking. Kate's mouth was everywhere—on her mouth, on her the soft rise of her stomach, on the inside of her thigh. She sucked just a little too hard, and when Delia cried out, instead of easing up, Kate chuckled and continued. Kate's fervor was almost too much, almost too painful, but Delia wanted more. Sensations of pleasure flashed through exciting shocks of pain. Suddenly, Kate seemed to calm herself, and she gently pushed Delia's legs apart. "I want to touch you here," she whispered, drawing her finger slowly through the wetness of Delia's cunt. When she reached Delia's clit, she drew slow, maddening circles around the tiny swollen bud, and Delia shuddered from the intensity of the sensation. It made her head buzz pleasantly, and by the time Kate slowly pushed her fingers inside her, she cried out and clung to her, lost in an orgasmic storm.

The city still burned, though not as furiously as before. Taking their prisoners from among the remaining people who could still walk, the invaders had gone back to their long canoes. The night sky glowed fiercely, like the coals of a dying fire.

Dead bodies were strewn throughout the city, but the central plaza was the scene of the most ghastly massacre. Limbless torsos, dismembered arms and legs lay in a vile soup of blood and gore. Women who escaped the bloodbath ran wildly into the center of the city, screaming and wailing as they tried to find their children amidst the carnage. Men with horrible wounds straggled into the square and stood around staring, with stupefied expressions at their dead children and weeping women.

The triumphant invaders screamed as they ran to their war canoes, and they escaped down the river. Some of the young men argued angrily among themselves about pursuing the invaders, but such talk died quickly in the face of the gruesome scene before them. They failed to protect their city, their women, and children. They failed their leaders: their war chief, the Tattooed Serpent; and his sister, the priestess who wore the serpent on her face—the two most revered personages among them. It was from the children of their union—of the Tattooed Serpent and his sister-priestess—that the future spiritual and religious leaders of their people would have come. With the loss of their leaders came the loss of their future, and their realization caused a deeper, more devastating, sense of communal grief.

Delia awoke from the dream and lay still, waiting. Something had awakened her. She listened, and then she heard a noise from outside the trailer. She touched Kate's shoulder and gave her a little shake. Kate's eyes opened slowly and she smiled, reaching for Delia. But Delia put her finger across her lips and whispered, "Someone's outside. I'm going to check it out. Watch me through the window."

Delia stood up and began dressing. She crept slowly down the hallway, carrying her boots, not putting them on until she reached the living room. Then, she looked outside.

The clouds of evening had cleared and the moon, huge and orange as cantaloupe, was high in the star-strewn sky. It provided enough light to illuminate the scene outside, and in its light Delia saw two men coming over the bank of the river. She watched as they walked across the moonlit field, noting that one of them wore his baseball hat backwards. They each carried long metal probes, shovels, and flashlights and they were headed for the mound.

Delia stood still, waiting until the men reached the mound. She watched as they flicked on flashlights. Then, she opened the front door of the trailer and quietly slipped outside. She counted to ten and began to edge her way toward the wooden bride, keeping just inside the shadows that the trees cast on the bridge. When she reached the middle, she looked over the edge and saw a bass boat with a small outboard motor tied to a tree halfway down the riverbank. She crossed to the other side and stood quietly, still keeping in the shadows, knowing that if she made a sound they would see her clearly.

One of them held a sheet of paper, which they both consulted. The other pointed to a spot away from the collapsed mound, and the two men began walking again.

Delia watched them, puzzled. They appeared to be pothunters, maybe the same ones who looted the site before. Maybe the ones who broke into the locked room at the university to steal the copper plates and other artifacts. Pots were the easiest artifacts to locate, and they generally brought the most money on the black market, depending on their condition.

Delia waited until the two men were well away from her before she started following them again. She circled to the left of their path, which took her near the tree line and the shadows under which she successfully concealed herself again. She followed the two men for perhaps an eighth of a mile before they stopped beside another small mound. Then, turning off their flashlights, they began to probe the ground. A few minutes went by before Delia heard the unmistakable clink of metal against something hard under the soil. When the men lay down their probes and picked up their shovels, she stepped out of the shadows, turned on her flashlight and trained it on their faces, hoping not only to take them by surprise, but also to blind them temporarily.

"Looking for something in particular?" Delia asked.

Both men jumped at her voice and stopped digging. She kept her flashlight on their faces and watched as they shielded their eyes from its glare.

"Why don't you take that light outta our faces?" One of them said, more a direction than a question.

Delia walked over to them and moved the beam of her flashlight away from their eyes. "Kinda late to be out trespassing, isn't it?"

"Hey, little lady," the man wearing the battered baseball cap said. "That ain't very friendly talk comin' from such a pretty gal."

The two men started walking toward her, carrying their shovels with them, and the shorter one picked up the big metal flashlight but didn't turn it on.

"What're you looking for in the middle of the night?" Delia asked.

"We're just here to dig up some pots. Make a little extra money. Lotsa people do it around here. Ain't no harm done." He grinned. "We thought this was old Buck's property."

"Buck's dead and you know it. It belongs to me now. You're breaking the law by digging here. This is a burial site."

"Who the hell put you in charge?" said the short one.

"I'm the archaeologist on site," Delia said. "I'm Hollis Whitaker's granddaughter. I have permission to excavate this site."

"Well, la-de-dah," the little man said belligerently. "I'm all impressed as hell."

"Aw, hell, Brad. Ain't no need to be rude to the pretty lady," the man with the baseball cap said. "These folks don't mind us takin' their pots, ma'am. They ain't got no more use for 'em."

"Oh, for Chrissake, why don't you just hand over my driver's license to her?" Brad said angrily.

The man with the baseball hat looked baffled for a moment and then grinned. "She don't know if that's your real name." He turned to his taller friend. "I just said that to throw her off."

"Sweet Jesus," Brad said, shifting the flashlight to his other hand. "She can tell just by lookin' at you that you ain't that smart."

At this, Brad motioned to the other man, who then began moving to Delia's left. She recognized the tactic and said, "Whatever you're thinking of doing—I wouldn't. It won't work."

The two men looked at each other and drew together again.

"Look lady," Brad said in a hard voice. "We've talked to you politely and all, but both sides gotta give. Why don't you just go back home and mind your own damn business? Then maybe I won't have to do somethin' unpleasant to you."

Delia was about to reply when she heard Kate's voice behind her. "Is that you, Pete Marshall?" Kate directed her flashlight at the man in the baseball hat.

The man put his hand up and shaded his eyes from the beam of light. "Aw, shit. Katie?"

Kate stepped forward to stand beside Delia, who noticed she was carrying the old Remington.

"You son-of-bitch, murdering rat bastard." Kate's voice was devoid of emotion.

Delia looked from Pete to Kate and back again. Surprisingly, Pete looked a bit uncertain now. "Now Katie, you know that ain't true. I never had nothin' to do with whatever happened to Buddy."

"You obviously know these two," Delia said to Kate. "Who are they?"

"They're a couple of low-life scum-bags," Kate said flatly. "They work for Bob Noland. They do his dirty work."

Delia tried to read Kate's expression. It was too dark.

"What are you doing out here?" Delia asked them again.

"Look, we told ya, we're just out here seein' what we can turn up for a few extra dollars." Pete Marshall glared at Kate. "And you're a crazy woman. We didn't kill your asshole brother. Some other upstanding citizen did us the favor."

Kate didn't look at Delia, but she handed her the rifle and said: "Shoot off his goddamn kneecaps. I don't trust myself not to put one in his head."

In response to Kate's request, Delia took the rifle from her and lowered it to Pete's knees.

"Hey, now this ain't funny," Brad said. "You better put down that gun before you hurt somebody."

"Oh, hell," Pete interrupted. "She's probably never even fired a gun before. Probably couldn't hit the broad side of a barn."

"We ain't kiddin' around here," Brad warned. "Y'all just go back and leave us to our diggin'. We won't be long."

"Shut up, Brad," Kate said, in the same emotionless voice she used before.

"I think you two better clear out before I call the sheriff," Delia said. "Trespassing, destruction of human remains, interfering with government operations and its agents—they'll lock you up for a long time. Most of those are federal charges, too."

"You can't prove we done any of that," Pete said uncertainly. "We just wanted to dig up some stuff."

Brad shook his head. "Shut the fuck up, asshole. Don't say another word."

Delia turned to Kate and said, "Give me your cell phone." Kate reached in her jacket and pulled out her phone.

"Now, wait just a minute. There ain't no reason to get the law involved here," Brad said. "Look, we'll just be runnin' along."

"I don't know, Brad," Kate said. "I was kind of enjoying the idea of Delia shooting your kneecaps off."

"You little bitch." Brad started to move toward her when suddenly he stopped, and Delia saw the surprise on the men's faces. Then Delia and Kate both turned around to see flames and smoke pouring out of the Whittaker farmhouse.

Chapter 13

"Go!" Kate yelled at Delia. "I'll take care of these two."

But before Kate could do anything, Brad and Pete took off running across the field toward the Buck's house.

"Let them go," Delia said. "Come on!" She and Kate ran back to the trailer and when they reached it, Delia jumped on the ATV. Kate threw herself behind Delia, and they sped toward the house. Bouncing over the uneven planks of the bridge, ignoring the road, the four-wheeler went bumping wildly across the uneven field. Once Delia nearly turned the machine over, but she managed to right it before it went completely out control. She slowed down a little after that, but as the flames began to shoot from the windows of the first story, she gunned the engine again and went careening across the field.

When they were close to the house and could feel heat from the flames, Delia saw with dread that there was no one outside. The thought that Eunice and her grandfather were still inside galvanized her into action. With Kate on her heels, Delia jumped off the four-wheeler and ran to the back door. She pushed it open and was greeted by thick, black smoke. She immediately crouched down and began crab-walking her way across the kitchen. When she reached the living room, she saw Eunice staggering through the door of the guest room, pulling her nightgown and robe up to her cheeks and over her mouth as a shield from the smoke.

Delia ran to her and putting her arm around Eunice's shoulder she yelled, "Let's get out of here!" Leading her out of the living room, Delia stumbled back into the kitchen where Kate took Eunice's arm and said, "I'll get her outside."

Delia grabbed Kate and handed her back her cell phone. "Call 9-1-1. I'm going upstairs to get Granddad and Wally."

Kate nodded and ran through the black smoke, dragging Eunice with her. They were quickly lost in the thick haze. Delia rushed through the smoky kitchen, to the sink, and found a dishtowel; quickly wetting it, she covered her nose and mouth. Then, keeping as close to the floor as possible, she felt her way through the house and up the stairs, using the railing as a guide until she reached the landing. There was a window, but at that level the smoke was too thick. She began choking and ducked her head toward the floor. After sipping some relatively clear air, she peered up from her position and saw that no flames had yet reached the second floor. Still, the pine planks were hot to the touch, and she knew that she had to move more quickly to escape the heat. The intensity of the flames on the first floor would soon break through and set fire to the second story, too.

She reached the top of the stairs and lowered herself against the baseboard so she would know when she reached the doorway of her grandfather's bedroom. The heat and smoke were becoming more intense and even the air near the floor was practically unbreatheable.

"Granddad," she choked, pushing through the door. She strained to listen for her grandfather's voice, but she could hear nothing above the growing roar of the hungry flames below her. The floor in front of her was beginning to smoke, and she knew she had only seconds to find her grandfather and his dog and make a quick retreat.

When she crossed the doorway of her grandfather's bedroom,

she crawled to his bed and saw him, struggling to sit up. Wally had Hollis's pajama shirt in his teeth and was trying to pull him out of bed. Delia rushed over to the bed and helped her grandfather up.

"Granddad, we've gotta get out of here. Can you walk?"

He merely nodded.

"Okay. Just hang on to me and don't let go." She pulled one of his arms over her shoulder and held his waist firmly. Then, grabbing Wally's collar, and she began leading the two of them toward the door of the bedroom.

The hallway was full of smoke and Delia yelled, "We're going to have to crawl, get below the smoke." She helped her grandfather to the floor and then, removing the wet handkerchief from her face, wrapped it around his. The cast on Hollis's wrist hampered their progress as they crawled toward the window that over-looked the front yard. But Delia managed to help him to the win-dowsill. Worried that Wally would try to bolt and run into heavy smoke, or directly into the fire, Delia tightened her grip around his collar, and he came willingly. She raised her head slightly to look outside the window, but the smoke was pouring up from the first floor through the air vent beneath them, and she began to choke. Trying to look out again, she saw two things. There were no firemen or trucks on the front lawn. The second thing fright-ened her more than the first—the roof outside the window was on fire.

She could not use it as an escape route, and when she turned back to the doorway, she saw that the fire had finally broken through the floor.

The entire hallway was engulfed in flames and the staircase was unreachable.

The fire was roaring; it sounded exactly like a train. Suddenly, one wall of the bedroom burst into flames. The old wallpaper was dry and highly combustible; it burned quickly and added to the already impenetrable smoke. Pieces of burning wallpaper and wooden lathe rained on them all, and she frantically tried to brush the burning bits off. Her grandfather had lost the wet rag she put over his mouth and was choking; Delia knew that the smoke was close to overcoming them.

So far, Delia had not allowed herself to feel fear; she had been in many dangerous situations in her life. She had even been in a burning building before. But the smoke was so thick; she could neither see nor breathe. She had to find another way out.

Delia lifted her head a little, and when she took her next breath she inhaled nothing but smoke. Choking until tears came to her eyes, she saw Hollis try to raise his head so she quickly cupped the back of his neck and pushed his face against the floorboards. He began to gag, and Delia knew if she didn't get him out soon, he would die.

She lowered her forehead to the floor again and cautiously tried to take a little breath of air. This time, she was able to breathe without coughing. The pine wood floor beneath her was growing hotter to the touch, and tendrils of smoke were coming up through the cracks between the planks. She realized that they had very little time left before the floor beneath them caught fire. Then they would either fall to the story below or be forced to jump out the window onto the burning roof.

Neither alternative would get them to safety.

Wally kept his head on the floor, between his paws. He lay perfectly still, as if waiting for Delia to make up her mind. Her grandfather looked up at her, his eyes questioning.

"I'm thinking," Delia yelled so he could hear her.

He motioned to Delia to come closer and whispered something in her ear. Delia nodded eagerly. Her grandfather's suggestion gave them a chance; not a very big chance, but more than any other options.

Delia began crawling again, dragging Wally and her grandfather behind her. They slid and crawled across the hot floorboards until they reached the end of the hall.

"Okay, you two, stay here while I get the ladder," she said. She opened the closet door and was relieved to see no smoke inside. She stood up cautiously, grabbed the piece of rope that was attached to the trap door in the ceiling and gave it a hard yank. The door dropped open, and the ladder unfolded itself. It was a steep climb but only a few feet to the attic. Delia called, "Come on, Granddad. We're getting out of here."

First, Delia helped her grandfather up the ladder. It was a hard maneuver, but he managed to make it to the top of the stairway, and then he turned around to help her with Wally. She put the dog's paws on the first rung of the ladder and put her hands on his hindquarters, expecting that she would have to push him to take the steps. But to her surprise, he nimbly hopped up toward the attic and began licking Hollis's face when he reached the top.

"Good dog! Boy, I wish I could do that," Delia said. She quickly ascended the stairs, then reached down and pulled the ladder up into the attic. While there was no visible smoke in the space, she smelled a noxious burnt odor, and the attic air was hyper-heated. When Delia drew a breath, the dry, hot air seared her nostrils and stabbed her lungs. She coughed violently and sank to her knees. The heat in the floorboards was so hot that she couldn't stand in any one place, so she bent her head, grabbed her grandfather's hand and moved quickly to the window. By the time she reached the small louvered window, she could hear people shouting to each other below. She peered through the wooden slats and saw firemen running across the yard, dragging a hose.

At first, she tried to break the slats with her elbow, but they wouldn't give. She tried to push through them and finally pounded them with her fists. They still wouldn't give.

The air in the attic was hotter and thicker now. She turned around to look at her grandfather, and he pointed to the trap door. Though it wasn't burning yet, smoke was seeping in around its edges. The heat was nearly unbearable. They had to get out. The whole house was going to burn down.

Looking around frantically, she saw an old metal Christmas tree stand under the eaves. Knowing it would be too hot to touch; Delia pulled off her shirt and tore it into two halves. Wrapping the strips around her hands, she grabbed the stand and swung it against the louvered slats. This time, they gave way with a satisfying crack. Delia punched and pried at them with both the tree stand and her hands until the window was clear. She looked down at the back porch roof and was relieved to see that it wasn't on fire. Craning her neck, she looked back into the attic and saw that she didn't have any time left; she had to act now.

The roof of the old farmhouse was burning and, as she watched, part of the ceiling—over a gable to her left—collapsed. Sending fiery chunks of shingles into the air, the debris from the collapse shot through the open windowpane and onto the roof of the back porch. The roof began smoking in the places that the burning pieces of shingles landed. Delia reached down, helped her grandfather to his feet.

"Let go of Wally, Granddad," she instructed him and pulled the dog from his arms. "Don't worry, I'll bring him with me." And with that, she unceremoniously pushed her grandfather through the small opening. He landed with a heavy thud on the roof and yelped as embers from the house fire landed on him, burning through his pajamas to his skin. Delia wasted no time turning around to grab Wally. She shoved him through the opening too. Then, scrambling through the window herself, she joined her grandfather and his dog on the roof.

She walked to the edge and looked down to see if any firemen were there, but she could only see an abandoned hose in the back driveway. No one held it or directed it on the flames that lapped around them; no water came from it. Delia wondered if they were having trouble getting it to the fire. Behind her she heard a loud whoosh and felt the back porch roof shudder beneath her feet. It swayed for a second or two, and Delia knew that more of the roof must have had collapsed.

She had to get them to the ground—now.

Stepping around the parts of the porch roof that were burning, Delia peered over the edge and noted with relief that her grandmother's trellis was still standing. Turning around she helped her grandfather to his feet. His eyes were closed. His eyebrows and eyelashes were singed. She pulled him to her and shook him. "Granddad, you've got to get off the roof. Go down the trellis." She half-pushed, half-pulled Hollis to the edge of the roof nearest the trellis and then helped him turn around.

"Find the first step!" She yelled at him and hoped that he could hear her because the fire was so loud that she could barely hear herself. As her grandfather lowered himself toward the trellis, she held his hand tightly, and then she heard him croak, "Okay, Sis. I got a foothold!" She held on to him as long as she could and then turned back to get Wally. He was behind her, parts of his fur burned and singed. She called him and he came, limping across the hot shingles. She looked toward the ground and saw her grandfather, yelling and waving his good arm at firemen who were now looking up at her. Sliding over the edge of the roof, she slipped her foot inside the first square opening she could feel. Then she held out her arms to Wally. He approached cautiously, and Delia said, "You're going to have to trust me, big dog. I'll have to carry you down now."

He pawed at her outstretched hands and crept closer, dancing first forward and then taking short sideways steps back until he seemed to decide that he was going to trust her. Holding him tightly in her arms, she maneuvered the dog until he was slung over her shoulder, his front paws and head hanging down her back. Delia was glad he hadn't backed away or refused to come with her. It would have been impossible for her to manhandle him down the trellis.

The weight of both Delia and the dog, however, was simply too much for the old latticework. The wood was old and rotten. When she put her full weight on the structure, she heard an ominous crack. Tightening her grip on the dog with one hand and clutching the trellis with the other, she gulped deeply and stiffened. The back porch was burning and smoke engulfed her as she fell out and away from the house. She felt Wally leap from her shoulders, and she tried to twist her body so she wouldn't land on him.

Delia hit the ground; her head bounced on the hard, cold earth, landing heavily on her side. She felt something in her side crack and give way. A rib, maybe two, she thought, before the gray curtain of unconsciousness claimed her.

Chapter 14

When she regained her senses, Delia was lying in cold water and looking up at a fireman. She opened her mouth to tell him she was cold, freezing, but when she tried to speak, she began to cough.

"Ma'am? Do you hurt anywhere in particular? Are you burned anywhere besides your arms?"

Delia again tried to speak but was only able to turn her head away from him and vomit a stream of black liquid—part soot, part ropey mucous. A white-hot spear of pain stabbed into her side and she cried out.

The fireman leaned closer, and she managed to croak, "My side...hurts."

"You probably cracked a rib falling off the roof," he told her. "I know it hurts. The paramedics are here, and we're gonna move you outta here as soon as they check you over and get some oxygen started. You just hang in there, okay?"

Delia closed her eyes and concentrated on not coughing. When she opened her eyes again, she saw the fireman was gone, his face replaced by a ridiculously young female paramedic with blond hair and freckles.

"We need to get her off the ground," she yelled to someone

behind her. Delia could still hear the roar of the fire and felt some of its heat, but she could not stop shivering.

"Cold," she whispered, grabbing the sleeve of the paramedic. Stabbing pain from her side accompanied each cold shiver.

"We're going to get you warmed up in a minute," she said; then Delia felt herself being lifted up and onto a gurney.

"Okay," the paramedic said. "We're going to transport you now. If you'll let us get a blood pressure and listen to your lungs, we'll get out of here."

Then she was on a gurney, bumping across the uneven ground. Feeling the broken ends of her rib grinding against each other, Delia wanted to scream, but she could only groan. The blood pressure cuff was too tight, and the constriction of the blood vessels in her arm made the wounded hand that she battered on the slats of the attic window throb. Splinters from the broken louvers were driven into the side of her hand, and as her adrenaline dissipated, the pain was excruciating.

"Hand hurts," Delia whispered, though she doubted anyone could hear her. Voices were shouting all around her; she wondered briefly where Eunice and her grandfather were.

Finally, the gurney bumped against the back of an ambulance. Its legs folded and she was inside the vehicle. She was shivering so violently that the gurney shook. The paramedic said, "I know you're cold. I'm going to put an oxygen mask over your mouth and nose now, to help you breathe better. Here it comes." Delia felt a cool stream of oxygen coming through the mask, and then Kate was beside her.

"It's going to be okay, Dee," Kate said, close to her ear. "We're all going to the hospital."

A moment later, someone tucked a warm blanket around her, and Delia closed her eyes. Concentrating on breathing the cool, clean oxygen, she tried hard not to cough or throw up again. She heard the engine start up, and then they were speeding down the road.

"Everybody quiet now!" One paramedic demanded. Turning toward the front of the ambulance, she yelled, "Delmar, turn off the damn siren. I need to be able to hear breath sounds." The siren abruptly stopped, and the paramedic listened intently.

"Okay, good breath sounds. Delmar, turn it back on."

The paramedic leaned over Delia and asked: "Can you hear me, ma'am?"

Delia nodded.

"I'm starting an IV in case they want to give you any medicine in the ER; we'll already have a line going. Hold real still while I do this."

Delia nodded and looked over at Kate.

"I bet you want to know about your grandfather and great aunt, huh?" Kate said.

Delia nodded.

"Eunice is fine. A little smoke inhalation. Your granddad is on his way to the hospital too. He's got smoke inhalation also. But they're going to be okay. You're going to be okay, too." Kate stroked her cheek gently.

Delia turned to the young paramedic who nodded in agreement. "Your lungs sound pretty good," she said, removing her stethoscope from her ears. "Blood pressure's okay." She grinned. "Just lay still and take it easy. You've done enough for one night."

Delia smiled weakly, but the effort cost her; the skin of her face hurt, and she realized that the heat from the fire scorched her cheeks worse than a bad sunburn.

"Are you in any pain?" the paramedic, whose nameplate read "Brandi," asked.

This time, Delia managed a whisper, "My side."

"She landed on her side when she fell off the trellis," Kate said. "They'll X-ray her when we get to the ER."

Delia winced, and Kate leaned down again. "Hang in there."

Delia closed her eyes and tried to breathe shallowly. She felt herself drifting off and reached for Kate's hand. A few minutes later the ambulance rocked to a stop, and a second later the sirens were still. The driver hurried to the back, and then Delia felt herself being lifted out of the ambulance. People were shouting orders and someone, presumably the doctor, leaned over her asking. "Can you talk to me?"

"Yes," Delia spoke in a rough, uneven voice. "But it hurts."

"I know. I just have a few questions." He came around so she could see him; she noticed that his white coat was too long for him. He wore a stethoscope around his neck. "Can you tell me how long you were inside the house?"

"Four or five minutes."

"Okay, good." She felt him pick up both her hands. "It looks like you have some splinters in your hands. We'll get those out after we take care of the more serious things." He paused and then said: "Do you hurt anywhere else?"

"My side hurts," Delia whispered. "My head. I fell."

"How far did you fall?"

"Back porch roof. Eight feet?"

"Okay, I'm going to check you for burns. We're going to roll you over now and take a look at your back."

When they turned her over, Delia felt a wave of vertigo wash over her; she began to cough and vomit again. Warm hands held her head while the doctor barked, "Somebody get a sample of that sputum . . . *before* it hits the floor. And get those pants off her. Cut them off. The bra, too."

Then the doctor's voice spoke to her again, "You have a few minor burns . . . nothing serious. The nurses are going to get blood from you. We need your blood gas, and we have to get it from the artery, so the stick will probably hurt. I'm going to listen to your lungs and insert a little camera scope down your throat. We'll put you out for that. I know it's hard, but try to relax. We're going to take good care of you. Okay?"

Delia nodded. The next few minutes passed quickly.

"I need a large bore IV line," the doctor ordered. "An arterial blood gas, CBC, Chem 7. Let's give her 20 milligrams of morphine. Somebody call down to X-ray. I want a CT scan on her head and X-rays of her ribs." He turned to Brandi. "Did she lose consciousness?"

"Yes," Brandi said. "She was unconscious when we found her in the back yard."

"Okay, let's get the scan ASAP, and then I want to intubate her."

Delia nodded, feeling comforting warmth spread into her arms and across her chest. Then, she was floating above the pain, and the voices faded away.

Chapter 15

Something was in lodged in her throat. Delia tried to fight whatever was choking her, but her hands were tied down. Whimpering and struggling to escape her bonds, she heard Colleen's voice trying to calm her.

"Dee, stop fighting the tube. They put it in there so you can breathe." She felt a hand push damp hair away from her forehead. "Wake up, Dee. Look at me. Open your eyes."

Delia blinked a few times and opened her eyes cautiously. The window curtains were open, and the room was flooded with sunlight; Delia squeezed her eyes shut. When she opened them again, the first thing she saw was Colleen's face, calm but concerned above her.

"Don't try to talk," Colleen said. "The swelling in your throat has gone down; they're going to take the breathing tube out this morning."

Delia tried to lift her arms and looked imploringly at Colleen when she discovered they were in restraints. Her hands were lightly bandaged, and they throbbed with pain; then she remembered breaking out the louvers in the attic window.

"They didn't want you to try to pull the tube out while you were asleep. Do you want me to call the nurse to take them off?"

Delia nodded.

"I'll be right back," Colleen promised.

She came back with a nurse who gently released Delia from the restraints. A few minutes later a doctor walked into her room. His nameplate identified him as James Jordan.

He smiled and came within reach of her bed. "Hi, I'm Dr. Jordan. I saw you in the ER a couple nights ago. I don't know if you remember me? You're a lucky woman. You look a lot better than you did when you came in. Can I listen to your lungs?"

Delia nodded, and he rubbed the end of his stethoscope with his hand before placing it between Delia's breasts, a frown of concentration on his face. He had her lean forward and, with his stethoscope on her back, listened again. When he finished, he nodded his head approvingly.

"Right. They sound a lot better." He flipped open the chart in his hands. "Dr. Carmichael is your doctor. We'll see what he has to say about releasing you when he gets here."

He tucked his stethoscope back into the pocket of his white coat. "We looked down your windpipe the night you came in—you were lucky. It was pretty swollen, so I intubated you because I was afraid your throat might swell more over the next few days, making it hard for you to breathe."

He turned toward the door as another man in a white coat entered the room. "This is Dr. Carmichael now. I was talking to your patient, Mike. Told her she was a pretty lucky lady." He handed Delia's chart over to Mike.

Dr. Carmichael was a tall, slender, black man with a shaved head. He had a wide, open grin and turned it on Delia as he approached the bed. "Good morning. Are you ready to get rid of that tube?"

After Delia expressed herself in the affirmative as best she could, Jordan and Carmichael, with the assistance of a nurse, removed her breathing tube. The movement of the plastic against the back of her throat caused Delia to gag, though she avoided throwing up.

Swallowed experimentally a few times, she felt how sore her raw throat was. "How long have I been here?" She spoke softly through clenched teeth.

Dr. Carmichael looked quickly at his chart. "You came in . . . uh, night before last. So this is the beginning of your second full day. What do you remember?"

Delia tried to recall anything that happened since her arrival in the ER and failed. "Have you been here before?" she asked tentatively.

Carmichael laughed. "Okay," he said, briefly touching her arm. "We gave you a powerful sedative to keep you quiet while the tube was in . . . it's just easier that way. But we stopped that early this morning. I think your lungs are okay. The sputum sample we got the night you came in showed there wasn't any cause for concern. But I'd like to keep you until tomorrow."

Delia began to protest, and he held up his hand. "Just wait a minute. I don't feel comfortable releasing you today. You took a pretty good fall and hit your head. You also cracked a couple of ribs. We did a CAT scan on you when you came in, and everything looked okay, but you just woke up and I want to observe you a bit longer." He gestured to her bandaged hands. "Your hands are fine. We pulled out a few large splinters, but there was no serious damage. They should feel better in a couple days." He looked at her chart. "Do you have any pain?"

Delia took a quick inventory of her body and said, "My ribs. It hurts to breathe deeply."

"That's not surprising. They'll hurt for a while. Have you ever taken hydrocodone before?"

"I think so . . . a long time ago."

"I'm going to prescribe some for you to take with you when you go home. Remember to take your pain medication on schedule.

Take it *before* you're in pain. The nurse will give you a little device that will help to clear out your lungs . . . she'll show you how to use it. Do the exercise for about a week or so."

"So I can go home tomorrow?" Delia asked hopefully.

"Is there anyone to take care of you for a few days, until you get back on your feet?" Carmichael asked.

"Yes," Colleen said, glancing at Delia, who nodded. "I've come down to work on the excavation—I'll keep an eye on her. I've had some nursing experience."

"Great," he said. "Do you think you can do without the morphine?"

"I don't know," Delia admitted. "Let's find out."

"Okay," he said. "I'll have the nurse disconnect you and then we'll start on the hydrocodone. Remember, when you do get home, to take it easy for a few days. No more rescuing dogs or people from burning buildings, okay?"

Delia promised and watched while a nurse freed her from the morphine pump and removed her IV line. After the nurse showed her how to use the device to keep her lungs clear, she left. Colleen sat down in the chair beside Delia's bed.

"I can't believe I have to stay another day and night. How long have you been here?" Delia asked hoarsely.

"Kate called me the first night you were here. I drove down the next morning and relieved her. Last night I slept in the recliner," Colleen said, pointing to an uncomfortable looking chair in the corner of Delia's room.

"What about Granddad and Eunice?"

"Your great aunt was released the same night. Your grandfather is still here . . . he's going to be fine. He's been sedated and intubated just like you. But he's older . . . and so they say he will need more time to heal."

"Will they let me see him, do you think?" Delia asked.

"I can't imagine why not." Colleen smoothed Delia's hair from her forehead. "We'll ask them after a bit."

Delia yawned painfully and felt sleep tugging at her. "I'm so tired . . . and I stink like smoke."

"They told me they cleaned you up a little, the blood and some of the soot," Colleen told her. "But they couldn't move you around very much because of the breathing tube."

Delia looked down at her bandaged hands and saw her nails were dirty. "I want a shower."

"You need to rest, love." Colleen leaned over and kissed her gently on the lips. "When you wake up, you can ask a nurse to help you bathe. I've a few errands to run. The Jeep needs petrol. Perhaps I'll pick up a few things at the grocer's," she said. Colleen leaned down and kissed Delia again, gently on the forehead this time. "I'll be back tomorrow morning to pick you up."

But Delia was already asleep.

By morning, the surviving priests and temple dignitaries gathered on the top of the tallest mound in the city. They were with the body of the young warrior chief. No one was able to find the body of the Serpent Woman. The ceremony of burial was elaborate and lavish; his funeral dress and wealth were assembled in a hidden chamber of the Temple Mound. No one but the most high priest, the closest advisor to the Sun King, knew the location of the chamber; luckily he survived the massacre. The Tattooed Serpent's body had been prepared during the night; his head was badly misshapen from the blow he suffered but there was a large necklace, made from hammered copper discs and drilled mussel shells, around his neck.

The funeral party carried his body on a lavishly decorated litter down the center street of the smoldering city; every home's thatched roof was burned away, the poles that supported them were mostly charred; some still smoked. Above the stench of charred wood and thatch was the sickly sweet smell of burned human flesh, mixed with the coppery smell of blood that now dried in the sunlight, blood that would soon turn putrid in the harsh sun.

Only the dignitaries assigned to the funeral party were allowed in the burial chamber, a room whose floor was covered with thousands upon thousands of mussel shells strung on necklaces. The ceiling was lined with logs, as were the walls of the tomb; logs split down the middle, the smooth face wedged against each other, paneled the entire tomb. The young warrior's body was placed on a small raised platform constructed of wood and covered with the brightly colored feathers of exotic birds brought from the jungles of Central America thousands of miles away. Other items in the tomb included necklaces made of wolf and bear teeth, copper axes, silver jewelry, pottery in the form of turtles, fish and other creatures that inhabited the waters and woods around the city.

Only the torches held by the funeral attendants lighted the chamber. The smell of the smoke combined with the odor of raw earth permeated the small space. The Tattooed Serpent's body, beginning to swell with putrefaction, made the air inside the tomb nearly unbearable; many of the attendants discretely covered their mouths and noses with scented cloths. One young attendant, barely into his teens, staggered away from the group and vomited in a corner.

Chapter 16

Delia awoke, drenched in sweat. Sunlight still poured through the curtainless window, but it was no longer morning. She closed her eyes again, but opened them when the image of the tomb and the body of the Tattooed Serpent came back to her. She looked around the room for a telephone and found one on the bedside table. She wanted to talk to Eunice.

When there was no answer at Eunice's house, Delia sank back down against the pillows and was about to ring the nurse to ask when the door opened and Eunice stepped inside. "Delia!" she exclaimed and hurried over to the bed. She kissed Delia's forehead and said, "Lord, child, I have been so worried about you. I've just been up in Hollis's room."

"How is he?" Delia asked. "People keep telling me he's going to be okay. Is he?"

"Oh, yes," Eunice stated emphatically. "Doctor told me he'd take the breathing tube out tomorrow if your grandfather keeps improving. How are you doing?"

"I'm good," Delia told her. "Hungry."

"Well, I imagine you are," Eunice told her. "You haven't eaten for days. Let's ring the nurse and see if we can't get you some food. A person can't get well unless they eat." She found the buzzer and pushed it. "I'm not sure if this thing is even hooked up to anything," she scowled. "It takes them forever to answer."

"How's Wally?" Delia asked.

Eunice snorted. "He's just fine, the old flea-bitten hound. Thinks he's due some special consideration since the fire . . . when I left, he was up on my divan asleep."

"That's great, Eunice," Delia said. "Doc says I can go home tomorrow."

"Are you coming to stay with us or will you stay out at the site?"

"I'll stay at the site," Delia told her. "I'll be fine out there."

"Sure you will," her aunt said sarcastically. "After all—we've only been shot at and burned down . . . what else could happen?" She paused. "Dee, listen . . . I'm worried about you going back there."

"I know, but really . . ."

"No, let me finish," Eunice ordered. "I had the strangest phone call yesterday. That no-good Bob Noland called me, wanting to talk to Hollis."

"About?"

"Well, it was peculiar. He was as sweet as pie, saying how he was so sorry to hear about our bad luck . . . he said something about duck hunters. Suggested that they must be pretty bad shots to think Hollis was a duck. And then he mentioned what he called the 'radical Indian group' that left those silly poles and feathers and the note. . . ."

"Wait a minute," Delia interrupted. "How could he know about those things?"

"Oh, I'm sure someone in the sheriff's department told him," Eunice said. "Or he might have read it in the paper."

"Oh, God," Delia groaned. "Has it been in the paper?"

"Of course it's been in the paper—a good house fire is always reported in the newspaper."

"Did the article mention the site?"

"Yes, it did." Then seeing Delia's upset, she asked, "That's not good, is it?"

"No," Delia said. "Now every pot hunter in the county will be out there." She paused. "What else did Noland say?"

"He said the reason he called was to offer us a place to *stay*. Said he had a rental house over in Tuckerman we could stay in ... until we decide whether or not to rebuild the house."

"*Whether* or not we rebuild?" Delia asked. "What's that supposed to mean? Is there some doubt Granddad won't?"

Eunice sighed. "Dee, honey, we have to be practical now. Before ... I would never have suggested that he move into town with me. But now that the house is gone, and Hollis isn't farming anymore ... well, what's the point of him living way out there? I've been there a lot since his tractor accident, but all my friends live in town. My canasta club, my church, the classes I've been taking ... it just seems more practical."

"Hmmm," Delia said thoughtfully. "I see what you mean. You aren't suggesting that he *sell* the place are you?"

"Lord no! That land has been in a Whitaker's name since 1879. It always will be. I know Hollis will miss living out there, but he's in no shape to be out there alone."

"What else did Noland say?" Delia asked. Her ribs were beginning to hurt, but she put the pain out of her mind.

"Well, if you can imagine the nerve of that man ... he asked if Hollis would be willing to sell the farm to *him* ... along with the Buck's sixty acres."

"What did Granddad say?"

"Oh, for pity sakes," Eunice said scornfully. "I haven't told Hollis anything ... if he knew Bob Noland called for any reason, let alone offered to buy the farm and the other property ... Hollis, well ... I don't like to think what he would have said."

"Well, I think it's pretty suspicious myself."

"So do I," Eunice said. "First Noland offers to buy the land after someone took a shot at Hollis and Kevin. Then the house burns down around us, you're almost killed..."

"Do you want to call the sheriff and tell him what you told me?" Delia asked her.

"Oh, I don't know, Dee," Eunice demurred. "It was just a feeling I had. Besides, Noland is a slippery one. I know he has the sheriff in his back pocket, and probably a deputy or two. None of them would believe me."

"You're probably right," Delia admitted. "Have they figured out where the fire started yet?"

"Not yet," Eunice said. "I'm going to go on home now. I'll stop at the desk and tell the nurse you want something eat." She looked at Delia critically. "Try to get some rest and *be careful* while you're at the farm. Call Kevin and have him come out there to help, you hear?"

"I don't want Kevin out there...it's too dangerous. Until we figure out who's behind all this stuff, I don't want anyone at risk. Colleen is taking me back to the site, and I'm going to ask her to stay with me for a few days, until I get back on my feet."

"Well, I'm glad you have a friend to stay with you. Call me when you get home, if not before."

After Eunice left, Delia sat for a few moments. Thinking over what her great aunt had told her, she crawled out of bed and walked unsteadily over to the sink. She found some soap, a washcloth, towels, and even a small bottle of shampoo to wash the smoke and dirt from her hair. After drying herself with one of the clean towels and wrapping herself in another, Delia was tired and sat down on the edge of the hospital bed. The effort of washing herself and shampooing her hair left her exhausted. She lay back on the pillows, grateful to be free of the IV, and was about to ring the nurse again when one came into the room bearing clean towels.

"Hi, how are you doing today?" she asked.

Delia nodded. "I'm okay; I'm just so hungry, I could eat a fried gopher. Could I get something to eat?"

The nurse laughed. "I don't think gopher's on the menu today, but I saw some extra trays in the hall. It looks like French dip sandwiches and fries. Will that do?"

"Absolutely," Delia said. "It sounds great."

"Okay, I'll get someone to bring you a tray," the nurse said, picking up the towels Delia had discarded. "I'll get you a clean gown, too."

A few minutes later, an aide arrived and set Delia's meal on the wheeled tray at the foot of her bed. Rolling it over, she adjusted its height and also laid a clean nightgown beside her.

"Thanks for everything . . . especially the food. I'm really hungry," Delia said, taking a huge bite of her sandwich.

"Everything okay now?" the aide asked.

"Great," Delia said, wincing through her first swallow of food but spearing some French-fries energetically. "Thanks again." It only took a few minutes for her to finish off the food and, when she was done, she pushed the tray away. She wondered where Colleen was and what she was doing. She remembered Colleen saying that she sat by her bed through a night and thought about the kiss she gave her before leaving.

After a few minutes of pleasant reverie, Delia turned her attention to review the events she experienced since her arrival in Arkansas—seeing the log tomb, meeting Kate and then Colleen, deciding to excavate, hearing Bob Noland's story, learning about Buddy's disappearance, and most important, having disturbing dreams every time she slept. She wondered what Buddy's role was in them. She tried to establish connections between everything. Believing that some of them were definitely connected while others seemed random and inexplicable. Her scientific mind didn't want them in her life. They confused things. Could she trust something that came in a fevered sleep?

She sighed. She wanted to see her grandfather. She wanted to talk to Kate. But she was tired again. She shook her head. It would take less energy to call Kate on the phone than to try and find her grandfather. She dialed Kate's number and waited.

"Dee!" Kate said when she heard Delia's voice. "I came to see you this morning, but they said you were sleeping and wouldn't let me in."

"Sorry," Delia said. "Listen, have you got a few minutes?"

"Sure," Kate said. "Are you okay?"

"I'm fine," Delia said. "I'm going home tomorrow...Kate, do you know what happened to those men we found on the property?"

"Sure do. Those bastards are in jail," Kate said firmly. "I went down to the sheriff's office this morning after I came to see you, and guess what?"

"What?"

"They charged both of them with trespassing and disturbing a burial site...basically, the things you told them the feds would get them for. Except they're using the Arkansas law to hold them."

"Will it stick?"

"Who knows? But *they* must think it will because they rolled on Bob Noland."

"You're kidding."

"I'm serious. They said *Noland* set the fire as a diversion, so while we were occupied with the fire, they could get access to the tomb."

"But...they weren't even looking at the tomb. They were probing a smaller mound."

"I know. I told Pettit that and when he questioned them, they said Noland wanted a mound that was untouched. He wanted grave goods."

"That doesn't make any sense," Delia countered. "It would take them more time to open a new mound than it would to loot an open one."

"Dee, the plan was that they would probe the mound that night and then come back later with a small backhoe, tear off the top, take what they could get and get out."

172

Delia thought a moment. "Did they say that was why Noland wanted to buy the land?"

"Pettit didn't tell me everything, Dee. You know he and I don't like each other very much."

"Yeah, well, Eunice needs to talk to Pettit, too. She came to see me today and told me something really strange." She related her conversation about Bob Noland to Kate.

"That rat bastard. He's such a vulture. Well, that's just one more nail in his coffin."

"So Pettit thinks he has enough to charge Noland?"

"He didn't say. I just figured out most of what I'm telling you by what he said to me. He's interviewed me twice since the fire. I'm sure he's still gathering evidence and interviewing people. But I can tell you this—he was *really* pissed off about the fire and the fact that you and your granddad got hurt. He said Noland knew that someone would get hurt . . . he was counting on whoever was in the house being in the hospital or even dying so he and Brad and Pete could come back and tear open the mound. Maybe tear open more than one."

"Well, let's face it; he did a pretty good job of getting rid of us—if that's what he intended. Granddad and I are still in the hospital." Delia paused. "Have they questioned Noland yet?"

"I don't know," Kate admitted. "Pettit wouldn't tell me. But I'll tell you one other thing I found out while I was down at the sheriff's office."

"What's that?"

"I saw Kevin in Pettit's office. I got the impression that he was questioning Kevin."

"You didn't tell Pettit about seeing Kevin talking to Noland did you?"

"I didn't have to," Kate said, a little defensively. "Somebody else must have seen them talking. If that's even why Kevin was there. I mean, I don't know for a *fact* that Pettit was questioning him . . . I just saw Kevin in his office."

173

"Okay, take it easy. I'm trying to think this through. Something doesn't add up."

"I think it fits perfectly," Kate said. "Noland found out, from someone, about the site and wanted the artifacts. I told you when we first talked; Mississippian grave goods are very valuable. So, he tried to buy the land from your granddad; and, when that didn't work he started doing stupid shit, like taking a shot at your granddad and Kevin; putting those stupid feathers and poles down at the site."

"Do you also think he stole the copper plates and the other stuff from the cage?"

"It's not out of the question. Like I said before, maybe someone told him. Or maybe he just figured it out...if somebody told him about the copper plates and other things you picked up, he could have figured we'd lock the stuff somewhere...the archaeology department would be a logical place to look. You've seen the caliber of security we have over there."

"And you think it was Kevin who told him about the excavation," Delia stated.

"Not necessarily," Kate said. "Maybe Kevin told John Ed and he told Noland."

"Hmmmm," Delia muttered. "I didn't think of John Ed. I just can't believe Kevin would do that...I thought he had better judgment than that."

"Maybe it wasn't him. Maybe when they bring Noland in to question him, he'll tell them how he found out. The important thing is—*they got Noland*. They'll get him for arson, and if they can prove he meant to hurt your granddad and Eunice, maybe even attempted murder. That would make me *very* happy."

Delia was quiet.

"What's the matter?" Kate asked.

"It's nothing," Delia assured her. Then relenting she confessed. "I've had some weird dreams since I got here. Some of them were about someone who looked like Buddy."

174

"You dreamed about Buddy?"

"Well, sort of," Delia said reluctantly. She paused. "Can I ask you some things about him?"

"Like what?" Kate sounded puzzled.

"Does anyone know what he was wearing when he disappeared?"

"Probably his dark gray suit. And I know he had on a blue Oxford shirt—that's all he ever wore...I used to tease him about it—and probably his black wing-tip shoes." Kate paused. "Why do you want know?"

Delia didn't answer right away.

"You must have some reason for wanting to know those things about Buddy. Tell me. I want to know," Kate insisted.

"Well, it's pretty long and complicated, but basically, ever since I got here I've been having these horrible dreams...about a massacre."

"Massacre?"

"Yeah," Delia confessed. "An invasion and a massacre. You—someone like you—were in the dream too."

"Me?" Kate didn't speak for a moment. "You saw Buddy and me in your dream?"

"Yes."

"What were we doing?"

"Kate, it was just a *dream*."

"I don't care. I want you to tell me."

"Okay, okay." Delia briefly recounted the dreams she had since arriving. "You were both rulers of this city that was burning. You had a serpent tattoo on your face."

"Like the one on the pot?"

"Exactly like the one on the pot."

"And what about Buddy?"

"At first, both of you were standing on top of a mound, watching the massacre. Later, Buddy, well, the warrior that looked like Buddy, was killed by the invaders...Kate, you were even wearing

175

and holding some of the artifacts I found *before* I met you."

At first Kate said nothing. Then, she finally said, "That's hard to believe."

"You think I don't know that?" Delia asked. "But I did dream it, nonetheless. And listen to this—Buddy was buried in a log tomb . . . like the one we uncovered."

"What are you saying? That you think Buddy's buried in the log tomb?"

"Of course not," Delia said firmly. "I never said that."

"Well, okay. Because that's just . . ."

"Crazy? Hare-brained?"

"Not exactly the words I'd use," Kate said hesitantly. "Buddy and I were probably in your dream because . . . well, because we've been on your mind since you got here."

"Damn, I feel like the pieces to the puzzle are all there, but I'm too tired to figure it out."

"The pieces to what puzzle?" Kate wanted to know. "We know, or mostly know, who was behind all this shit now . . . it's just who Eunice said it was. Noland and his idiots."

"But you don't know for sure that they'll stay in jail. They might get out on bail. And Eunice told me she was sure Pettit was in Noland's pocket. So maybe he was just saying all that stuff to placate you. He might not arrest Noland . . . I want to talk to Kevin and find out what Pettit said to him, find out what he was doing talking to Noland." She paused. "I just don't think it's safe at the site now. I don't want you to go out there . . . just in case."

"I've known Brad and Pete all my life," Kate said. "They're a couple of blowhards who couldn't pour piss out of a boot with directions written on the heel. I'm not afraid of them."

Delia chuckled at Kate's colorful expression. "That's all well and good. But I still don't want you or Adam or Paula out there until I get out of the hospital. I don't want anyone else getting hurt. So . . . promise me you'll stay away until we know for sure who was behind it."

"I promise," Kate said grudgingly. "Goodbye, Dee."

"Goodbye, Katie," Delia said.

After hanging up, Delia felt a wave of exhaustion wash over her. She closed her eyes and began to drift toward sleep. She was vaguely aware of someone coming to take the food tray away, but soon after that, she slept.

At the entrance to the burial chamber, someone screamed; it sounded like a young girl's shrill, high-pitched shriek of terror. The source of the scream was soon evident as a slim, pre-adolescent girl dressed in a white cotton shift tumbled into the chamber. She scrambled across the floor of the tomb and threw herself into a corner where she cowered. The men dragged her to the base of the burial platform. The faces of the men showed no emotion as the high priest raised a stone club and, in one swift movement, silenced the girl forever. Blood gushed from her head onto the floor of the tomb as the body fell forward. The young funeral attendant who had turned away to vomit earlier, turned back to the ceremony; but at the sight of the battered girl lying in a growing pool of blood, he went back to his corner and began retching again.

When Delia awakened, it was fully dark. Someone had come in and closed the drapes. A nightlight burned over a small desk in the corner of her room, but it only served to accentuate the unease that Delia felt in the aftermath of the dream. She knew that the only way to dispel the horror of the images in her head was to move her body. Forced inactivity from the past few days wore on her; she was unused to such idleness and now longed to be out of bed. Swinging her legs over the edge of the mattress, she looked around and saw that the nurse who brought her night-gown also left her some socks and a thin cloth bathrobe. Donning both, she padded out to the nurses' station. She was drawn to the bright lights and the bustle of people going about their jobs. Delia finally caught the attention of one desk nurse and asked where her grandfather's room was located. As she walked along the hall to the elevator, Delia found that she felt much stronger and more energetic than she had that morning.

When she found Hollis's room, she half-expected to see Eunice or perhaps Kevin, even Kevin's father   , but he was alone. The light of the muted television flickered, and his breathing machine made an oddly comforting, rhythmic pumping noise.

Delia approached her grandfather's bed cautiously and, as she reached his side, she saw how drawn and pale this latest assault left him. She pulled a chair up next to the bed and picked up his thickly veined, liver-spotted hand, holding it gently. His eyelids fluttered, but he didn't open his eyes; and she wondered if they had sedated him as they had her. Then, in a gesture that would have been unthinkable to her a week ago, she rested her cheek against the rough, worn skin of his hand and closed her eyes.

When she opened them a few moments later and looked up, Hollis's eyes were open and he was smiling at her. He moved his hand from under her cheek and rested in on her head. Peace and contentment, feelings she mostly associated with the serene beauty of her home at Half Moon Lake, settled over her and the dream of death was forgotten.

Chapter 17

By the time Colleen returned the next morning, Delia was awake and ready to leave. She hated to admit it, but the extra day had been good for her: She felt stronger than she had the day before. Her ribs still hurt, but everything else was tolerable. Colleen had stopped by Delia's trailer and picked up some clean clothes for her to wear on the trip home.

"Well, it looks peaceful at the site," Colleen told her as she watched Delia dress. "There were some men from the electric company working there when I arrived; they assured me the power will be on by the time we get home. I hope so because I put away some things I bought at the grocer's."

"Thanks for doing all that," Delia murmured as she buttoned her jeans. "I really appreciate it."

Colleen kissed her quickly on the lips and stood back. "Quite all right...I'll go down to the nurses' station and see about the paperwork."

"Did you stay at the trailer last night?" Delia asked.

"No, I didn't," Colleen replied. "It was a tad chilly and dark...a bit gloomy, so I went to a hotel."

When Colleen returned, she picked up the plastic sack that contained Delia's belongings and said, "While I was talking to the nurses, a woman came up to the desk and identified herself as a reporter from Jonesboro. Said she was following up on the fire and wanted to talk to you. Apparently it's a slow news day."

Delia groaned. "Well, that's just great. That's all we need...the media crawling all over the place. I wonder if there's a back way out of here."

"We have a few minutes before she finds out you're here." Colleen's smile was very self-satisfied.

"We do?" Delia asked. "How so?"

Colleen peeked outside the door. "She's walking in the other direction," she told Delia. "Let's go while we have the chance."

As they slipped into the hall, Delia turned around to Colleen. "Why's she going the wrong way?"

"Because I told her I had just seen you down in the cafeteria."

Delia laughed and then put her hand over her mouth. "You are a devious woman, aren't you?"

Colleen grinned mischievously and took Delia's arm. "Me? Devious?" She began walking briskly down the hall. "Perhaps a wee bit."

By the time Colleen and Delia reached her grandfather's farm, it was almost noon, and her ribs were aching. She tried not to breathe too deeply, but each bump in the road made the ride definitely uncomfortable. One particularly hard bounce of the Jeep's unyielding suspension elicited a groan from Delia.

Colleen reached over, took her hand and squeezed. "Can you hang in there until we get to the trailer?"

"I'm fine," Delia said through gritted teeth.

"I'll brew you some tea that will help you sleep when we get to the trailer." She looked at Delia. "It's so much easier on you than synthetic codeine."

Delia merely nodded. She felt short of breath and incredibly, profoundly tired. Her spirits, which had been lifted temporarily at being released from the hospital, were starting to sag. "How are we going to get to the trailer?" she asked, her voice hoarse with pain.

"I'm going to drive us down there in the Jeep," Colleen said. "It's going to be a bit uncomfortable for you—the little road that goes down there is badly rutted, but it won't be as bad as trying to get you down there on the four-wheeler. How does that sound?"

Delia closed her eyes. "Fine, just let me brace myself."

Colleen reached over and touched her shoulder. "Just hold on a few more minutes." She paused. "Unless you think you need to go back to the hospital?"

Delia shook her head vehemently. "No, I'm fine . . . just drive."

Colleen nodded. "I'll drive as slowly as I can."

By the time they reached the trailer, the sun was high, and the day had turned warm. The men from the power company had been as good as their word, for when they pulled up beside the trailer, Delia could see there was a power line attached to her trailer. She was glad to have heat and light.

Colleen gathered Delia's bag of soiled clothing and got out of the car. She went to the door of the trailer, opened it, and went inside. After a few seconds she reemerged and came back to the Jeep.

"I cleared a few things out of the way and turned down your bed." She offered Delia her arm, but Delia waved her away.

"I can make it," she said and, swinging her legs out of the Jeep, she walked slowly to the trailer. Despite Delia's objections, Colleen helped her up the steps to the trailer's door and opened it for her. Once inside, Delia stopped and stood for a few moments.

"You're doing great," Colleen said. "Just take it slowly."

When they reached the bed in the tiny backroom, Colleen helped Delia peel off her clothing, leaving her naked.

"Do you have anything you want to wear to bed?"

"Look in that drawer," Delia pointed to a built in dresser. "I put

181

some clean pajamas in there the night of the fire."

Colleen pulled out the flannel pajamas and said, "Here, sit down, and I'll help you get these on."

Delia sat down on the edge of the bed, vaguely realizing that she was naked in front of this incredibly attractive woman. She put her hands on Colleen's shoulders to steady herself.

Colleen first helped Delia aim each foot through a leg hole and then pushed the pants up to her knees saying, "I don't think I've ever been this close to a woman's privates before and not had something else entirely in mind." She looked up at Delia and smiled. "Despite the fact that you're an invalid, I'm sorely tempted."

"Before you make any decisions, I think you should kiss me," she said softly and lowered her mouth to Colleen's.

After a second or two, Colleen took Delia's face in her hands and very gently, began to return her kiss. It was the slowest, gentlest of kisses. Colleen put the barest amount of pressure into her kiss, letting the passion build, and then she pulled back a few inches to look into Delia's eyes.

"You're in no condition to be kissing, but it feels bloody marvelous."

"No more talking then," Delia murmured, pulling her up again and covering her mouth with her own.

Finally, Colleen broke their kiss and patted Delia's face. "You really should get some rest now, love. You sleep while I make tea." Delia nodded and gently lowered herself to the bed. "Okay, maybe just a nap..."

The next moment, she was dreaming again.

The Serpent Woman was gone, as was the burning city, replaced by the familiar surroundings of her excavation site. Although the night was dark, there was a full moon, which allowed Delia to see a figure standing at the edge of grave-sized hole. It was indistinct, but as Delia got closer she could see that the figure was definitely masculine. As she went closer still, she saw he was holding a large flashlight, using it to peer down into the grave.

"Who are you?" the dream Delia asked him.

As the man turned toward her she saw his face and instantly recognized him as Buddy Treadaway.

"I need your help," he said.

"What do you want from me?" Delia asked him.

"I want you to protect my sister," Buddy said. "Protect Kate. Don't let the past become her future."

"Who?" Delia asked. "Noland? Is it him?"

Buddy shook his head. "No. Go help her. She's out there. Now, look."

He turned away and shined his flashlight down into the tomb. "Look at me."

Delia looked at his face and then down into the tomb. It was a sight that though she had seen many times, she had never become accustomed to.

The skull was crushed, but it still had hair. A gray pinstriped suit was mostly gone, but Delia could see a scrap of a blood stained blue material. At the same moment that Delia felt sure she knew that the person in the grave was Buddy, she felt a hand push her down. Then, she cried out, both from pain and surprise, as she fell into the open tomb.

Chapter 18

Before she landed beside the skeletal corpse of Buddy, Delia awoke in Colleen's arms, crying and whimpering indistinctly.

"What, love? What is it?" Colleen was completely naked. Delia allowed herself to be patted and soothed until the fear from the dream was past. Then she pulled away from Colleen and began coughing, which quickly led to gagging. Colleen got out of bed and came back quickly with a paper towel which Delia held over her mouth.

"Cough up as much of that as you possibly can," Colleen instructed her. "You must get rid of it sooner than later."

A few moments later, Delia wiped her mouth and looked embarrassedly at Colleen, who accepted the towel. "I'll dispose of it, love. Don't worry—I've seen worse."

Delia lay back in the bed, exhausted from her coughing.

Colleen stood over her. "Do your ribs hurt?"

"Not too much," Delia replied.

Though she was in pain, Delia appreciated the fact that Colleen was naked. Delia gazed at her body, reached out her hand and pulled her closer.

Her breasts were large and generous with perfect brown nipples. Delia noticed razor thin white scars down the middle of each one. She ran her fingertip down one of the scars and looked at Colleen questioningly.

"I had a biopsy on each one—many years ago," Colleen said. "No cancer, thank the goddess." She looked down at her stomach, and traced a wide scar down the center that disappeared into her dark pubic hair. "That," she said, "is my Caesarean scar."

"You have children?" Delia asked.

"Indeed," Colleen replied. "I have three—Michael, Megan and Scott. Michael's twenty-seven, he's a pediatrician in Cambridge. Megan is a graphic designer. She's twenty-five, married, and lives in London with her husband, Spencer. Scott is my youngest, he's just turned twenty-three. He goes to school in Fayetteville." She wrinkled her nose. "In archaeology."

"I remember Kate telling me that now," Delia said. "So, you were married?"

"Oh, yes, I was married for nearly twenty years," Colleen replied.

"Do you miss your children?"

"Terribly. But I go home at least once a year—usually during the summer and sometimes for Christmas. This year I'll stay a bit longer as Megan is pregnant, and I want to be there when she delivers my first grandchild. I see Scott frequently. I go over to Fayetteville, and he comes here. We're very close. He's my baby."

"That's so wonderful," Delia said. "I wonder if someday I'll regret not having children."

Colleen sat down on the edge of bed. "I consider having my children the best thing I've ever done—more than my education or any other accomplishment. They are such wonderful, interesting people. Scott is coming to visit me in a few weeks. I told him about your dig. He's mad to see it. He'll probably try to talk you into letting him help."

"I'd love to meet him," Delia replied. "We can use all the help we can get."

Colleen smoothed Delia's hair away from her forehead. "You're a bit feverish. I'll get you some more tea to bring it down. Much easier on the stomach than aspirin or Advil."

"God, you are gorgeous," Delia said hoarsely. "I wish I wasn't so weak. I'd do something about it."

Colleen smiled and pulled on her pants. She touched Delia's shoulder and gave her a quick kiss on the end of her nose.

"Perhaps if you lie in a different position, the change would ease your pain . . . on your stomach?"

"Is that medical advice?" Delia asked. "Or sexual?"

Colleen laughed. "You're a wicked one, aren't you?"

Delia laid her head on the pillow and closed her eyes. "I'm too tired to be wicked."

Colleen's tea did indeed ease the pain, and Delia tried to listen to her explanation of what the tea contained. But the sound of her lilting voice and the relief that came from the cessation of the pain in her ribs was too seductive, and soon she was dozing again. She awoke to the sensation of Colleen's strong hands massaging her calves and feet.

"Oh, that feels so heavenly," Delia groaned.

"Awake are we?" Colleen asked. "How do you feel?"

Delia turned her head to see Colleen sitting against the trailer wall at the foot of the bed. She was wearing a pair of white cotton drawstring pants and a tank top.

"I feel better. My lungs seem clearer. They don't hurt as much, and I don't feel like coughing anymore. What you're doing to my legs and feet is wonderful." She murmured her pleasure.

"I tried to wait to touch you until you woke up," Colleen said, not at all penitently. She released Delia's leg and crawled to the top of the bed. "This bed was not made for two full-figured women," she complained, as she kissed Delia's bare shoulder. She stood up beside the bed and took off her clothes, then crawled back into bed. The sensation of naked, warm flesh against her side gave Delia a shiver of pleasure.

Colleen leaned in to kiss her, but Delia held her back. "There's something I have to tell you before ... before we make love."

"Oh?"

"Yes, I feel like, well, I just think you ought to know that I slept with Kate the night of the fire."

Colleen smiled. "I suspected you might."

"It doesn't bother you?" Delia asked.

Colleen shrugged. "Well, I can't say that I'm not a bit jealous, but then again ... I did decline your invitation to come and work. Nothing I said led you to believe we would ever see each other again." She kissed Delia's shoulder. "Kate's a lovely woman. Very persuasive when she wants something." Then she began kissing Delia's shoulder again.

Delia relished Colleen's lips on her shoulder and later, her teeth gently nibbling the top of her shoulder. Although she tried to turn over to return the gesture, Colleen held her down on her stomach.

"Stay there," she instructed. She brushed her lips across the back of Delia's neck and began kissing more firmly. "Besides, I like this submissive posture. It's one of my favorites."

Delia found the facedown position unfamiliar but exciting, and then Colleen's lips were at her ear, whispering something that made Delia groan with anticipation.

"I promise I won't hurt you, if you simply trust me a bit," Colleen whispered, kissing behind Delia's ear. "Just relax and let me make you feel good."

Delia closed her eyes and felt Colleen's warm hands kneading her lower back, moving down to her buttocks, lightly tracing the curve of her ass.

"God, I love your bum," Colleen said, giving it a harder squeeze. Then Delia felt Colleen's mouth at the juncture of her thigh and butt.

"Oh, god, I love that."

"May I fuck you?" Colleen asked in a mock formal voice.

"God, yes," Delia moaned.

In answer to her request, Colleen slipped her hand between

Delia's legs and parted the folds of warm, slippery flesh. She probed gently, and with her fingertips she drew slow, maddening circles around Delia's exposed clit. Delia arched her butt into the air and into Colleen's touch.

"I want to be inside you," Colleen said in her ear.

"Please," Delia responded. "Please. Just do something."

"Spread your legs for me," Colleen instructed her, pushing Delia's legs apart. Then she felt Colleen's fingers inside her and then outside, on her clit, then inside again and then outside circling her clit. She was throbbing. Colleen's fingers continued their maddening pattern and soon, at Delia's pleading, increased their tempo, faster and then, Delia urged, "Deeper, please."

Colleen pushed harder and reached to pull Delia up onto her lap, holding her around the waist and letting Delia ride her fingers. She helped Delia to lift herself up and then grind her pelvis against her hand and fingers. Colleen whispered encouragement in her ear.

Delia gasped out loud, "Oh, god, oh, yes. It feels so good, don't stop, please."

Finally, Delia felt her orgasm coming at her like a wave and cried out as Colleen's fingers continued to pound into her. She pushed backwards—hard and with abandon, matching the rhythm of Colleen's thrusts.

Afterward, she lay gasping into the pillow, and then she felt the weight of Colleen's body on her butt.

"Am I too heavy?" Colleen asked.

"No," Delia said. "What're you doing now?"

Colleen settled herself onto Delia's rear end and asked: "You sure I'm not too heavy now?"

"Of course not," Delia said. Then she felt Colleen grasp her shoulders and begin a gentle rocking motion against her back-side. The motion pressed Delia's ass down into the bed and caused her butt cheeks to part slightly; she could feel Colleen's pubic hair—first against her butt and then between her cheeks.

"I'm not hurting your back, am I?" Colleen asked.

"God, no. Just keep doing what you're doing."

She could feel Colleen's growing wetness between her cheeks; the sensation was delicious. Colleen continued rocking, groaning a little and then tightening her grip on Delia's shoulders.

"God, I love this," Colleen gasped. Her rocking motion had begun to push Delia's clit against the sheet and the friction of the sheet with the rocking motion of Colleen's body pushed her to orgasm again. Finally, she could feel Colleen's slickness directly on her asshole and that sensation, combined with her clit's contact with the sheets pushed her over the edge; she began to raise herself in unison with Colleen. Incredibly, they both reached orgasm at the same time, and when Colleen fell off Delia they turned to each other and grinned.

"Wow!" Delia gasped.

"Indeed," Colleen said. "Quite remarkable."

Delia pushed Colleen's hair away from her face. "Imagine that. Simultaneous orgasm. You don't experience that every day."

Colleen closed her eyes. "I'm wondering if I've ever experienced it—certainly never the first time."

"We're suited to each other," Delia murmured, nuzzling her neck.

"I believe you're right," Colleen agreed. They were both quiet for a moment, and then Colleen said, "Stay awake now and tell about the last dream you had."

Delia cleared her throat and took a sip of the now-lukewarm tea Colleen had brought her earlier. Then she told Colleen about her last few dreams.

"And you're sure the figure was Kate's brother, Buddy?"

"I've only seen his photograph on Kate's desk. But the person in my dream looked *like* him. His head was crushed, and he was buried in a log tomb, or I presume he was. Oh hell, I don't know. I can't figure it out; I'm too tired. But in the latest dream, he pointed a flashlight into the log tomb ... our log tomb and showed me a body."

"Whose body was it?"

"I guess it was Buddy's because he said, 'Protect Kate. Don't let the past become her future. Go help her . . . or something like that.'"

Colleen nodded. "Fascinating."

"Yeah," Delia said, her eyes closing with exhaustion. "I wish I wasn't so damn tired. I want to go out there and look at the tomb." She pushed herself up off the bed and tried to sit up. "I've slept more over the past three days than I usually do in a week."

Colleen pulled her back down. "You need to rest, love. The tomb will still be there when you wake up."

Delia sank down onto the pillow again and murmured. "Maybe just a short nap."

She closed her eyes and, after a few minutes, Delia heard Colleen's breathing deepen but she was unable to drift off. She got out of bed quietly and padded down the short hallway to the front room. The tea that Colleen had made her earlier was warm, and Delia poured herself a cup. As she sipped, she idly looked out the little front window of the trailer. It was completely dark now and the moon was positioned mid-way across the sky.

There was a light along the tree line by the river.

Delia stood for a moment, considering what she ought to do. She barely needed to guess who was carrying the lights. The most likely possibility, Delia decided, was looters. The story in the newspaper about the Whitaker house fire and the reporter Colleen overheard at the nurses' station indicated that the location of the site was now public knowledge.

Thus, even though Brad and Pete might still be locked up, they were just the tip of the looter's iceberg. Pothunters were notorious for their brazenness, and the rewards for a single night's work were great enough to overcome many people's fear of getting caught.

Delia knew if she wished to protect the site from looters, she would have to do it herself. And this time she would not go unarmed.

Chapter 19

Dressed in black jeans and a black turtleneck, Delia again peeked through the window and thought more about the lights. They were in approximately the same spot where she and Kate surprised Noland's men. As she put on her father's duster, Delia felt a surge of anger. Whoever it was down there was damaging the integrity of her excavation.

Before leaving, Delia checked on the package that Shawla sent and looked through it until she found what she was looking for; it was a piece of equipment that she relied on during her wilderness treks. Setting up camp in the dark was always difficult before she saw the gizmo offered in the L.L. Bean catalogue—a high-powered LED light on an elastic strap designed to be worn around the head. It illuminated a large area, while allowing both her hands to be free. Now, she fastened it on her head, picked up the old Remington and slipped outside. After moving a few yards away from the trailer, she checked the position of the light again.

It hadn't moved.

As she began walking toward the light, Delia's steps slowed momentarily. The thought that she should awaken Colleen, tell her where she was going or take her cell phone, briefly crossed her mind. However, it was unlikely that pot-hunters posed any real threat. Besides, she reminded herself, she had a weapon. She shrugged off her reservations and continued walking.

As she had done a few nights previously, Delia crossed the bridge and continued along the outer perimeter of the site, finally entering the stand of trees that bordered the river. Again using the shadows cast by the moonlight to hide her approach, she walked carefully to avoid stepping on dry branches that would betray her presence. Somewhere nearby she heard the squeak of a small animal as a night-hunting owl carried off its captured prey. In her right hand she carried the Remington, one cartridge in the chamber, and nine others waiting in the breech.

Fall's night air had a crisp bite and, as she made her way just inside the line of trees, Delia flicked the safety off the Remington; still trying to keep to the shadows, she moved as silently as she could. Occasionally, she stood still and listened. She heard the constant rush of the river beside her, nothing else. As she drew closer to the light, Delia suddenly saw a shadowy figure moving ahead of her but off to the right. She stopped and strained to make out what it was. Pressing herself against a big pin oak tree, she stood motionless and waited. After a few moments, she began to think that the figure was a merely a branch or bush moving in the wind. Then, it moved again. In the light of the moon, Delia saw that there was someone just ahead of her. As the person moved on through the trees, Delia caught a glimpse of coppery hair in the full moonlight. It was Kate.

Moving quickly through the shadowy woods, Delia gave a low whistle, and Kate turned around. Delia stepped out from behind the tree and motioned to her. Kate stood still for moment and then began walking toward her. When Kate was right in front of her, Delia suddenly heard loud rustling a few feet from where Kate had been. Delia reached out and grabbed her, pulling her close so the large oak hid them both.

"What are you doing here?" Kate hissed angrily.

"I saw a light down by the mound where we found Brad and

Pete," Delia whispered. "What are *you* doing here?"

Kate shook her head impatiently. "Not right now. Did you hear that noise?"

"Yes," Delia said. "Did you see anyone up there?"

"No," Kate answered.

"Well, someone's up there with a light," Delia said. "How did you get past the trailer? I didn't hear anything. Why didn't you stop?"

Kate looked away and didn't answer. Then Delia understood. "Oh, shit."

"Yeah, Delia. If I'd had a truck I could have hooked up the god-damn trailer and dragged it down here and you two wouldn't have noticed."

"Oh, God," Delia said softly. "I'm sorry, Katie. I didn't know."

"I saw her Jeep. I was going to come by to tell you what I was going to do and why, but when I got there . . . when I walked up to the door . . ." She looked at the ground and Delia realized that she was crying. Delia reached out her hand, but Kate pushed it away. "I heard what was going on. I heard you two laughing and talking and . . ."

Neither of the women spoke for a few seconds, and then Delia said, "I *am* sorry, Kate. I didn't know it was going to happen."

Kate sniffled a little and shook her head. "It's okay. It serves me right for creeping around."

"So . . . what are you doing here?"

Just then both Delia and Kate heard the thrashing noise again, louder than before. Someone else was definitely in the woods and was making no effort to be quiet.

"What do you think it is?" Kate whispered.

Delia shook her head. "I don't have a clue." She paused. "We'd better go check it out."

Kate looked down and said, "Well, at least you have the gun this time."

"Why don't you go that way?" Delia pointed to the left. "And I'll

193

go around to the right. Be careful."

Delia watched as Kate made her way quietly through the trees and then she began moving herself. The noise was coming from a tangled thicket that grew beneath the stand of pine and oak trees along the river. Delia strained to see into the brambles, but the moonlight wasn't strong enough to illuminate whatever was making the noise. As she grew nearer, Delia heard the noise again, and this time she heard something that definitely sounded like a person moving around.

Out of the corner of her eye, she saw Kate coming, and they both converged on the thicket at the same time. As they stood looking at other, they heard a muffled sound from within, like someone trying to talk. Delia motioned to Kate, they each grabbed a handful of vines and pulled.

"Mother of God," Kate said loudly, staring at the man sitting on the ground. Bound to one of the trees, he had duct tape over his mouth. His face was bloodied; there was a gaping cut over his left eye, which was swollen shut, and his broken nose was smashed flat against his face. As they stood looking at him, he started to thrash around, kicking out, and twisting his head from side to side.

Delia looked from the man to Kate. "What?" she asked. "Do you know him?"

Kate continued to stare at the bound man and then said, "Oh, yeah. I know him. That's Bob Noland."

Delia clicked the rifle's safety on and leaned it against a nearby tree, then watched as Kate knelt down and ripped the duct tape off Noland's mouth, watching with satisfaction as the pain of having his battered face even further insulted crossed his features.

"I don't know who did this to you," Kate said, tossing the bloody tape aside. "But they get my vote for mayor."

Noland spit out a bloody mouthful and immediately began babbling. "We've gotta get outta here now. Right now. C'mon, untie me. Let's go. He's gonna kill me."

"You're not going anywhere, you weasel," Kate snarled.

"What're you talking about?" Delia asked. "Who's going to kill you?"

Noland shook his head and looked around frantically. "Look, ladies. We don't have time to chat. He'll be back any second. He's digging a grave for me." He paused. "And he'll be more than happy to make it big enough for all of us. Now, stop shittin' around and untie me."

"For a man who's tied up and beat up, you sure have a lot of demands," Delia observed mildly. "Now, who's trying to kill you?"

Noland began twisting and thrashing around again. "Goddamn it, get me the fuck outta these ropes. We're sittin' ducks here. He'll be back."

To Delia's surprise, Kate slapped Noland across his face, and a fine bloody spray spattered across her face.

"Jesus, Kate," Delia said fiercely. She grabbed Kate by the arm and pushed her away from Noland. Then she turned back to him and grabbed the front of his coat. "I think we should just leave you here," she said softly. "I don't really care who's trying to kill you. From what I know about you, it could be just about anybody around here."

Noland shook his head. "No. No. Look, I'm sorry, okay? It's just . . . he'll be back. He's got a gun and . . . look what he did to me. He tied me to this tree and beat the tar outta me. Then he left me out here, in the goddamn woods." He twisted his body in another attempt to free himself.

"Tell me who he is," Delia said.

Kate came back and fell to her knees. "I'll shoot your fucking kneecaps off if you don't tell us, you murdering bastard."

"Okay, okay." Noland looked around, searching the dark woods furtively. "It's Kincaid."

Kate fell back on her rear end, her expression one of disbelief. "Kincaid? What's he got to do with any of this?"

"Oh, wake up, Kate," Noland hissed. "He's the one who stole

those artifacts from the college. He killed Buddy, not me."

"Bullshit!" Kate said. "Why would he do any of that?"

Noland spit in disgust. "Aw, shit. I swear, I'll tell you everything. Only we gotta go *now*."

"Too late," Kincaid's voice sneered from a dark area ahead and to the right of Delia. "It's a shame none of you will be around to find out 'everything', as Mr. Noland puts it." Delia swung around to face the direction of Kincaid's voice and heard the unmistakable sound of a bullet being chambered. She looked around frantically for her rifle.

"Don't even think about reaching for it," Kincaid. "I'll shoot you right where you stand."

Kate stood up and started walking toward Kincaid. "What are you doing here?"

Just then, Noland kicked out with his legs, and Kate yelped in pain, grabbing her ankle. Then she threw herself on Noland and began pummeling him with her fists. "You son-of-a-bitch. Goddamn murderer," she cried. "I'll kill you."

Delia pulled Kate off Noland. "Kate, calm down now," she whispered her in ear. "We've got to think."

Kincaid moved closer to them. The shadows of the tree branches cast his features in a silver-gray light, reminding Delia of an old black and white movie. A horror movie. His expression was eerily calm. In that instant, she knew without a doubt that he would kill them all without any qualms.

Chapter 20

"But...why?" Delia asked Kincaid. "What's so important about this site?"

Kincaid pointed his gun directly at her. "Don't think about trying to distract me. You take one step, and I'll shoot you."

Delia held up her hands. "Okay, okay."

"He won't tell you the truth. He's a liar," Noland blurted. He twisted his head around to look at Kincaid. "I'll tell you something else...he's an addict. A gambler. He owes me money."

Kincaid moved closer to them. "I should've killed you a long time ago, you piece of shit. I've given you enough artifacts to stock a museum." He stopped.

Noland looked up at Kate. "You see, he admits it. Hell, they couldn't print enough money to equal what he owes me. So he gave me artifacts...from the digs he supervised. He got people to give him artifacts, too, that he said would go into museums."

Kate looked from Noland to Kincaid. "You know what? I don't give a fuck what he did. So he's a gambler...so he owes you money and gave you artifacts to pay off his debts; he's guilty of a lot of shit. *But he didn't kill my brother!*" She held out her hand to Kincaid. "Give me the goddamn gun, and I'll shoot him myself."

Noland thrashed violently. "I didn't kill Buddy!" he yelled. "I swear I didn't."

"Shut up," Kate snarled. "Just shut up."

"No, wait," Delia said to Kate. "Wait a minute." She glanced at Noland. "Why would Kincaid kill Buddy?"

"Don't you get it?" Noland was frantic now, his words barely intelligible. "I didn't have any *reason* to kill your brother...he couldn't hurt me. He couldn't prove anything. He was just blowing off steam when he went on television."

"But...he could hurt *you*," Delia said softly to Kincaid.

"What are you talking about?" Kate asked.

"Listen, Kate," Delia said. "Think about it.   If Buddy kept his promise to go after Noland for the disappearance of those two men, Kincaid's relationship and debt to Noland would have been exposed."

"Damn straight," Noland said.

"That's what worried you," Delia said to Kincaid. "You knew if Buddy investigated Noland, he'd find out about your arrangement. You'd have been ruined...your reputation, your career...everything."

"You killed Buddy because of *money*?" Kate asked Kincaid in disbelief. "Because you owed this sorry piece of shit some money?"

"You make it sound like nothing," Kincaid spat. "It wasn't nothing. It was *everything*." He pointed the gun at Delia. "You think I wanted to end up like her? Reputation ruined? Fired from my job? Just because I gambled a little?"

"Where's my brother?" Kate asked Kincaid. She began moving towards him. "What did you do with him?"

"He buried him," Noland said eagerly. "He buried him in Buck's field, in that little burial mound."

"What he neglects to tell you is *why* I buried Buddy out there," Kincaid said placidly. "Would you like me to tell you why before I shoot you?"

Delia reached out and grabbed Kate to keep her away from Kincaid. If she could keep Kincaid talking there was a better chance that she could think of a way to distract him.

"I'd like to know," Delia said, holding Kate close to her.

"I performed an intrusion burial," Kincaid said smugly. "Noland buried his buddy and the gaming commissioner in that little mound. Of course, at the time he didn't think anyone would ever dig around out here because his relative, Buck, owned the land. So when I killed poor old Buddy, I figured—why not bury him in the same place? That way if anybody ever discovered the bodies..."

"They'd think all three people were killed by the same person," Delia finished for him.

"That's ridiculous. There'd be forensic evidence," Kate objected. "Different bullets, different rate of decay, different fibers..."

Kincaid laughed in genuine amusement. "Thanks for pointing that out, Kate." He paused. "See, I buried Buddy right in there with the ones Noland murdered. It was a little messy, but I assure you—everybody is mixed up down there."

"How did you know where the bodies were buried in the first place?" Delia asked.

Kincaid glared at Noland. "Because he came to my house the night he killed his partner. Said he needed a hand with something important. I didn't want to help him, but he said he'd kill me if I didn't."

"Why would he let you know he killed his partner?" Kate asked. "That would give you something on him. You could have gone to the police."

"Not without implicating himself," Noland said proudly. "I made him help me both times so he'd be an accessory to murder if anyone ever found out."

"Did Buck know what you were doing on his land?" Delia asked quickly.

"Hell, yes, he knew," Kincaid said irritably. "He owed Noland money too. Noland knew as long as Buck owned the land, no one would ever disturb the grave. That's why he buried them here."

"*That's* why he was so mad when Buck's widow sold the land to Granddad," Delia said. "He was afraid."

"Got that right," Kincaid said. "And then, when you came in to my office and showed me those pictures—" He grinned. "I told him about the pictures . . . I started working on him. Told him you'd dig up those bodies, sure as anything. So he tried to . . . dissuade you from digging here. Plus, he wanted whatever grave goods he could get. When I told him about those copper plates and the head pot, he was even more excited. He's a fool."

"You'll never get away with this," Delia told him again.

"Well, I guess we'll see. I've been lucky so far," Kincaid said. "And it won't hurt that when the cops find Noland's car, inside they'll find the copper plates and the head pot. Maybe a gun or two, just to confuse things some more . . . like I said before, it will be a forensic nightmare. Six different bodies, different burial times. They'll never sort it out."

"That's crazy," Kate said, her whole body straining towards him. "Crime scene analysts can do anything these days."

"You've been watching too much television," Kincaid said. "Do you know how far behind the State Crime Lab is? Eighteen months and getting worse by the day. They've had budget cuts five years in a row now. They've got evidence and bodies that are over two years old. Besides, who says any one will ever find your bodies anyway?"

"Hey," Noland said to Kincaid. "Hey, come on, Jim. No hard feelings. We'll call it square, buddy. We can sell the stuff and you can have the money."

Kincaid laughed. "I'm going to sell the stuff anyway, Noland. I don't need you anymore." Nolan gave one last desperate kick, making Kincaid stumble and fall to his knees.

From that position, with shocking abruptness, Kincaid aimed his pistol at Noland's head and pulled the trigger.

A spray of blood, brain matter, and pieces of skull flew in all directions. Delia grabbed Kate and pulled her into the thicket. She burrowed through the thorny mass, tearing her hands and knees. "Come on," she hissed to Kate. She had thought to lead them to the river, but the thicket was so tangled that she lost all sense of direction. Delia could hear Kincaid cursing and tramping toward them. She tried to fight fear that crawled up from her stomach and into her throat. She felt pieces of Noland's head drying on her face and in her hair; she pushed down the urge to stop and wipe off the gore.

She couldn't tell if Kate was behind her or not; Kincaid's pursuit of them was too loud, so she continued clawing her way through the thorny brambles. Hoping that, when she emerged, there would be some cover for them to use in their escape, Delia held firm to her tendril of hope because it was all she had.

Her strength was nearly gone when she emerged from the thicket and found herself at the edge of the field. Inwardly cursing, knowing that Kincaid would have a clear shot at them now, Delia gathered herself and stumbled forward. She could hear someone coming behind her but whether it was Kincaid or Kate, Delia couldn't tell.

Then, suddenly, it didn't matter anymore, as the ground dropped out from under her, and she fell down into a hole. She lay there, trying to catch her breath. After the initial shock of falling wore off, she struggled to stand. It was then that she realized she was standing in an open grave. She reached up and switched on her LED light to examine the scene around her.

Kincaid had done his work well. It was impossible to tell one body from another. Bones, still covered with bits of cloth, were jumbled together. It would take months of work for forensic specialists to piece the skeletons together and to match the skulls to the bodies. It would be a miracle if they were able to determine if Buddy's body was here among the mud-covered, scattered bones and scraps.

As she stared at the partially exhumed corpses, Delia heard Kate's voice asking, "Are you really stupid enough to think that the authorities won't suspect you?"

"Now why would they suspect me?" Kincaid asked.

"Oh, I don't know," Kate returned sarcastically. "Maybe because you'll be the only one left."

"I'll be long gone by the time anyone figures out where either one of you is buried. I planned for this day, just in case I ever got out from under that bastard. Noland told me, after some persuasion on my part, where his collection is; I've got an overseas buyer. I'm flying out of Memphis tomorrow night; I'll be in Amsterdam before your corpses are even cold."

"The police already know about your involvement in the fire and the stolen artifacts," Kate insisted. "Noland told them. They've got Brad and Pete's statement too."

Kincaid laughed. "I got to Noland before Jack Pettit did," he said. "My step-sister's kid, Adam Bernstein, kept me well-informed about what was going down here. He was very helpful."

Kate cursed at him, and Kincaid laughed again. "I don't know what you're so upset about, Kate. You've got what you wanted. Can't you smell it?"

"What are you talking about?" Kate asked him.

"Go on," Kincaid called to Delia. "Tell Kate who's down there with you. Better yet, go on down there with your brother."

Kate landed in a heap beside Delia and immediately stood up and screamed at Kincaid, "You bastard!"

Suddenly the knowledge that they were about to die and that he intended to bury them in the unmarked grave hit Delia squarely. They might not ever be found. She felt a surge a rage and began climbing out of the hole. Somehow, Delia managed to get to her feet but, when she was close enough to touch him, Kincaid shoved her. She staggered backward and Kincaid followed her. At the edge of the hole, Delia slipped and started to fall back into the grave. She saw Kincaid's boot coming toward her face; it was too late to dodge it, and his foot smashed into her face.

Pain exploded inside her head. Blood and mucous gushed from her broken nose, along with tears of pain, blinding her. Kincaid's boot also split her lips; it felt like every tooth in her mouth was loose. She tried not to let the scream in her throat escape. She lay on her back, staring up at the moon. The pain, at least temporarily, was immobilizing. In addition, the pain of her cracked ribs returned with a vengeance.

Delia groaned as her nose and eyes began to beat with pulses of their very own.

Holding her hand over her face, she crawled over to a corner of the grave to get away from the rotten corpses. As she did, she realized that there were other unearthed bodies in the grave. She felt more bones under her hands and knees, and the smell of wet earth mingled with the faint odor of corruption. Nausea washed over her, both from the smell and the pain in her face. She struggled not to vomit and tried to think of some way out, but the pain in her face was so overpowering that she simply knelt while blood pooled in her palm.

Kate screamed again at Kincaid and when she did, an idea to distract him came to Delia. It wasn't the best idea, but it was the only thing she could come up with at the moment. She hoped that it would work because, if it didn't, she and Kate would both soon be dead. She looked up at him and concentrated on speaking. Her words were unintelligible, and Kincaid came closer to the edge of the grave opening.

"What're you trying to say?" Kincaid asked, looking baffled.

"Why is his head crushed like that?" Delia repeated, enunciating carefully.

He walked even closer to the edge of the opening and shone his flashlight down into the dark grave. "What the hell are you talking about?"

Behind her Kate was crying and repeating Buddy's name. Delia started to move toward Kincaid when suddenly, Kate stood up. As

203

Delia watched, all the anger, frustration, and bitterness that Kate had felt since they unearthed Buddy's body came boiling to the surface. Her expression grew dreamy, as though she were drugged, much like the Serpent Woman's face on the head pot. Kate's earrings trembled as rage possessed her, reminding Delia of the many piercings along the Serpent Woman's ears.

Seconds later, Kate threw her head back and roared her rage to the sky. As the past and the present coalesced, Kate's face and the Serpent Woman's face became one.

Before she could react, Delia watched as Kate, in one unbroken motion, launched herself up out of the hole at Kincaid, grabbing the shovel that he had left in the mound of dirt beside the grave. Kate stood before Kincaid, fearless and completely possessed by fury. A puzzled expression replaced his grim face; then, Kate lifted the shovel over her head. As she swung with all of her might, aiming it at Kincaid's head, Kincaid raised the gun and shot Kate in the center of her chest.

Chapter 21

The force of the bullet drove Kate backward into the grave, and her body fell heavily on top of Delia. She could feel Kate's lips at her ear, struggling to speak, but though she strained to hear, she couldn't make out her words. Two deep shuddering breaths later, Kate stopped moving, and Delia felt a warm gush of blood on her neck.

She quickly rolled Kate's body off her own and began trying to open her shirt. The light was dim inside the grave, but she turned her head so the LED light would illuminate Kate. Ripping open her shirt with both hands, she exposed Kate's chest.

The bullet had blown her chest open; in the bright LED light, Delia saw the terrible damage. The ghastly, open wound revealed a mass of mangled tissue and shards of ribs. The flow of blood was so heavy that it quickly filled Kate's chest cavity, pooled, and spilled over onto the ground.

Delia could hear Kincaid shouting something at her, but she ignored him and focused on Kate. Her face was pale—the color of wax paper; blood streamed from her nose and mouth. Taking off her duster, Delia tore off her own shirt, folded it and put it over the horrendous wound. Then she used her duster to cover the lower part of Kate's torso. Her blood soaked through the shirt almost instantly, but Delia kept up a steady pressure on the makeshift bandage.

She looked up at Kincaid. "We need an ambulance. She's bleeding to death."

Kincaid regarded her from the edge of the grave in disbelief. "Are you crazy?"

"If you call an ambulance now, you can leave before it gets here," Delia told him. "You'll have a big head start on any police that show up. Call them."

Kincaid shook his head. "You know, I'm glad you came down here. You're a genuine entertainment," he said happily. But as his smile faded, he pointed the gun at her. She heard the sound of a bullet being chambered. She closed her eyes and waited for the impact.

Then, Colleen's voice echoed from the edge of the tree line. "Drop the gun, Kincaid. I've got you right in my sights."

He turned in surprise and when he did, Delia stood and flung herself up over the edge of the grave. She frantically grabbed at his legs and managed to yank him to the ground before he brought the butt of the pistol down on her forehead; she felt her skin split open as blood began pouring down her face, blinding her.

She cried out, but kept a tight, unrelenting grip on his pants legs. Ignoring the pain in her face and head, she continued to drag him down into the grave opening. Though he tried to kick her away, he couldn't keep her from pulling him over into the hole. He landed on top of her, the gun wedged between his and Delia's body, and his weight drove the air from her lungs. Gasping for air, Delia heard the muffled sound of the gun as it went off.

She felt a searing pain in her right hip and screamed. Rolling away from him, she began frantically groping for the gun. He had the same idea, and just as her hand touched it, he grabbed it and leaped triumphantly to his feet. His grin was maniacal and, when he pointed the gun at her, Delia knew she was going to die beside Kate and Buddy.

In desperation, she grabbed the shovel that lay next to Kate's body. She raised the shovel over her head, a shot rang out, and Kincaid, without a word, dropped dead beside her.

Once the ambulance was underway, and the paramedics were treating her hip, Delia started to sob. When she started, she could not stop. Her clothes and hands, covered with the dried remains of Noland's brains and blood, were now stained with her own, Kincaid's and Kate's blood. The paramedics worked swiftly, and Colleen remained beside her, holding her hand. Kate and Kincaid's bodies were in the coroner's van.

"I shouldn't have let her jump up there," she cried. "I knew he was going to shoot her. Buddy warned me; he asked me to protect her and I didn't."

"I'm going to give you something, hon," one of the male paramedics said, as he injected the contents of a hypodermic needle into her IV. "It'll help with the pain and calm you down some. Just relax now, and let the medicine do its work," he said softly.

As she lost consciousness, Delia had one last, terrible thought—Kate was dead and it was her fault. The dreams had talked to her and she hadn't listened.

Chapter 22

Archeologists from three states attended Kate and Buddy's funeral. Members of the American Prosecutors Council, American Bar Association, and many of Buddy's friends from law school as well as those he knew from the Naval JAG Corps were there, too. Kate and Buddy's parents flew in from Louisiana. They stood huddled together, their faces stunned by grief and loss. Sheriff Pettit, his deputies, and Paula attended, too. Delia spoke to them politely.

Everyone tried unsuccessfully to evade the cameras and reporters.

Delia had checked herself out of the hospital against her doctor's strident objections. The orthopedic surgeon had told her that she was risking further injury to her hip if she didn't stay in the hospital. Looking at herself in the mirror before leaving for the funeral, she hardly recognized herself. A portion of her head was shaved clean when they stitched the gash from Kincaid's bludgeoning. Yellow, black and green bruises covered her face. The flesh around her eyes was swollen until they were mere slits. Talking was excruciating because her lips were still swollen, and one of her front teeth was chipped. Her ribs and hand hurt. Everything hurt.

Colleen and Eunice had tried to talk her into staying in the hospital, but Hollis chased them out of her room. He had helped her dress, and he pushed her wheelchair when she left the hospital. Later during the funeral, as she sat glassy-eyed and numb from painkillers, she clung to his hand.

After the funeral, Delia sat on the enclosed back porch at Eunice's house while some of the other people who had attended the funeral mingled in the front room. She stared into space, her hip and face throbbing despite the powerful painkillers she had taken, wanting more than anything else to be home in Utah.

Then, she heard a noise beside her and looked up. It was Kevin. Dressed in a dark blue suit and white shirt adorned by a thin tie, he stood looking down at her, his face solemn.

"Dee? Can I talk to you for a minute?" he asked softly.

"Sure," she said, using her uninjured leg to push a chair towards him. "Have a seat."

He sat down but didn't speak for a few moments. "I wanted to tell you some things about what happened with Noland."

"Okay," Delia said. "Shoot.... Damn, poor choice of words, huh?" she asked bitterly.

"I know you saw me that day with Noland. I saw you wave and all, but...well, dang it, I'm kinda embarrassed by the whole thing."

"Hey, listen, I understand. Working for Noland and washing trucks with your good buddy John Ed must have seemed a lot more exciting than working at the site with me," she said sarcastically. "I completely understand."

"No, look, it wasn't like that, okay? See...I thought that I could, I don't know, investigate Noland if I worked for him. I heard all the stuff people like Eunice and Kate were saying about him, how he was a bad guy. I thought I could find out if he was the one who killed Kate's brother. I didn't know any of them until you got here." He paused. "Kate was a good person. Anyway, I started

209

thinking that maybe Noland was responsible for all the stuff that was happening. When your granddad and I got shot at, well, it really pissed me off."

"So you decided to, what, go undercover or something?"

Kevin blushed. "Basically, yeah. I called him up and asked if I could talk to him about a job, doing whatever. Unloading trucks like John Ed. I thanked him again for the dog and lettin' us hunt on his land...you know?"

The sincerity in his voice and the impulse behind his actions suddenly broke through Delia's hurt and anger. She reached out her hand and took his. "I'm sorry, Kevin. I'm really sorry."

"No, it's okay," he assured her. "Really. I shoulda told you...or somebody...what I was gonna do. I know it musta looked pretty suspicious to you, to see me with him. I figured later that you mighta thought I was tellin' him things. That I was in on it with him. But that's not what it was. I was tryin' to help." He looked at the floor. "Didn't work out that way, I know. But that's what I was tryin' to do."

"Did you tell Sheriff Pettit this?" Delia asked.

"Yeah. That day Kate saw me down at the sheriff's office...I mean, I didn't find out anything. Noland was kinda distracted when I talked to him. He said he'd call me, you know...blah, blah, blah."

"I understand," Delia said, letting go of his hand. "At least you tried to do something constructive. I just..." She couldn't finish. Tears welled up in her eyes and spilled down her cheeks. Kevin reached in his coat pocket and took out a clean, white handkerchief and handed it to her.

She took it and wiped her face. "I didn't know men even carried these anymore," she said, laughing a little.

"Look, Dee. I really liked getting to know you and everything. I'm real sorry about Kate...that she got killed. I should've been there with you instead of trying to play detective. I mighta been able to do something."

"Well, at least you have an excuse—you weren't there. I was, and I didn't do a damn thing to save her."

"That's complete nonsense and you know it," Colleen said from the doorway. She came and sat down on a wooden bench facing them.

Kevin stood, leaned down and kissed Delia's cheek. "I'll drive you to the airport, okay?"

"Sure," Delia said, patting his arm. "That'd be great."

Kevin nodded at Colleen and left.

Collen leaned forward and took Delia's undamaged hand in her own. Cocking her head at Delia, she appraised her.

"You should be in hospital," Colleen said. "I can't believe you're risking your health by doing this. Kate wouldn't have wanted it." When Delia didn't answer, Colleen said: "Love, you did your best to save her."

"I might as well have shot her myself," Delia said bitterly. "He told me to keep her safe. For her not to die like she had in the past. But my scientific mind..." she trailed off bitterly.

"Dreams are imperfect; it can be hard to know what they mean," Colleen said. "And sometimes even if you do know, you can't change what will happen."

"It was there for me to see—I should have known. I should have changed it," Delia insisted. Her voice broke and she stopped. "I got her killed."

Colleen reached out and gingerly touched Delia's swollen, battered face. "I daresay you'll feel differently as time passes. I saw you, Dee. I saw you there kneeling next to her. You did try to stop the bleeding. You did everything humanly possible to save her."

"I should have started trying to save her *before* he shot her," Delia said stubbornly. "I should have seen what my heart and soul was trying to show me, not just my eyes. I turned away from the dreams, from what all those howling deaths were trying to tell me. One woman goes into an anguished frenzy over the death of her brother. But I didn't think that applied to Kate."

"Kate and Buddy repeated the past; it's not your responsibility to change the future. How could anyone know what was really going on inside of Kate?" Colleen asked softly. "Buddy disappeared ten years ago; he's been missing for a long time. Kate never came to terms with the fact that he was probably dead."

Delia raised her head and looked at Colleen intently. "But I took her there, to face Buddy's killer and his grave. I told her about the dreams before I knew what they meant. Before I thought about what they might mean to her. Why did I tell her? It was crazy."

"Yes, well . . . the dreams," Colleen said softly.

Delia closed her eyes and said, "Colleen . . . I saw him beside the grave opening . . . in my dream—before I went down there."

"Yes, I remember you told me," Colleen said.

"This whole thing. All the dreams I've had since I got here. You told me that I had to figure out what they meant."

"I did indeed," Colleen said. "And you did."

"Too late. If you believe any of it, and I'm not even sure I do, it was all about Buddy Treadaway. I think . . . but I'm not sure . . . that Kate was the Serpent Woman . . . brother and sister. Buddy wanted me to find him." She looked up at Colleen. "I know that sounds nuts."

"Don't try to discount what your dreams told you, Dee," Colleen said. "It's the best part of you. It's a spiritual gift."

"Oh, right. Some gift. A gift too late to save Kate's life."

Colleen didn't speak for a moment, as if she sensed that Delia could not be consoled about Kate. Then she said, "You know, finding Buddy was obviously part of the importance of the excavation. But it isn't the total sum of your responsibility here."

"What do you mean?"

"When you came to see me, you and Kate identified a problem with the age and type of artifacts you had uncovered. Remember? That's why you wanted to excavate the site in the first place."

Delia frowned. "So?"

"So," Colleen said patiently. "Don't you think Kate would want

212

you to finish the excavation? Solve the rest of this mystery?"

"She was excited about it," Delia admitted. "But I don't have the heart for it now." She paused. "Based on what I dreamed and what we found so far, I think there's probably a simple explanation. Maybe as simple as intrusion burials. Or, that the people who were taken as slaves simply brought their own Mound Culture with them. That would account for some of what we found." She shrugged. "You take over the dig next year. I'm sure the grad students and volunteers would be glad to help. It's not my problem anymore."

"It's too bad you feel that way," Colleen said. "I'm sure your grandfather is disappointed. He and Eunice were excited as well ... not just about the dig, but having you here with them."

"Yeah, well, it's what I do, you know? Disappoint people," Delia snarled. "It's my real gift."

Colleen stood up. "When you've had time to think about it ... to grieve and accept that what you did was right, you'll stop feeling sorry for yourself. Whatever else happened ... call it what you will. Fate. Destiny. It's something *you* don't control." She leaned down and kissed Delia softly and added, "When you're ready to talk sensibly, call me."

Delia sat, staring at the backyard, listening to Colleen's fading footsteps. She didn't turn around to watch her leave.

Two days after giving her deposition at the coroner's inquest, Delia boarded a plane for Salt Lake City.

Chapter 23

Late on Christmas Eve afternoon, Delia opened the door to her Grandmother Ruth's hogan with an armload of pinion pine firewood. A foot of new snow piled into drifts and crept up the sides of her home. Neji was sprawled in front of the wood stove and looked up as she entered. Before walking across her grandmother's new linoleum floor, she kicked off her snow-covered boots. She hung her duster behind the door and stuffed her gloves into one of its pockets. Only then did she cross the room and dump the wood into a box by the stove. She limped to a straight-back chair where her grandmother was sitting in front of the loom. Earlier in the day, Robert had left. He was on his way to his aunt's house for the evening, leaving Delia in the care of her grandmother.

Eight weeks earlier, Robert had picked her up at the Salt Lake City airport: his face grim and determined. He had an ambulance waiting.

"I don't know what happened to you in Arkansas to make you this crazy," he said. "But I will not allow you to hurt yourself like this." Delia found that she didn't have the energy to argue with him. And, the next day, surgeons inserted pins into her damaged hip. After recuperating at Robert and Lilah's house in Bittercreek for the next two months, Delia went with them to spend the holidays in Mexican Hat with her grandmother, Robert's mother. They arrived four days before Christmas.

Delia gazed at the beautiful Two Grey Hills rug her grandmother had worked on since she arrived. "The most beautiful one yet."

Her grandmother allowed a ghost of a smile to crease her face, which at eighty-seven was still unlined.

"You say that about every one that I make," she said softly. She continued to push the wooden shuttle up and down without looking at Delia. "Your leg is hurting . . . go sit by the fire and rest."

Delia walked stiffly to the worn red armchair in front of the stove and sank into its cushion gratefully. Neji looked up and Delia motioned her to come. When the dog was within reach, Delia began stroking her ears. "A friend of mine in Arkansas has a chair that looks exactly like this one," she told her grandmother.

"Your friend in Arkansas . . . you miss her," Ruth finally said.

Delia stared out the window by her grandmother's head. "Sometimes." She looked around the room. "Do you like the linoleum yet?" She asked.

Ruth shrugged. "It's hard to get used to, but I suppose I will . . . someday."

"You miss the old dirt floor," Delia teased her.

"I don't miss it," Ruth said. "I was *used* to it, but sometimes change is good."

Delia nodded. "Yes. It is." She straightened out her leg, grunting at the sharp pain in her hip. She was stiff from sitting in one position too long. Earlier that afternoon, she cleared the road leading from her grandmother's hogan to the main road; now her hip and leg ached from pumping the clutch of the mini-plow. Delia tried to put the throbbing out of her mind. She stood up, stretched her back, and said: "I think I'm going to take some Advil, get my heating pad, and go to bed. I'm pooped."

"You are still blaming yourself for that girl's death," her grandmother told her.

"It's not a question of *blaming* myself," Delia said hoarsely, feeling the sting of guilt in her words. "If I opened myself up to what the dreams were trying to tell me...if I protected Kate like Buddy told me to."

"What you did doesn't matter now. It is done. What matters is what you do *now*."

"I'm doing okay with it," Delia said flatly.

"That's what you say," her grandmother said, stopping her weaving and turning to Delia. "It does no good to carry death around with you, Granddaughter. It will poison you. This is why, when one of the Dineh dies, the house that he lived in is abandoned. Otherwise, the ghosts of the dead will come to live with you. You are still living with the dead."

In bed, later that night, Delia lay listening to her grandmother's gentle breathing from across the room. She felt deep sadness as she thought of Kate. She turned over on her side and let her hand rest on Neji's massive head, taking comfort in the soft fur of her coat.

She knew that her grandmother was right about the burden of guilt. She carried Kate's death on her shoulders. She knew she had to move on, but the memory of Kate's broken body, the smell of her blood seeping through her fingers, and the smell of the open grave would not leave her. Not yet. If time healed at all, it would heal slowly.

About the author

Jeane Harris lives with her dog Sweetie and cat Senor Lucchi in Jonesboro, Arkansas. She is a Professor of English at Arkansas State University. She is the author of two previous novels: *The Magnolia Conspiracy* (previously published as *Black Iris*) and *Delia Ironfoot*, and two short stories that appeared in *The Erotic Naiad* and *The Romantic Naiad*.

For more information about Bywater Books and to see our entire catalog, please visit our website, www.bywaterbooks.com or call us toll-free at 866-390-7426.